ATTORNEY AT LARGE

THADDEUS MURFEE SERIES

JOHN ELLSWORTH

SUBJUDICA HOUSE

Lincoln Mascari knew everything about the young lawyer, and he knew about the kid. Sitting hunched at his desk in Skokie, reading the article twice more, Mascari pounded the paper and threw it violently across the room. The *Chicago Tribune* was reporting the Desert Riviera Casino was worth $750 million and Thaddeus Murfee owned it 100 percent. Mascari wanted it back.

Maybe he would trade for it. The idea hardened in his mind like cement.

There could be a trade, the kid for the casino.

First he needed to lay hands on the kid. So he did what all good hoodlums do, he hired someone to grab her.

He summoned Arnold Goldstine to his office. Arnold was from Joliet and his grandfather was Al Capone. In fact, family legend had it that it was his grandmother who gave Capone the dose of syphilis that later killed him in prison. But that was a story for another day.

"This guy has got a kid," Mascari said.

"Then you got the wrong guy. I don't do kids."

Goldstine left.

So he sent out an invite to Dumas Lamoneti. Dumas was a made guy out of Miami. His resume had him the best torture guy in Florida. He was that good.

"This guy's got this kid," Mascari started in.

"I don't do kids," said Lamoneti. He spat on the cement floor of Mascari's Skokie office and turned on his heel. He was in the air and headed back to Miami an hour later.

So Mascari called Johnnie Getti in New York.

"Yo, Johnnie. Mascari in Chicago. Who you got will do a kid?"

"That's a tough one. But I'd say Ragman, out of LA."

"Got his number?"

"Don't got it to give out. But I'll make a few calls. Make sure he gets in touch with you."

"You do that."

They talked and promised to meet for golf in Scottsdale when the hawk flew and the snow blew. They wintered in Scottsdale and their golf course homes were only four strokes apart.

Mascari's operation was based out of an industrial park on the outskirts of Skokie, in a converted lube joint. Almost impossible to find. Three weeks later, a short, unremarkable man, clean shaven, three-piece suit, ambled into Mascari's office. When he learned who the man actually was, Mascari had no idea how he got there.

"They call me Ragman." He didn't offer to shake.

Mask stood up from his desk. "Please. Have a seat."

"Thank you. Now. How can I be of service?"

"This guy's got this kid."

"Okay."

Long pause. "You ain't gonna run out of here because I said it's about a kid?"

"You pay cash?"

"Totally."

"I'm not running. You found your man."

THADDEUS MURFEE HAD A KID. In fact, he had two—or so he had been told.

He also had a casino, another child of sorts. He had won the casino in a lawsuit. A lawsuit against the gangster who even now was hiring thugs to kidnap his daughter.

The casino was world class and was located on the Las Vegas Strip, smack in the middle of three hundred miles of sand. The deed said the name of the place was the Desert Riviera Casino and Hotel. He had kept the name because he was a pragmatic man and the word "desert" was spot on. The "riviera" part he was still looking for. That piece had him puzzled.

Thaddeus was prowling the gaming floor, watching for cheats. So far that night he had eighty-sixed four blackjack card counters and two cowboys with some sort of magnet they were using on the $100 slots. Idiots, he kicked them out. With the assistance of security, of course.

He was twenty-eight, single, and caught between two women. Two years ago he could hardly score a date. Now he had two women at once. So what had changed?

He decided he needed a drink. He needed to be still and think this through.

Luckily he didn't have far to go, because in his Desert Riviera Casino over 1,200 gallons of liquor were dispensed every day. Truth be told, Thaddeus would rarely take a drink. And he would never take a drink while he was on duty at the casino.

But tonight was different.

It was 10 p.m. and his limbs were heavy and his walk around the casino floor had slowed to a crawl. In part, it was the rigors of the job. But more than physical tiredness, the exhaustion was emotional and mental. He needed to make up his mind about the two women.

And he needed to do it now.

As in yesterday.

He headed for Rudy's serving station. He liked Rudy. Rudy liked him enough to let him drink a beer in peace.

The work problems never ended.

Thaddeus had just been handed a summons from some unlucky gambler out of Los Angeles who claimed that the Desert Riviera Casino had served him eleven White Russians while he was in a blackout and he had lost $500,000. He wanted the money returned, plus legal fees. Thaddeus and the casino could walk away from the mess for $625,099.45.

So far they hadn't paid off because, as Thaddeus put it to his legal staff, "We're a casino, not a slot machine. We don't pay off—ever."

Thaddeus couldn't believe the claim, but thankfully the casino had a comprehensive insurance policy that covered such outrageous jousts.

Another claim was being made by a twelve-year-old girl. The kid was claiming she was fondled by Klarice the Klown while reciting her Christmas list on Klarice's lap. Klarice had taken a lie detector test which came back negative. The casino attorneys had offered the same lie box to the little girl. But her parents were balking. No, they said, she won't submit to a lie detector exam. But she will accept $3,500 in damages to settle the case. Either cash or thirty-five black chips, thank you.

Then there was the cowboy who drove his new Chevy pickup into the water-park that surrounded the casino. He was intoxicated, of course, and the current had washed him off downstream. He had nearly drowned because he was too drunk to stand in the waist-deep water. EMTs had been called. They furiously jumped into the water and dragged him ashore.

The water was never more than four feet deep—Las Vegas City Code.

Plus, the water never moved faster than five miles per hour, thanks to the sophisticated pumps and tanks and computer-regulated valves buried underground.

While the cowboy nearly succumbed to the waters, he was further embarrassed by inner-tubing children who zigzagged past. They laughed while he flailed against the current and struggled to gain his footing.

According to his yellow-page attorney, the case was worth $25,000 plus lawyer fees. And, the cowboy hinted, he was connected, which could only mean he could call down some mob muscle if the Desert Riviera didn't pony up the funds.

Thaddeus needed that beer in a bad way.

He worked his way through the casino mob and finally emerged at Rudy's serving station.

The lounge reeked of alcohol, and with good reason. Anybody who didn't understand the service setup would have been astonished to see what all went into serving one lousy beer in a Vegas super casino.

Rudy, behind the bar, slid a frosted mug to Thaddeus.

Thaddeus took a sip and wiped his mouth with a napkin. "Nice," he said to Rudy, and hoisted the glass.

Thaddeus had no sooner swallowed, than Tim Mineers, assistant beverage manager, screeched to a halt beside him. He took the next stool and said, "You smell that?"

Thaddeus inhaled. "Smells a lot like a party going on somewhere. Airborne alcohol esters."

"My God that's poetic."

"I try," Thaddeus smiled and took another drink.

The odor was particularly strong because the area was connected by HVAC ductwork to the room above.

The upper room was the casino's pump room. Inside the dark room nearly 2,000 upside-down liquor bottles were standing at the ready on metal racks. They reminded Thaddeus of Russian troops amassed on the border of some luckless neighbor, ready to rush in at the slightest provocation—or, in this case, the touch of the tap by the bartender one floor below.

Liquids continuously fed into multiple mouths of a complex system of plastic tubes and spring pumps. When a bartender from one of the property's fifty-three drink stations triggered the system to zip a shot to a waiting glass, it sounded like an airlock from *Star Wars*. Bottles burped with bubbles. Same system for the beers, wines, and specialty spirits.

"Guy could get loaded just sitting here breathing," Tim said.

"Expect so. How's tricks?"

"We're taking in two semis of booze a day. There's still barely enough to go around."

"That's your job, isn't it?" Thaddeus asked.

"We haven't actually run out. Not yet anyway."

"Tim, do we have any good dark beers from local breweries?"

"Ask Rudy for the Desertmeister. Highly recommend."

"Thanks."

"You're drinking alone tonight?"

Thaddeus shrugged. "Every chance I get."

"Am I interrupting?"

"Yes. But glad for the company for a minute or two."

"So how's your love life, Thad?"

Thaddeus bore in on him with his dark blue eyes. There was no warmth there. "What, even the staff knows about my love life?"

"There's a lot of talk."

"Son of a— is nothing sacred around here?"

"When you've got kids with two women and unmarried, I'd say you're beyond sacred," Tim laughed. "I call it The Penis Chronicles."

He slapped his knee, delighted with himself but somewhat careless because Thaddeus was so young he seemed harmless.

Only then did he notice his employer wasn't laughing. Thaddeus shut his eyes and wished he were alone.

The so-called comedy was eating him alive and more and more he was using alcohol to take the lid off that pressure cooker.

For the umpteenth time that hour he kicked himself for creating his conundrum. Two women giving birth within a month of each other, fathered by him, and, as far as he could figure out, he was in love with them both. One more than the other, probably, but even that changed like the shifting winds across the Rockies over east.

He swore he would only have two drafts tonight, otherwise he would wind up drunk-dialing the women and creating an even bigger mess.

He pulled his cell from his shirt pocket and slid it across the bar. Rudy looked up.

"What's this?"

"My cell. Don't let me have it back tonight."

A knowing look crossed Rudy's face. "Want me to have the front desk disable the lines in your apartment too?"

"Guess not. Then I couldn't be reached at three a.m. when the drunks can't find their cars and the reports of grand theft auto start pouring in."

"Where's Mickey Herkemier, isn't he supposed to be managing all that?"

Thaddeus grimaced. "He keeps hours. Unlike me, all employees have hours around here. I only wish."

"So unplug the frickin' thing. Don't let it get to you."

"You're right."

Back to resolving his family problems.

He had three options.

One, he could do nothing and let the present miasma continue with him living with neither woman, neither child. That wasn't good for anyone, so that was out.

Two, he could marry Ilene and repay Katy by paying her way through med school. And he would support Sarai, their daughter—that went without saying. That created even more problems because he probably loved Katy more than Ilene.

Three, he could marry Katy, support Andromeda with Ilene, and get the two children together as often as possible. That had possibilities, because he was sure Ilene would be very liberal with visitation. There would be joint custody, primary custodian Ilene. Thaddeus could visit every other weekend.

He mused about the possibilities, turning them over in his head, while trying to ignore the chaos around him. It was Las Vegas insanity filling the air and swirling around his head. It was pure chaos created by the gambling arcade, an area about the size of two football fields wired with strobes and sirens.

Casino life was intense, and maybe it was more than he actually wanted.

Thaddeus had downed about half the beer when he felt a heavy sweat break out on his forehead.

For a moment the room was spinning, then stopped.

"Shit," he muttered and stood up. "Thanks, Rudy."

He slid the mug back across the bar. Then he felt as if a light had flashed on and off inside his head.

He suddenly had the desire to start running, to leave the service area, leave the casino, and run out into the night, away from all the bells, the clamor, the excitement, the winners and losers, and the problems that were over-whelming.

But instead of running he braced himself for several minutes. He leaned his back against the bar. He took deep breaths.

He watched the people pass by, some in a hurry, some casually strolling, taking it all in. Most had determined looks and seemed focused on one game or slot or roulette wheel. In fact, it occurred to him that he had never seen a more determined looking group of people.

He had to smile.

Whatever his own intense feeling was, it slowly loosened up inside.

Eventually a sense of calm returned and he pulled another napkin from the dispenser and used it to wipe his forehead.

Then he knew.

It was the two women and two kids in his life.

He had to have some kind of resolution. He was being

forced to make a choice and get on with one woman or the other, and let the other go on with her life.

But no matter which way he turned, he realized he would have one child with him every day and would be missing the other child every day.

He cursed himself again and grew angry with the mess he had created. "You and your misguided dick," he muttered, and the woman passing in front of him turned her head and stared right into his eyes.

He shook his head and said, "Just talking to myself, sorry."

"I'd kill anyone talked to me like that," she tossed over her shoulder and disappeared down a long army of slot machines.

Every square inch of the casino was designed to rip money away from people who damn sure couldn't afford to lose it. You're involved in one of the dirtiest schemes in the world, he told himself. Second maybe only to narcotics trafficking or human trafficking.

Suddenly he missed Chicago and missed Albert.

He missed the practice of law and missed Ilene and Andromeda.

Almost as quickly came the second flood of feelings and he found himself missing and desiring Katy Landers. And missing their daughter, Sarai.

Tears flowed, hot tears. He shut his eyes hard and thought about praying but he didn't know what to say. He dabbed his eyes with the napkin.

"Whew," he sighed, and tossed the balled up napkin over the bar and into the trash at the near end.

"Two points," said Rudy.

With a huge sigh he pushed away from the bar and headed upstairs to his apartment. Truth be told, he couldn't remember a time in his life when he had ever felt as lonely as he did right then.

He'd get some sleep and take the plane back to Chicago tomorrow or the next day, latest. Or maybe head up to San Francisco and catch up with Katy.

Whatever.

Then he froze in his tracks. He returned to the bar and held out his hand to Rudy. "Knew you'd want it back," the bartender laughed.

With the cell phone safely back inside his shirt pocket, he headed upstairs. This time, for real.

He had a kid, all right. Fact was, he had two.

And it was driving him crazy.

2

Two years ago Thaddeus was a nobody lawyer in small town Illinois, chasing cases. One day he fell into a murder case that resulted in a Not Guilty verdict. After that he sued the State of Illinois for the malicious prosecution of his client. He proved that the Governor and the Attorney General had conspired against her.

Result: he earned over ten million dollars in legal fees. Not bad, your second year in practice.

But then things headed south.

He had crossed the Chicago mob and they sent men after him. They wanted him dead.

Fair enough, he understood where their heads were at and he really couldn't blame them. He had messed up their ability to print dollars by illegal gambling, loan-sharking, prostitution, and drug dealing. He had lit them up with the spotlight of public clamor.

He got that.

But what they didn't expect was that he would fight back.

How did he fight?

With the only tools a lawyer had: he sued them. The experts told him it couldn't be done, that the mob couldn't be sued. But he ignored them. He sued the mob and won.

The defendants were a godfather, Bang Bang Moltinari, and his consigliere, Lincoln Mascari.

Thaddeus must have done something right, because—long story short—he took away their casino. And he took a bunch of money from them. Money they had stashed in Swiss banks.

Now he owned the Desert Riviera Casino and Hotel in Las Vegas and he had millions in the bank.

After the casino case concluded, the FBI went after the godfather in its own conclusive way.

They had the Air Force fly a drone over the Don's estate in Mexico where he was hiding out, and fired a Hellfire missile into his bedroom. End of godfather. Which, Thaddeus had to admit, helped him breathe a whole lot easier.

But there was one glaring problem left unsolved and that was Lincoln Mascari, who was still very alive and well. Mascari had stepped into Bang Bang's shoes in Chicago.

The largest Chicago mob family now belonged to him.

3

Two weeks later, he was back in Chicago, trying a medical malpractice case for the death of a newborn. He and Albert represented the parents.

The long courtroom windows admitted early evening dark and the glow of Chicago street lights when closing arguments finally got underway.

The jury was exhausted but excited to hear the lawyers' summations. Before long they would be free to return to their families and normal lives.

Thaddeus wet his lips and swallowed hard. A final sip of water and he crossed from counsel table to the podium.

"Let me thank you for your jury service," he began, and he stepped from behind the podium and up to the jury. He wanted them close, wanted to see their faces, wanted them to see the pain in his eyes, the pain he felt for the dead baby.

Thaddeus was lithe and lean, wore round eyeglasses below the bowl cut of his hair, and that day was dressed in pinstripes and wing-tips—Chicago court haberdashery.

He moved with the athletic step of a college point guard as he made his way along the jury box.

At his collar his hair was just an inch too long for someone trying cases in front of juries, at least according to how old-school Chicago did things.

His face was what some would call "attractive" and others would call "brotherly." But his eyes were an icy blue that pierced and probed at witnesses, lawyers, jurors, judges, and the rest of the world.

Right then they were focused only on the jury. Eye contact bound everyone together as they tried to unravel the mystery of the baby's death. Was it medical malpractice or was the mother's lack of prenatal doctor visits what killed the baby Kim Ehlers? Soon, the jury would be making that decision. For right now, Thaddeus was doing everything in his power to guide them along the path to making what he wanted them to believe was the only correct decision.

He began slowly.

"Now, Doctor Jordan is a heck of a nice man. We can all agree on that at least. He is the father of seven children and the grandpa to eleven grandchildren. He is a member of the Moose, the Elks, and the VFW. Vietnam 1968-1969. He worked at delivering babies for twenty-eight years before taking medical retirement."

He looked the jury up and down, and nodded. "But Doc Jordan was a huge drinker—by his own admission. Remember Father Conroy's testimony? Doc Jordan told Father that he'd flunked out of AA no less than seven times. That he even remembered. And look at this"—holding up exhibit 67—"It's in the admitting hospital's own investigation report that Doc Jordan had ingested a fifth of vodka in the twelve hours before he entered the hospital to deliver little Kim Ehlers. Of course Doctor Jordan's wife, Cindy, claims she never told that to the investigator. Still, it's in the hospital's own records! How else did it get there if she didn't

tell them?" His piercing eyes addressed the jury and he let it
sink in.

"By the way," he began again, "how many drinks would
that be, for those of you unfamiliar with the ingestion of
large quantities of liquor? Well, let's see what the doc's wife
said Doc had in the previous twelve hours."

Thaddeus cut to the whiteboard and wrote: "1 Fifth of
Whiskey = 1/5 Gallon."

Then he turned to face the jury.

"A gallon has one hundred twenty-eight fluid ounces, so
one-fifth of that is twenty-five point six ounces, which tells
us there are twenty-five point six ounces in your fifth of
whiskey. The standard shot glass is one point five ounces, so
the fifth contains about seventeen shots. Which means Doc
Jordan had about seventeen drinks or one-fifth of a gallon of
vodka in the twelve hours before he arrived at Hudd Family
Hospital. And one-fifth is how much Cindy told hospital
investigators that Sam had to drink over the last hours
before he went into that delivery room. She also told the
investigators that she found the empty fifth in the kitchen
trash and that she knew it was from that day because the
fifth that Doc always kept in the freezer was missing."

Thaddeus returned to the podium and pretended to
study his notes while he let the math and admissions sink
in. Then he returned to his place before the jury.

"Here's another way of looking at it. If your car gets
fifteen miles to the gallon and you poured Doc's fifth of
vodka in the tank you could drive three miles on how much
Doc Jordan had to drink."

The jurors looked at Doctor Jordan to see how he was
taking this.

He was a gray-skinned man in his early sixties who
looked middle seventies. It had been a hard life for Doctor

Jordan, spending his best years with the bottle. His pallor and slump said it all.

He grimaced at Thaddeus' words. Another deep cut. A look of predictable guilt settled over his face.

The jurors looked away.

Thaddeus continued. "So when the baby girl Kim's fragile brain had its blood flow cut off by the twisted umbilical, she didn't have a sober doctor to rely on to save her life. Was that the baby's fault? Well, according to counsel"—he paused long enough to point at defense counsel—"according to counsel, the baby's prenatal vitamins and the mother's lack of prenatal examinations should be blamed for everything that went wrong that Christmas Eve. He wants you to forget Doctor Jordan's two solid days of drinking and look only at baby Kim and her mother. But here's what I need you to remember when you retire to deliberate...."

An hour passed, by the clock on the wall.

Soundlessly, as a ghostly apparition, the jury returned and assembled in the jury box.

All were standing, looking away from the doctor. His eyes retreated to the table top. He had seen all he needed to know.

Judge Brown said the magic words, spoken daily in courtrooms across America, "Has the jury reached a verdict?"

The jury foreman answered, "We have, Your Honor."

"Please read your verdict aloud."

The foreman pressed his half-shell glasses to the bridge of his nose and cleared his throat. It had been a long two weeks but there had been little bickering. The jury was of one mind. He read, "We the jury do find for the plaintiffs and against the defendants."

Thaddeus and the baby's parents stood up from their table like the phoenix from a very hot fire.

They had survived!

There was barely suppressed elation as they struggled to control their joy at having beaten the wealthy doctor-hospital syndicate.

They pumped hands all around and there were whispered thank-yous passed along to Thaddeus. They broke off in small groups and began packing briefcases and laptops.

The jury foreman approached Thaddeus and tapped his shoulder. "I think I remember you."

Thaddeus turned from his briefcase and faced the foreman. He smiled down at the man, who was much smaller than he looked just an hour ago in the jury box. "How's that?"

"Yes, I'm sure of it now. You were Georgetown's shooting guard, took them to the Sweet Sixteen. You guys would've won the whole thing if Drummond hadn't fouled out."

"That was eight years ago. You have a good memory. Thanks for your jury service. You've all done the right thing here today."

"You're the lawyer who sued the mob and took a casino away from them."

Thaddeus turned back. "You know about that?"

"Everyone on the jury knew about that. We discussed it."

Thaddeus shook his head, a wan smile on his face. "Well, that's why we have trials. You never know what a jury will do—or talk about."

Albert Hightower was exhausted from the two-week trial. But he was ready to fly Thaddeus back out to Las

Vegas. He touched Thaddeus' elbow and moved him away from the juror.

Albert said, "You up for this?"

"Flying out to Vegas? Are you?"

"Let me grab a steak and a pot of coffee and I'm as good as new."

"What if we eat on the plane?"

They were flying the new Learjet 85 and would call the cabin attendants with food orders before they left the courthouse. Chicago's Midway Airport was a half hour away and the general aviation terminal would be cleared out by the time they arrived. The plane belonged to the law firm so there was no schedule to meet, no deadlines, just a great weekend opening up for the lawyers. Albert would captain the flight. Co-pilot Bill Burrell would fly the right-hand seat. Thaddeus would sleep most of the way.

"I'll call in the orders. You want a steak too?" Albert asked.

Thaddeus stopped dumping files into his briefcase. "Two enchiladas and a green chili relleno. Con arrozo y frijoles."

"Done."

They would be airborne in less than an hour, shoes off, ties loosened, full bellies.

The jury had returned a six-million-dollar judgment. The lawyers had just earned two million dollars in legal fees, and they would be getting repaid their $150,000 in costs.

The parents would receive four million dollars for the untimely and horrendous death of their angel. It was never enough, it solved nothing, but it made a statement. The statement said the parents could sleep tonight, knowing that the doctor, not they, bore responsibility for the tragedy.

They thanked Thaddeus and hugged him and Albert again for the verdict and left the courtroom.

Thaddeus and Albert followed close behind, watching the clients disappear inside the elevator.

They knew that for those parents it would be a quiet ride back to their empty house.

He shuddered at their loss, which Thaddeus still felt clear down into the pit of his stomach.

Then it was time to move on, time to prepare for the next courthouse war.

But first he would look in on the casino.

Slowly—so slowly—they were coming on-line with better casino management, better security, and better staff all around as Thaddeus grew more intimately acquainted with his acquisition.

Still, the whole business was like a beast that was eating away at more and more of his time. He was beginning to have serious second doubts about his decision to keep it and run it himself.

He had hired Mickey Herkemier and placed Mickey between himself and the casino as the general manager and CEO, but enough problems still found their way through the wall he had tried to erect. Thaddeus reminded himself of what Truman had said: The buck stops here.

The taxi took them to Midway Airport, where they hurried through the general terminal, stepped outside into the early evening air, and clambered aboard the waiting jet.

4

Ragman was demanding $1 million cash up front Lincoln Mascari pulled out all the stops to get it for him. From his office in Skokie he demanded his troops take down banks and double-up the narcotics traffic.

They hit the First State Bank of Arlington Heights and brought in $85,000 cash, with change.

The Greenville Farmers Trust in Greenville was next; it netted them $55,000 on a Friday when soybeans were being sold and money deposited by the farmers.

Hunnicutt Mutual Savings and Loan in Joliet coughed up $125,000 and its branch in Forest Heights added another $35,000.

Narcotics sales skyrocketed.

In three short weeks the cash was assembled and placed in a black valise on Mascari's ancient oak desk in the refurbished lube joint.

"I need you to chain this to your wrist and fly it over to LA," Mascari told Zann Roget, his long-time hussy and mother of two of his kids. "Guy's name is Ragman and he'll be waving a sign at LAX says 'Salvation Army.'"

"That's it? Just 'Salvation Army'?"

Mascari shrugged. "I know. It ain't much to go on, but that's how he wants to play. Now get outta here."

So Zann flew to LAX on a rainy Thursday morning, white-knuckled as they rose up through the clouds, and then relaxing when they topped out, the sunshine blazing down. Soon, the Scotch wagon clattered up the aisle.

She was half in the bag by the time they touched down in LA., with the valise chained to her wrist.

The key had been FedEx'd to Ragman, care of a Mailbox USA.

Walking tipsily up the jetway, she located the sign and saw the small, nondescript man holding it. He was wearing a relaxed-fit business suit and a red carnation in his lapel. "Hold still," he told her. He inserted the key.

Two seconds later she was free of the bag and he was gone with the outgoing crowd.

She waited three hours for her return flight and drank coffee the whole time. At 4:05 they took off, her with a headache, the 777 with a tailwind.

5

S he had graduated from UCLA, turned down several
guys who wanted to settle down and make babies
with her, and headed to Las Vegas to count cards.

The first couple months she had spent practicing her blackjack in the off-Strip casinos where nobody noticed her.

She soon graduated to the super casinos along the Strip, where she began to turn heads.

Slowly at first they began watching her, then she became a suspect, one who was probably counting cards.

So she had to refine her game, become less noticeable. She learned she had to suffer some losses in order to make them believe she was just an amateur who happened to be having a lucky streak. So she lost a few bets every night, here and there. Then when the deck shifted in her favor she would hit it big, scoop up her winnings, and move the party to the next casino on the Strip.

Before long she was earning $1,000 each time she went into a casino. It became easy to win and she was loving her life.

Then came the attack and everything changed.

The night of the attack, Thaddeus had been back in Las Vegas one day following the Kim Ehlers baby trial.

On returning to the casino he had shut the door to his office and begun learning everything he could about the casino on paper.

He had examined the books, studied the management records with Mickey Herkemier, studied staffing requirements and available staff, discussed security with the chief of security. On the second night back, he was going to take time to snoop around the floor of the casino. He believed in hands-on management and he believed that studying the players and the dealers was the best way to spend some time when all else was put to bed.

He noticed her right away.

There was something familiar but fleeting about her.

Maybe it was her hair, he guessed, or how she carried herself.

She was facing away, studying the blackjack tables, and he was unable to get a good look. But he stood by and watched. Something had made him look at her a second time.

Kiki Murphy was four months in Las Vegas when she walked into the Desert Riviera that Thursday night. She was alone coming in and she planned to be alone going out. She was attractive in a TV personality kind of way, well-muscled arms and legs, spray-on tan, looking like maybe she had at one time been a gymnast but gave that up when she grew six inches too tall.

Her healthy looks and blond wedge haircut would have easily landed her a job as a First Report news anchor, but that wasn't her. She was trying to remain anonymous on the Strip.

Her outfit was extremely ambiguous: khaki slacks, navy golf shirt with the Polo pony, ankle boots, sorority necklace and eyeliner only.

This was her fourth night in a row working the tables, where she was winning her $3,500 mortgage payment, due in two days.

The Desert Riviera staffers wouldn't know it until later, but Kiki was also packing heat.

Hidden in her Coach bag was a nickel-plated S&W .38 snub-nose.

She had zero intention of pointing it at anybody, much less shooting anyone—it was all about self-defense. There was just too much money flooding through the casinos. Sooner or later someone would see her win big, see that she was alone, and rob her.

So she bought the gun.

A purse model.

Like all gamblers, she was hedging her bets.

It just so happened Thaddeus was snooping the high-stakes tables when Kiki came through the rope.

He watched as she marched up to the blackjack dealer and plopped down $900 in black chips.

He watched the interplay between Kiki and the dealer.

She was adorable and Thaddeus could see the dealer almost smile. He guessed the dealer probably gave himself ten hands to clean her out. You could just see it in his eyes—his tell, his giveaway.

From where he stood Thaddeus had a pretty good view of four blackjack tables. He was looking for card counters. She was playing at the blackjack table closest to his left, table 11 (there was no table 13—gamblers know all casinos number their tables. They would never wager a bet at a table number 13).

Much to the dealer's dismay, after an hour she was still flush—$500 ahead, in fact.

Thaddeus couldn't stop smiling at the look of consternation on the dealer's face. He had found that she was an expert gambler. And maybe, just maybe, she was counting.

So Thaddeus continued watching.

If she was counting, out she would go as casinos abhorred card counters and routinely bounced them out the door.

Plus...there was something about her. Something familiar that he couldn't quite conceive into a full thought.

So he watched and watched.

Card counting was a mathematical exercise where the practitioner gave a +1 to some cards, a -1 to some cards, and a 0 to some cards. In that way the counter could knowledgeably estimate what card the dealer would turn over next. The more cards that were dealt, the more accurate the knowledge became and the more self-confident the bets. When the count reached +4 to +8 you would see the heavy bets come pouring onto the table. But when it submerged to a -1 to -8 the card counter might be betting one chip per hand—just so they weren't too obvious, which they would be if they stopped betting altogether.

So it was the timing of the bets Thaddeus was watching.

Plus that face.

He couldn't quite make it out, not from his angle.

Card counting wasn't illegal. He just didn't like it going down in his casino.

Neither did any of his competitors along the Strip. Get caught counting and they banned you. They emblazoned you with the modern-day equivalent of the "A" for adulterer. They ruined you by mailing your photo to every corner of the globe where there was a casino.

Which spelled ruin for the counters.

The other casinos reciprocated with the pictures of counters caught in their nets. Together, everyone avoided significant losses by their ad hoc network. It was a kind of quality control where the owners made sure everyone had a little fun, but not too much.

Kiki was a graduate of UCLA with a degree in mathematics and a minor in communications. Her honors thesis had been mathematical probability, so intellectually she was a universe above everyone who was being paid to catch her. But she was doing graduate study in the school-of-hardknocks with a major in card counting. Her plan was to become a top blackjack player and travel. She planned to live an opulent lifestyle and gamble in the cities where gaming was legal. She was even thinking of opening a 401(k). If she put in $1,000 a day she could retire in three years. That was as far as she had thought out any kind of plan. Win big, save big.

She won a $200 bet and leaned closer to the table, which, to Thaddeus, might be her tell, her giveaway.

So he watched her closely.

Before heading to Vegas, Kiki had turned down three proposals from hopeful young men in college.

First there had been the academician, whose brilliance ran to microbiology and grad school. This was the man her father favored.

Not Kiki. She knew she would wind up supporting him for seven years while he pursued a Ph.D., so she declined the fellowship.

Then there was the athlete, a wide receiver for the Bruins who stood 6-4 and tipped the scale at 205 and could out-leap a gazelle. But he had wrecked his knee against Stanford and she didn't care to spend her life hearing about what might have been, while he coached Pop Warner and ate his heart out.

So she put him on waivers.

Then there had been the musician, a guitarist whose riffs reminded everyone of Eddie Van Halen. But he couldn't keep his privates in his pants, so she declined to wager her perfect health against HIV every time she got it on with him.

In the end, she had packed up her Bug convertible and headed north the day after graduation, in search of her own success.

Now she played only the super casinos.

One night she would hit the Mirage, the next night Mandalay Bay, then the Bellagio, Circus Circus, Luxor, MGM Grand, and Thaddeus' place, the Desert Riviera.

She knew it was owned by Thaddeus Murfee.

She knew everything about him.

And she knew that he was watching her. Only he didn't really know why, but she did.

She started winning after an hour, raking in earnings more often than giving up wagers. Not enough to draw attention, just enough to keep the lights on and the cat happy with connoisseur tuna.

He saw that she was doing what card counters did best. She was placing small bets and counting cards while waiting for the percentages to change. When the percentages changed the light flipped from yellow to green. Then the big bets would be placed. The counters would step up and bet amounts as large as $500 a hand, then $750, then $1000, then $2500.

He wouldn't let that go on very long.

He would eighty-six her first.

With studied ease, she slid a stack of black chips worth $500 across the green felt.

Twenty feet away Thaddeus watched her place the bet and it immediately caught his eye.

The floor shift manager next to him, he could feel him stiffen, too. His job was to spot card counters, just like Thaddeus, and just like the dealer.

They knew that normally the casino had a two percent edge on blackjack, but that the capable card counters could quickly turn those odds around until they climbed as high as eight percent in favor of the player. Such odds were intolerable in casinos not just in Las Vegas but worldwide.

Thaddeus tried not to gawk at the young woman's play.

Like all good snoops, he was tall, 6-3, and even from a distance he could look down on her cards. She was showing a jack and a king on the $500 wager.

When she looked away he took three quick steps toward her.

It was not the amount of the bet that caught his eye and the eye of the shift manager. She was only betting $500 on the hand—a very small bet inside the rope.

And they had seen them all, from the $100 a hand to the $200,000 a hand gamblers, truckers to oil sheiks, and the size of the bet meant nothing.

But what piqued their interest was the timing of the young woman's bet.

Until that bet, she had bet the table minimum of $100 per hand, occasionally $200. Whether she won or lost didn't seem to matter, for she bet one black chip and only one.

Until now.

Now she had shoved out $500 and was trying to make it look as casual as checking out at 7-Eleven. Casual she wasn't. She twirled the sorority charm. He smiled.

She wasn't even aware of it. The touching of the necklace, the twirling of the charm, was her tell, her giveaway.

Which meant there was blood in the water. The odds had shifted her way and Thaddeus and the shift manager were guessing she knew it.

Thaddeus moved in on her.

6

I n most casinos the game of twenty-one is called blackjack.

It is the most popular casino game in America.

The object of blackjack is to get blackjack (twenty-one) without busting.

A player gets blackjack by receiving cards that add up to twenty-one. Face cards count ten, the ace can be one or eleven—the player's choice—and all other cards count at their spot value. Five spots and it is a five; nine spots and it is a nine, and so it would go.

And there was one other important rule. The dealer had to hit sixteen and had to stand on seventeen or above.

In other words, if the dealer had a face card (ten) and a six, he had to take another card.

What would he get?

A high card that put him over twenty-one and a loss?

Or would he get a low card that totaled him up to twenty or twenty-one?

Here was where card counting entered in.

Kiki Murphy knew when the odds were high for a high

card to be dealt, and she knew when the odds were high for a low card to be dealt.

By wagering these odds, she was increasing her chance of making the mortgage payment before Friday.

He was still watching and had just about made up his mind. She was just the kind of player he definitely did not want taking swings inside the high-rollers rope.

From his vantage point, it appeared certain that Kiki, with two face cards, was about to win her $500 bet. She was showing the king of hearts and the queen of clubs. One of the dealer's cards was face down—this was his hole card— and his other was face up. It was the six of clubs.

The worst possible hand for the dealer was a six. Whenever a dealer had a six showing, veteran players knew he was probably going to exceed twenty-one points because he had to hit sixteen.

So Thaddeus knew that if the dealer had a face card down, he would have to flip it over and then hit the sixteen, which meant if he got over five he would bust.

Plus he knew that the odds of going over five were higher than the odds of going under, because there were more cards above five than below.

Blackjack was only a game, but it relied on mathematics and right then Kiki's bets held the advantage.

The question for Thaddeus remained: did she know she had a mathematical advantage or was she only hitting a streak of good luck? Good luck was always temporary. Card counting could eventually break the bank.

And Las Vegas management never wanted to see the bank go bust.

Having the mathematical advantage was supposed to be the house's side, not her side.

So he moved a little closer.

Now he could smell her perfume.

It was a familiar smell, and his senses searched for a connection for another place, another time when he had come into contact with the perfume.

He kicked himself back to reality. Forget the perfume. If she were counting cards, she was about to be escorted out of the casino and told that she had been photographed and that she was never to return, under painful penalty.

He sidled two steps closer.

Then he made the fragrance: Balencia Paris, not a cheap stroke. So she enjoyed exquisite perfumes. Another two steps and he could reach out and touch her shoulder.

Which he did not do.

Instead he accepted a watery glass of Pepsi from a passing cocktail waitress, who was wise to his hustle and knew that he wished to appear to anyone watching like he was another cheap spectator out for a night of free drinks and some free gawking.

Then something incredible happened.

As he watched, Kiki split her cards.

This meant she moved the king next to the queen so they now lay side-by-side on the table.

The dealer looked up. He was surprised, like Thaddeus. "Are you splitting your cards?" he asked her.

"Yes," she replied.

Which caused Thaddeus even greater concern. The amateur would have stayed, showing twenty between the two face cards, and simply waited for the dealer to bust, raking in a pot of $500 on the hand. But not this gal. She was now playing two hands at once, by the split.

She slid five more black chips across the green felt to cover the second hand. She was betting $1,000 on the game.

The dealer dealt a new card from the shoe and placed it on her king.

It was the ten of hearts, which gave Kiki twenty points on her first hand.

Thaddeus watched her closely; her face—from the side —never changed expression. No tell.

This time she didn't twirl the sorority charm.

It was almost like her skill was improving as he watched.

She waved her hand across the king and ten, indicating she wanted no more cards there. She then waved her hand over the queen as if to say "come here," and the dealer dealt her a card for the queen. It was the nine of spades and Kiki waved her hand over these two cards, indicating she wanted no more for her second hand.

The hand signals were required because the eye-in-the-sky couldn't hear words, it could only pick up actions.

Somewhere up above, the prodigies in the surveillance room were watching all tables to spot cheating on either side of the deck. When Kiki put her cards side by side, the cameras knew she was splitting her hand. Eyes focused in on her. When she waved her hands over the cards the cameras knew she was ready to see what the dealer turned over. Every move was choreographed so the geniuses would instantly understand the drama playing out below their feet without anyone speaking a word.

She was now showing nineteen on one hand and twenty on one hand.

And it was time for the dealer to turn over his hole card.

He deftly flipped it up.

Queen of spades. Now he was showing sixteen, which meant he had to hit it.

Thaddeus watched her face and hands even closer.

Her expression never changed. Not a muscle moved.

There was no glee, which would have telegraphed that she knew she was about to win; there was no alarm, indicating trouble ahead. There was nothing. Just the look of a twenty-something who might be sitting through a college class taking notes in freshman statistics.

Thaddeus was puzzled but he wasn't ready to act.

Not yet.

Why?

She could still be innocent, unaware of the mess she was creating for the house. They gave her the benefit of the doubt.

The dealer dealt one more, the ten of diamonds, and he was bust. Twenty-six.

The dealer counted out five black chips and slid them out next to Kiki's ten black chips. He counted out another five black chips and slid them out to her second hand.

They lay there, twenty black chips worth $100 apiece, untouched by her.

Yet.

Instead of gathering in her winnings, Kiki slowly took a drink of iced tea and counted her four remaining chips—$400 to leave with if she lost the next hand; $4,000 to take home if she won.

She waved her hand, indicating she was ready to begin play. She was letting her winnings ride, so she was now betting $2,000; another win would net her $4,000.

They searched her name at that moment.

She had been greeted by the Desert Riviera hostess when she entered the high-limit gaming area. The hostess had tipped off the shift manager and he had entered Kiki's name into a wall-mounted computer at his station.

A flood of data on the young gambler was immediately returned.

Had Thaddeus seen it, he would have been shocked.

KIKI WAS TWENTY-THREE, single, lived alone in West Mountain Valley—an upscale condo development with all amenities—had no known means of support, owed $65,000 in student loans, $4,500 on a Visa charge used to purchase a sectional and coffee table for her living room, subscribed to HBO but not to Showtime or Cinemax, watched three hours of cable a night, and had her hair styled every two weeks.

Male callers were infrequent, although there had been one baccarat dealer who had stayed over twice, but since he worked at the Luxor there was no conflict.

Her Facebook page was the usual leftover college chums who were moving along with new lives and beginning to post birth photos of new family members.

Her favorite movies were action-adventure, and she had read *Divergent* and *Fifty Shades of Grey* in the past three months. She gave both books five stars.

Most important, she owed $350,000 on her condo. Her physician father had co-signed, and she had never been later than the ten-day grace period, though she had come close twice in the past eight months.

THADDEUS MOVED behind her and then to her left. He didn't want to be seen—he hoped he wasn't—but he needed a better view of her.

With $2,000 at risk, Kiki received a ten of hearts and the ace of diamonds.

Blackjack!

An automatic twenty-one points.

Which pissed Thaddeus just a little. That was too easy and it told him nothing about her skill.

The payoff on a blackjack is 150 percent, so she had won $3,000 in less than ten seconds. She now had $5,000 in the pot.

Despite Thaddeus' own efforts at staying poker-faced, he had to frown. This was not headed in a good direction. She could catch fire if the math was in her favor and she could quickly win twenty or thirty thousand dollars. Plus, winners magically attract other gamblers, which put the shoe—the remaining cards—at higher risk of paying off to even more people.

Now he closed up the last step.

He was at her shoulder and he could sense she was uncomfortable with him there. Still, crowding around a hot Vegas table was common, so she shrugged it off.

She left $2,500 on the table for her next bet and raked in $2,500.

Two more players bellied up to the table.

Obese thirty-year-old guys in new jeans, starched western shirts with the fold lines still in the fabric, and new cowboy hats. The stylistic implications of their clothing only went so far, as one was wearing white Nikes and one was wearing tasseled loafers. Not exactly cowpoke. They were out from Ohio for a three-day poker drive at the Desert Riviera and were down $2,000 in two days. The idea of a hot table reeled them in like starved fish.

Thaddeus paid them little attention. Nothing hip, slick, or cool going on there. Just drugstore cowboys looking to get drunk, win big, and be somebody.

The deal went around. Kiki got a queen. The drugstore cowboys hauled in a nine and a seven.

The deal repeated and Kiki got a second queen. The twosome got a queen and a jack, respectively.

The dealer now had an eight showing. Not a great look this time, either, for the house.

Thaddeus and the shift manager watched closely.

Would she again split her cards like she had with the exact same cards last time?

She suddenly waved her hand over her cards. She was going to stand on twenty.

Thaddeus wondered why she hadn't split this time. Was she that good that she had made him and was now looking like a rank amateur? Or was she just having a short run of luck?

The guy with nineteen stayed. The guy with seventeen took a hit, got a seven, and busted. He was out. He pushed off from the table and jiggled the watery drinks when he slammed his fist against the table. "Damn!" he cried and backed away, down another $100.

The dealer flipped over the hole card. Six of spades. Which, added to his eight, gave him fourteen points. He was required to draw another card. Four of hearts. Now he had eighteen and couldn't take another card, so Kiki's twenty won and the cowboy with nineteen won.

She raked in the $5,000. The mortgage was made; still...she should have turned and left, but didn't. The shoe was hot; the math gods were definitely in her favor.

Thaddeus could tell that she had gone beyond the hollow-pit-in-the-stomach feeling of losing her stake. So now what would she try?

What happened next would mean everything to Thaddeus and Matty Jones. Matty was a card counter himself. An expert. And such a prodigy that the Desert Riviera paid him to teach other dealers how to spot it. He had taught Thaddeus over the last couple of years, since Thaddeus had taken over. You couldn't have Matty's job without being a proficient card counter, the ruse was so common.

She continued playing—$100 bets, nothing big.

So Thaddeus began counting cards: +2, 0, -1, 0, +1, +3.

He noticed that when she should win, she usually did and when she should lose she usually lost. He also noticed that the count was in her favor when she would bet more than one black chip. When it was against her, she bet just one black chip.

It seemed clear that she was counting, but he still wasn't positive. The last thing he wanted to do was run off some amateur who just happened to be having a lucky night. That was very bad for business; word quickly got around.

What puzzled him the most about the whole past hour was how obvious she had been. She clearly knew who Matt was. Probably had figured out who Thaddeus was by now. And he guessed she definitely knew that Thaddeus was standing right beside her and watching her every bet. Yet she still played as if she were counting and didn't give a damn who knew it. She rocked along, never changing the expression on her face, never making eye contact, and drinking only iced tea.

Thaddeus was aching to get a good look at her face.

There was just something there, something he should know.

Finally the shoe ran dry, the decks were reshuffled, and the cards were again in favor of the house, as they always were on a new deal. The house had two percent on the players. That's the house odds in blackjack.

She bet one chip. Of course. He would have been shocked at anything larger. But he would also have been less suspicious of her if she had bet more.

She quickly lost $800 on $100 bets.

HAD Thaddeus only known how right he was—that she was an expert card counter—he would have bounced her right there. But he didn't know, and he wasn't positive she was counting.

He looked over at Matt.

He gave back a small shrug.

Which meant she was very damn good.

She suddenly scooped up her chips.

"Potty break," she muttered, and strode off toward the restrooms.

The wannabe cowboys looked heartbroken.

"Lady Luck," moaned one of them.

They ordered fresh whiskeys. When she hadn't returned in ten minutes they looked at each other. Agreement passed between them and they left the table.

Thaddeus figured they wanted to play at her table, wherever she had gone, and they were off to hunt her down.

The cowboys knew she was loaded, at least by their measure.

They grinned at each other. This would be easy.

THEY FOUND her at the other end of the high-limit floor. She was placing $1,000 bets on another blackjack table.

In fifteen minutes she racked up $15,000 in wins.

So the shift manager motioned Thaddeus down to that end.

Kiki's winnings had surpassed $15,000 by the time Thaddeus reached her table.

This time there was no doubt in his mind.

Thaddeus touched her elbow and whispered, "Can I get a word with you?"

She turned and looked. He was wearing the Las Vegas casino owners' mandatory navy Armani and Gucci loafers.

As she turned around, the eye-in-the-sky clocked her mug shot and, within seconds, thousands of casinos saw her face, learned her name, and were apprised of her game. Her school-of-hard-knocks study had officially come to a screeching halt.

At that exact same instant, Thaddeus saw who it was.

"What?" she said, all innocence now. With just a hint of indignation.

Thaddeus imagined that she had probably answered to Mom in this tone, with this attitude, in twelfth grade when she was asked how late she stayed out last night.

"Kiki?" he said. "Kiki Murfee?"

She frowned. "Kiki Murphy, Thaddeus. With a 'phy.'"

"What—what—"

"What, I can't gamble here? Because my brother owns the place? Is that a rule?"

"My God!" he cried. "I didn't know—you looked familiar, but it's been so long!"

"I started to send you an invitation to my graduation then didn't. You wouldn't have come anyway. So I came here."

"Pick up your chips and follow me," he said. The old protective urge drove him to get her away from all this.

"Well—who the hell are you?"

"I'm the owner. And you're counting cards in my casino."

"What the hell is card counting?"

"Let's not have a scene, Kiki," he said. "Just take your

chips over to the teller, cash out, and don't gamble here again. Or anywhere on the Strip. It's not safe for you."

She sniffed. "If you say so. But I still don't know what the hell you're talking about."

"Then you have nothing to worry about," he said. "Let's just leave it at this. I don't want your business and I don't want you gambling in my casino, whether you're counting or not. Maybe you're just too lucky for us. Now let's go sit down someplace quiet and talk. I'm glad you found me and I love you too much to just watch you walk out."

Her eyes narrowed. "I'll leave. But I'm telling all my friends about this place. They'll stay away in droves."

"I'll make a note of that. We'll have to increase our advertising budget to respond to your power, I'm sure."

He kicked himself. That last comment was unnecessary and snotty, but she was testing him.

"You do that," she grumbled.

"I will."

She turned in a huff and headed for the teller's cage.

"Kiki!" he shouted. Heads turned to look at him, but she continued on a direct path to where she could trade her chips for cash and leave.

Later, he would admit that he should have followed after her and maybe he would have noticed the two cowboys still on her tail. But he was unsure of where they were at as brother and sister, so he gave her some space.

She was young enough that she would take his orders and leave and probably wouldn't ever return. Which, he realized, wasn't what he wanted, so he motioned Matty over. "Have someone follow her," he whispered. "And for god's sakes tell them not to get caught."

Luckily for Thaddeus—and the casino—the CCTV

cameras watched the two dudes from Ohio shadow her outside.

From what he would later read in the police reports, she set out on the sidewalk between casinos. She was stamping along, head down, in a rage.

The two gentlemen came up on either side of her and grabbed an arm. A scuffle ensued and one guy got kicked in the groin. It wasn't a disabling kick and by now he was coming back at her with a full head of steam like a nut-kicked bull. But it had allowed her to break free and by the time he was within arm's reach, she had whipped the pistol from the Coach bag and had it pointing at the guy's heart.

He stopped, took two steps back, and began to raise his hands.

His hands were up to his shoulders when the gun fired. He was dead before he hit the ground.

The other guy froze but immediately raised his hands over his head.

She had enough presence of mind to tell him not to leave or she would shoot him too.

And she had enough presence of mind not to shoot this time.

CCTV along the Strip picked it up and three different cameras made three different recordings of the action from three different angles. Except they all missed the head-on shot, the angle from which the dead guy had observed.

The attack on Kiki Murphy was recorded and made available to the Las Vegas PD by the constant live feed their police system enjoyed. Long story short, the detectives had reviewed the film and the shooting before the patrol officers made it back to the station with her.

∼

CHARLES M. BERENSON, Director of Security at Desert Riviera Casino and Hotel, came into Thaddeus' office at midnight, a grim look on his normally blank face.

He slumped in a chair. It was late at night, two hours later than he normally hung around.

"We've got a problem," he said.

"Okay, go," Thaddeus responded.

"That girl you eighty-sixed, Kiki Murphy? Our guy John Voss started to follow her, like you said."

"I remember. What about her? Has she sued us already?"

"No, she shot and killed one of our customers."

"What! What the hell are you talking about?"

"Calm down. They weren't on our property when it happened."

"Okay, tell me exactly what you know."

"Evidently these two drugstore cowboys followed her outside. They tried to rob her, she shot one of them, nailed him in the heart. She's downtown at LVPD as we speak."

"You're sure they were our customers did this?"

"Our security monitors show them following her around our casino and then outside. CCTV street side shows the same two idiots taking her on. Evidently she was armed and they were clueless."

"Oh my God! Where is she, LVPD downtown?"

"I guess." He yawned. "Getting late."

"Do we know any great criminal lawyers?"

He spread his hands. "It's not our problem, Thad. Didn't happen on our premises. Let the cops sort it out. I'm going home to bed."

Thaddeus abruptly stood and began slipping on his suit coat. "I'm going downtown."

"Where? Why?"

"To talk to her. She's going to need a lawyer and I just want to make sure she doesn't give a statement before she's represented."

"Such as yourself?"

Thaddeus looked up. "Hey, did I say that?"

"Isn't that why you got yourself admitted to the Nevada bar?"

"Not hardly. I wanted to be able to represent the casino."

He smiled through tired eyes. "I know you. A lady in distress and all that."

"She's my sister. Take over here."

Thaddeus headed downstairs to executive parking.

There was no time to waste. His own flesh and blood was about to go through the horrors of hell in the criminal justice system, and he had to be there.

There was just no choice.

7

Traffic was nothing and he made it to the jail before 1 a.m. The Clark County Detention Center was located on Casino Center Boulevard, within a stone's throw of Goodfellas Bailbond and Blackjack Bond and Bail.

The receptionist studied Thaddeus' bar card, gave him two dirty looks—the second just for good measure—and buzzed him on through.

Inside he signed in at the main desk and was escorted to a meeting room. It wasn't much, just a blue enamel door, steel conference table, and six steel stools bolted to the floor. The fluorescent light gave the green walls a bluish cast.

He waited fifteen minutes.

They led her in, no cuffs no leg chains, and she took a seat opposite.

He was surprised to see she was still dressed in her casino clothes. No orange jumpsuit and flip-flops, no cuffs and waist chain, no leg irons. By now she was wrinkled, the clothes hanging limply from her frame.

Her eyes were red, bloodshot, her cheeks tear-stained.

She gave him a disgusted look. He could see she had been immediately disappointed.

"You. What the hell do you want?" she asked.

Her nose was stuffy and her hands shaky with fear. She managed to extract a cigarette from a hard pack in her shirt.

Remarkably, they had also left her with her lighter. Must be new people on shift tonight, he thought.

Her upper body shook while she lit up. She blew a hazy plume across the table.

He leaned away and she smiled.

"I just wanted to talk to you for a few. I'm sorry those two guys followed you from my casino. I should have picked up on them and I feel bad."

"Feel better now? You've made your amends, so get off."

"Kiki—you still go by Kiki, not Kassandra?"

A shaky hand brought the cigarette to her lips and she inhaled. "That's what I normally answer to. Until tonight. Now it's 'Hey you!'"

"I get that. Why did you come to Las Vegas?"

She shrugged. "Why did you?"

"Good question. It was kind of roundabout for me. But you came to gamble. Or did you come to find me?"

Another shrug. "I'm a gambler. Just like you. Except you're on the house side of the table. I'm on the players' side. But we're both playing the same game."

"Does Dad know you're here?"

"Sure. I called him already."

"What did he say? Is he going to help?"

She shook her head violently. He could see the rage in her eyes. "You know Dad: 'You got yourself into it, you can get yourself out.'"

Thaddeus shook his head. "Some things never change. Well...look. Will you let me help?"

"Do I have any choice?"

"There's always the public defender." He then remembered his most important message. "By the way, don't talk to anyone."

"I've seen enough TV. Don't give a statement, don't talk to any cellmates because they'll rat me out, don't fall asleep around the crazies they got me locked up with."

"You're not single-celled?"

"Nope. I'm in the drunk tank."

"Unbelievable. So. What's your name?"

"I told you. 'Murphy' with a 'phy.'"

"Why'd you change it?"

"Would you want to have your name associated with Mother?"

"I still use the family name."

"Yes, but you live way the hell gone somewhere else. Nobody knows."

"How'd you find me?"

"It was in the LA papers when you got the casino. It was huge news."

"And you came rushing up to Vegas to gamble in my place?"

She drew a deep breath. "Actually, something just like that, yes."

"Kiki, you shot and killed someone tonight. Has that sunk in yet?"

Her upper body shook. Her legs jiggled. She stabbed the cigarette between her lips and inhaled mightily. "You mean have I realized my life is over? Yes, I realize that."

"Maybe, maybe not. A lot depends on how you handle yourself in here."

"Like what is your best advice?"

He pursed his lips. Maybe he had found a chink in her

armor. "You do not talk to the police, the detectives, nobody. You hire the best criminal attorney in Nevada. If you'll do these two things, you've got a fighting chance."

"I already called Dad. He's still loaded with bucks, but like I said, he blew me off."

"Unbelievable."

"No, that's just how he is. You remember."

"Do I ever."

"Except I've now got ten grand to my name and that's not going to hire the best lawyer in Nevada."

"No, it's not. Someone's going to want at least a hundred grand up front before they'll touch your case."

"Agree."

"Look, why don't we do this," he said carefully. "Why don't I stand up with you before the judge in the morning? We'll come up with a motion for bail, which will probably be shot down because the district attorney will cry that it's a capital case."

"A what?"

"A death penalty case."

"They've got the death penalty in Nevada?"

"Capital punishment is legal in Nevada."

He could feel the hairs prickle along the back of his neck when he said that.

It was a terrible thought, his own sister sentenced to death for a fight that was not of her making. The old racehorse was starting to warm up.

Still, he neither wanted to be involved in her legal problems nor did he have the experience for it. Plus there was something about not representing a loved one, wasn't there? Some wise saying?

"So you would do that? You would stand up with me?"

"I would. But I've only defended a handful of murder cases. I'm not the guy you want long term."

"But it would be something for me to have you in the morning. The public defenders are never in your corner. At least not according to all the TV shows. They're always on overload and just want to plead you guilty and move on to the next file."

"Maybe that's true, I don't know about Clark County. Tell the truth, I've never appeared in criminal court here. I should really obtain another attorney to help me with this initial stuff."

"So you're tossing me to the wolves?"

"I'm trying to save you from the wolves. If you'll let me."

Tears flooded into her eyes despite her effort to appear immune from her life. "You know, I always had, like, this mystical dream of finding you. Like we would be siblings again and it would all be okay. And now it feels like you're going to abandon me again."

"Right now you don't need a brother for your lawyer. You need the best lawyer money can buy. And I can do that for you. I'm going to do that for you."

She looked past him, crying silently. "Whatever."

He tried to catch her eyes, but she wouldn't look at him.

He sighed. "I'll be in court in the morning and I'll have the top lawyer in the state with me. I promise you that."

Nothing.

She was gone again. It was no use to pursue her.

He knocked on the door and got the guard's attention. "We're done in here," he shouted.

He retreated down the hallway and was finally buzzed outside. It was cool and he was free.

It was time to make some calls.

8

Back at the office he was suddenly run over by exhaustion. He had been hitting it hard for eighteen hours. He called downstairs and ordered a pot of coffee and a cheeseburger.

His hands were shaking. He didn't know if it was from a protein low or from the reconnection with his sister. It was going to be a long night. Plus he realized he had missed supper.

Something inside tugged at him about Kiki Murfee— Murphy—the thought of her sitting back there in a cell surrounded by drunks and toughs, absolutely at a loss about what everything meant, without any help from anyone. Except for him. Right then he was all she had. Bad thought, he decided, and turned to his computer to find help.

He liked to say that his office was exactly what you would expect from a guy who owns a super casino on the Vegas Strip. It was loud, garish, and very gangsta because it had been decorated and outfitted by his predecessor, Bang Bang Moltinari, who was, in fact, a gangster. Everything was purple and orange, not Thaddeus' favorites, but at least it kept him awake that night.

It was like a Jimi Hendrix "Purple Haze" video just to walk in there. Three white leather sofas arranged around a slate coffee table the size of Vermont, his enormous kidney-shaped ironwood desk where a fourth sofa would have completed the square, thick luxurious carpet that had originally been white like rabbit fur but now wouldn't quite come clean and forever remained a tasteful shade of beige, Western art depicting horses, Indians, cows, and red mesas and violet sunsets, a wet bar along one wall, and two walls of CCTV screens that kept him updated on every square inch of the Desert Riviera Casino and Hotel.

The hotel occupancy rate was hovering at mid-eighty percent, the shops and restaurants were enormously profitable, and the casino was a money machine.

In his wildest dreams as a law student he had never imagined an actual river of money flowing through his life. But that was the casino business. And he kept it all legal.

The casino manager, Mickey Herkemier, was a transplanted CPA who had represented Vegas casinos all his life and he knew exactly, to the penny, how much came in and how much went out. Beyond that, it was all refinement, with reports and sub-reports and sub-sub-reports, the kind of financial analysis that makes CPAs very happy. They were a hugely profitable going concern, employees were happy, and the employee turnover rate was the lowest on the Strip because their wages and salaries were the highest on the Strip.

He turned to his computer with its three screens and Googled "Criminal Defense Attorneys."

Immediately the main screen filled with sponsored listings and the highest-ranked organic listings.

His immediate reaction was that Vegas was a hotbed of criminal activity, based on the number of lawyers clamoring to be noticed among the dozens and dozens of listings. So how to choose one to pry out of bed in the wee hours? Simple, look for the 24/7 listings. And while he was at it, make it a female, because it's a female defendant and male attackers. Might as well make it about the strong versus the weak right out of the gate, he thought, hating the sexist aspect of his thinking but recognizing that the system thrived on it. No offense.

Which brought him to someone named Priscilla X. Persons.

At first he thought the name was made up, so he browsed over to the Nevada Supreme Court attorney listings and, sure enough, there she was. It was evidently a real name of a real person—no pun intended.

So Thaddeus dialed her number.

A very sleepy voice mumbled, "P.X. Persons speaking. How can I help?"

"My name is Thaddeus Murfee," he said, "and I have a client in trouble with the law."

"What kind of trouble?"

"Homicide."

The voice perked up. "Really? Can he afford an attorney?"

"It's a she, and yes she can. I'll be helping with that."

"And who are you?"

"Thaddeus Murfee. I own the Desert Riviera Casino and Hotel."

Long silence. "Is this a joke? Is this really Thaddeus Murfee?"

"You've heard of me?"

"No, I just can't imagine the owner of a casino calling

me. I've never done any work for your company before, have I?"

"Not that I know of."

"What are you looking for, lead counsel?"

"I think so."

"Is she incarcerated? Strike that, obviously she is."

"Clark County Detention Center. Since tonight."

"Has she given a statement?"

"No, and I've warned her not to. I'm a lawyer too."

"Excellent. Let's hope she listens to you. What do you say I hop in my car and run over to your office?" She obviously had come fully awake now.

"Tonight? That would be fantastic."

"I assume she'll be appearing in court at nine in the morning. We need to get started right away."

"You know, I couldn't agree more. I'll have my people bring you right up when you get here."

"See you in sixty."

They hung up and he put his feet up on the huge desk.

Room service delivered the coffee and cheeseburger and he clenched his eyes shut and chomped the USDA Grade AAA beef. It was delicious and the coffee resuscitated him. Just what he needed. The fries were fresh and hot, not greasy. He didn't allow greasy anything from the seven kitchens.

As he sat there he thought about the other women in his life, Katy and Ilene.

Right then they seemed like they were a million miles away, and they might as well have been.

Katy was twenty-two and doing her first year in med school at Stanford. Sarai, their baby, was two years old.

Ilene was thirty-two, the mother of Eleanor, previous marriage, and now Andromeda, by Thaddeus. Andromeda was age two. They were living on a small horse farm in Illinois.

Both infants were by him.

It was a part of his life that seemed to shape itself on its own, and he just didn't seem to be able to get all the sides of it nailed down at once. He thought it was like setting up a tent in a windstorm. Fasten down one side and the other side flops up. Go around and nail that down and the first side flies up again.

That's what it felt like. Or like he was in a blender and his feelings were being pureed. It wasn't comfortable and he had no clear insights into any of it. Still, it was reality and it was his reality to deal with.

"Keep your dick in your pants," was his mantra.

He must have reminded himself a thousand times a day.

Before Ilene there had been one girlfriend in college and two dates in high school. He was learning, fast, about women and about himself. Las Vegas was home to the most beautiful women in the world, but that hardly touched him. His dance card was already way full. He was already over the limit on catches.

He had everything he needed in his suite. Just off his office, there was a penthouse with living area—two story—loft, and three bedrooms. The master with the Italian Carrera marble was his own.

He lived at the office.

Two other bedrooms were kept in reserve for visitors. So far there hadn't been any visitors, at least none that he would want that close by.

He went into his bedroom and lay down. The sheets were high thread count and satin, also courtesy of Bang Bang. That would all change, in time.

Maybe there would be time for ten minutes of REM sleep.

He had just closed his eyes and started to drift off thanks to his full stomach, when the phone buzzed. The operator told him that P.X. Persons was waiting to come up. He said to bring her on up.

Priscilla X. Persons looked as outrageous as her name. She had quickly brushed out her flaming red hair. Her face was friendly with freckles. She looked large-busted, though he couldn't be sure, because she was wearing a gray pinstripe suit. On her pinky was a diamond as big as a salt shaker.

She looked every inch successful, and when she shook his hand it felt like being in the grip of an NCAA wrestler. She meant for that grip to say it all about her, and it did. Tough, aggressive, tenacious.

He immediately felt she was for real.

"Please, sit down," he said, and they each took the center of a sofa, staring at each other across Vermont, probably twenty feet apart. There was nothing cozy about Thaddeus' office arrangement and it wasn't meant to be. He didn't like long visits. He wanted people to come in, say their business, and leave. There was just too much on his plate to fraternize over the course of the ordinary day. So he kept it impersonal, spread wide apart, and that worked just fine.

"Did you say you own the casino?" she asked.

"I did. I do. It's a long story."

"Impressive. What should I call you?"

"Thad. And you?"

"PX. I go by my initials, although some people call me Pixie, my close friends."

"I'll stick with PX and we'll see where it goes."

"That's perfect." She withdrew a tablet from her briefcase and attached the keyboard. "So, what can you tell me about the incident involving—name?"

"Kiki Murphy. That's M-U-R-P-H-Y."

"And you're Murfee, M-U-R-F-E-E?"

"Yep."

"Coincidence?"

"She's my sister. It's a long story, but she no longer wants to use the family name. Can't really blame her, where she's coming from."

"Fair enough. We can look into that later."

"Good."

She smiled and sat up. "What happened with the shooting?"

"Maybe it would be better if I showed you the CCTV feed."

"Go ahead. Let's see what they have against her."

Thaddeus clicked a button on the remote and a screen rose up out of the coffee table. It jumped to life and a recording played.

Kiki could be seen walking away on the sidewalk, when two men hurried up behind her and attached themselves to her arms.

She immediately kicked at one of them, caught him partially in the groin and upper thigh, giving herself just enough time to open the Coach bag.

The incoming assailant could be seen screeching to a halt and raising his hands, as if in surrender.

The video had no sound, but you could see when the shot was fired because the victim immediately fell face-down to the cement walk.

The other perp was almost comical as he reached for the sky and froze in his tracks.

She trained the gun at him and, for an instant, Thaddeus saw a look on her face that told it all. It was taking everything she had not to pull the trigger a second time. The guy was lucky to escape with his life.

At the corner of the screen, a bystander punched numbers into a cell and within minutes a squad car was on the scene.

The Strip was heavily patrolled, marked and unmarked, and a cop was never more than three minutes away. Never.

Three uniforms disarmed her and pushed her down in the back of a patrol car.

"So she shot the guy," PX said. She made a note on the tablet. "Not much to say there. She did the shooting. Now the question is, was it intentional or did the gun just go off. Is it self-defense? It sure as hell doesn't look like self-defense to me. The guy appeared to surrender. There's got to be a back story to this. Did you ask why she shot him?"

"No," he said. "And I don't know Nevada law that well. I don't know jack about self-defense."

"Nevada's 'Stand Your Ground' law goes back a hundred forty years. Never forget, this is still the Wild West. If you're attacked and in reasonable apprehension of great bodily harm or death, you're entitled to pull the trigger. That's what happened here, looks to me, if the guy keeps coming. But he didn't, he stopped."

She brushed a comma of red hair from her forehead. Her lipstick was bright red, which made her refrigerator-white teeth sparkle. Her nose had probably been toned down by the surgeon's knife, he could tell, because everyone in Las Vegas did "enhancement," as they called it. She was all in the game, 100 percent.

He liked her already.

So he decided to move forward.

"So can you help?" he asked.

"Can I take it on? Depends."

"On what?"

"On you."

"You mean will I pay for her lawyer?"

"Exactly."

"I will."

"I need one hundred grand up front. Tonight."

He stood up. "Come on over to my desk. I'll write a check out of our general account."

"Good enough."

"Will you attend the first appearance in the morning?"

"Absolutely."

He wrote the check and pushed it across the glass top.

"Thanks," she said, and folded it once. She carefully tucked the check inside a suit pocket.

"Okay, then," he said. "Past my bedtime."

"Do you stay here at the casino?"

He pointed at the far double doors. "Right in there. Saves travel time."

She smiled. "Incredible."

"It's a good life, I'm the first to admit."

"Holy shit. And how old are you?"

"Twenty-nine. Almost."

"Do you have a girlfriend?"

He shook his head. "Don't even go there."

She smiled slyly. "I was just kidding."

No, she wasn't.

She recovered from her lapse. "Okay. I'll call you after the initial appearance."

"Fair enough. I'll wait to hear."

"Good night. I can find my way back downstairs."

"Security is waiting right outside the door. They'll escort you."

"Got it. Can't be too careful."

"Something like that. House rules."

"And the house always wins."

"That's the general idea, yes."

"I thought so."

"So long, PX. Thanks for coming."

"Thank you."

Then she was gone and he was in the grip of total exhaustion.

He went straight to bed without even bothering to shower.

It had been a long day, but he was just about on the other side, and it was good.

9

The Desert Riviera was exactly what the original architects intended it to be. Which was an eye-popping edifice of architecture meant to inspire great visions of entertainment to anyone who ventured inside.

And it did exactly that.

The first year Thaddeus owned it, over eight million people came through the front doors. It was on the cover of *Newsweek* magazine and there was even a piece in *Esquire*, for the discerning gambler.

Initially, the forty-story model of a desert mesa facade was supposed to be covered with sixty square football fields of pink tinted glass. But partway through the build-out they decided the pink was going to break the bank and about halfway up they went with black instead. Now it was said it depicted the desert hues, night and day. It worked well at that.

If you checked out the casinos along the Strip—the so-called super casinos—you would see that each one of them featured a front entrance that was meant to overwhelm and impress the entering guest. Each one meant to make mom and pop forget their personal financial situation and be ready to spend whatever it would take to be a part of the glitz.

In Thaddeus Murfee's casino it was a diamond-walled cave with four-story ceiling, stalactites and stalagmites included at random (they all supported slot machines), all surfaces covered with tiny glass beads cut like diamond facets, backlit, that exploded with shimmering light when you entered the mammoth cavern.

Some people immediately slipped on sunglasses when they came inside.

It was blinding and it was incredibly beautiful.

The entire left-side wall was a thundering waterfall that created four-foot waves that ran across the rear and outside, where a flock of wave-riders waited, young and old.

It ran out for 300 feet and gently emptied back into a tributary that ran back inside the casino, along a hidden tunnel, and ended up gliding along behind the waterfall until you came to a dock where you could get out.

It was dramatic, expensive, and caused "Ooohs!" and "Aaahs!" from everyone who came inside.

If you came in and went directly across the cavern and up over a bridge that modeled the Golden Gate Bridge, you then took an escalator down into the casino itself.

It was all wildly gaudy, didn't hang together in an aesthetic sense, but emptied wallets and checking accounts by its impressive scale and the challenge of getting as rich as the casino owner. Everyone, in short, was there to break the bank.

Fat chance.

10

Ragman took the first $1 million—there would be another bag, after the job—and hid the money off-shore. All except for $20 thousand cash that he hid.

He shopped the second-hand stores for clothes. If somehow he lost or left behind a shirt or pair of shorts, he wouldn't want it traced. Same for the tools he would need—the knife, the pliers, the wrenches—all came second-hand.

From his condo in North Hollywood, he made his plans on MapQuest. Then he hit the Greyhound Bus Lines website. Routes were planned and times and distances committed to memory. Escape routes were laid out and tickets bought in advance.

He would have the kid within sixty days.

The tickets would still be good then.

And he would have the second million.

After that he planned to head to Costa Rica or some other banana republic and let his feet grow roots. He would never have to move again, and that was very appealing.

There would be women—lots of them. Tall ones, short, slender, obese—he had plans for all of them.

He had a yard sale and disposed of everything he owned. He vacated the premises, turned off all utilities, and moved to Fresno. He paid cash at the Twiliter Motel on Washington Street, kept to the shadows, and allowed his trail to grow cold.

He spent the days alone, flitting about unseen, and he avoided places like bars and restaurants where anyone might try to strike up a conversation or where the exchange of words would be necessary. He wanted no one to remember his face.

He bought an Amtrak pass after two weeks in Fresno.

He rode the train mindlessly, sitting at the windows, staring at everything and seeing nothing.

He tried to change trains every eight hours, always heading in some unexpected direction.

In Phoenix he dyed his hair blonde.

In Dubuque he purchased cosmetic contacts and changed his eye color.

Through it all, he paid cash, never once used his real name on any piece of paper, application, or ticket, and spoke to no one.

He was very practiced at this kind of thing.

He had to be.

After this one there would be no other job for a man like him.

A man who got hired because he had no limits with children.

Mickey Herkemier had all the tools necessary to manage a Las Vegas super casino.

He was thoughtful but bold, forward-thinking yet a student of economic history, a politician yet beholden to no man, and a calloused supervisor who deep down had a heart of gold.

The only problem was, the gold wasn't his.

It belonged to Thaddeus, but larger and larger chunks were missing, thanks to Mickey.

Mickey was involved in the time-honored Las Vegas tradition called skimming. For an experienced CPA the setup was simple.

Skimming wasn't a financial mystery. It didn't require a specialized knowledge of computer software, and a close circle of cheats was never recruited. Skimming required only a briefcase and a couple of minutes alone in the count room, where the money was taken from the cashiers and counted before it rode off on the Brink's truck.

At shift change, 11 p.m., Mickey hustled those two minutes alone.

In the room.

With the uncounted money.

A quick flip of the wrist—once, twice, three times—and $30,000 went home with him.

Three nights a week and Mickey was a golden boy.

Skimming meant that Mickey took a share of the winnings out of the casino before the IRS knew it was there.

And before Thaddeus knew it was there.

Mickey had been hired by Thaddeus soon after Thaddeus came into ownership of the casino. Mickey snagged the job thanks to his twenty years in casino management and casino accounting and casino compliance audits.

Thaddeus had immediately clothed Mickey with authority to do just about any job that would arise around the property.

In part this was because Thaddeus was a practicing attorney and away quite often, but it was also because Thaddeus made the greatest mistake anyone involved in a cash business can make.

He trusted.

Thaddeus had trusted Mickey to keep one and only one set of books.

Thaddeus had trusted Mickey to record and report all income, to keep things on the up and up, and to make sure the net profits went to the owner.

Which was Thaddeus.

Mickey at first responded like a saint.

The funds were tracked and traced and recorded in the $700,000 accounting system as only a CPA could do, and that was fine. The IRS stayed away. Thaddeus made a profit, and Mickey took home a sizable paycheck every two weeks.

Slowly a change came about. The American economy took its horrendous nosedive and people started losing their jobs and homes. Panic-stricken, they flooded Las Vegas for a final go at accumulating a large nest egg so they might ride out the worldwide calamity of real estate values down by 80 percent, unemployment hovering at 10 percent, and layoffs of hundreds of thousands of workers every week. But rather than winning a nest egg, they lost it in Las Vegas. Which meant the casinos boomed. During the recession, the Desert Riviera Casino and Hotel saw its income actually double and then triple. Weekly nets surpassed $3 million.

And it was all cash.

Mickey sized up the new boss. Mickey saw a young guy who didn't know up from down, and Mickey's inner angel lost its way. The skim took hold, slowly at first and then snowballed.

Soon he was skimming $100,000 a week and nobody was the wiser.

He opened an offshore account in St. Lucia and began flying down there every two weeks with huge gobs of cash strapped around his waist and legs. Deposits were made in three different safe deposit boxes inside the vault, as one wouldn't hold all the $100s and two soon filled up and three would soon be stuffed as well.

Still, nobody was the wiser.

Except for the one federal agency that referred to itself —lamely—as a service. The Internal Revenue Service immediately knew the skim was in at the Desert Riviera when net profits fell off by one percent against adjusted gross.

The IRS computers operated off an algorithm known as DIF—a way of comparing baseline values across entire industries. Brother, when 99 percent of the industry was earning an 11 percent profit, you better not be reporting a mere 10 percent because if you do, the IRS is coming for you. So Mickey knew better.

But still he kept at it.

That one percent was all it took to launch a massive IRS audit.

Soon the feds were backing up semi-trailers to the casino's loading dock and hauling away millions of pages of financial records. This massive garbage mound was fed to the IRS Crays where it was canned, analyzed, matched, and cross-matched. Projections were drawn and compared against actuals. Finally the numbers were reported to revenue agents who met in windowless offices and created strategies based on what the algorithms told them.

The Desert Riviera tell was simple. Money was being diverted and tax was going unpaid.

That was all it took for Mickey's betrayal of Thaddeus to take the worst kind of turn. Not only was Thaddeus losing money—thanks to Mickey—but his very freedom was about to be taken away. The IRS bullies were on it.

A grand jury was convened at the Lloyd D. George Federal Courthouse in downtown Las Vegas.

An Assistant U.S. Attorney named David Fisher walked the jurors through a labyrinth of slick accounting practices implemented by Mickey Herkemier and attributed to Thaddeus Murfee. Fisher wrongly claimed that Thaddeus used those slick practices to funnel off revenues before the IRS got its juice.

After ten solid days of whiteboards and complex CID testimony, the grand jury returned a true bill.

Thaddeus Murfee was indicted on twenty-two counts of tax evasion, perjury, and filing false tax returns.

The indictment was kept secret because Thaddeus was known to have access to huge sums of money and it was feared around the halls of justice that the casino owner would flee the country if he became aware of the indictment before an arrest was made and bail was posted.

The key condition to bail in these cases was always the passport.

They knew he had a jet. They wanted his passport.

Without a passport he could only fly to the fifty states.

And the IRS and the FBI and the U.S. Marshal's Service had offices in all of them.

Two special agents from the Criminal Investigation Division of the IRS were assigned the task of making the arrest and working in concert with the U.S. Attorney to guide the case along to a guilty plea.

Little did the IRS know it had indicted the wrong person.

What's more, it wouldn't have cared even if it had known.

The point with these cases was to stand up a corpse where a businessman had once stood and point at it for all the other business folk to see and to have the living daylights scared out of them. Cash businesses reported cash —most of it—for this very reason. Thaddeus Murfee was to become an IRS poster child for what happens to business proprietors who cheat on their taxes.

They expected he would eventually plead guilty on three or four counts, rot in a federal prison for eight years day-for-day, and emerge a broken man, penniless, with even his law license pruned away by the state bar association.

The casino would be sold to pay the tax, interest, and penalty on the civil side, where interest would be accumulating almost as fast as the billions owed to the Chinese by this same government.

A perfect result for a tax cheat.

Hollywood personalities and TV hosts had trod this path before him and now it was Thaddeus Murfee's turn.

The press releases were written, AP was given a heads-up, and CNN assigned an investigator to track the case even before it was officially announced.

The IRS was calling in all the publicity it could drum up.

It was time for Thaddeus to go down, down, down.

Or so they thought.

12

Ragman traveled Greyhound to Palo Alto.

He watched the condo where Thaddeus Murfee's daughter lived.

After the mother drove off to school, he entered the condo. Her routine coming and going was known by now. She lived on the clock and was totally predictable, which made her an easy mark.

The kid's name was Sarai. There were photos of her everywhere: refrigerator, living room (seven above the couch, horizontal, the baby in various poses for the photographer while lying on her stomach with a blanket covering part of her head, and again, another with her sitting up, reaching for a bright red ball, and on and on in the typical poses preferred by the photographers commissioned to photograph two-year-olds).

There were signs of Thaddeus Murfee himself everywhere.

Ragman had established that Murfee visited the condo every other week, and, when not there, mama and the kid would go out to the airport and board Murfee's jet for Vegas, where they would spend the weekend. It was obvious the little girl was adored—even idolized—and Ragman knew it would require very little persuasion for Murfee to turn over his net worth when the kid went missing.

He walked around the neighborhood where the mother and child lived, considering whether he might want to take the child from the Palo Alto area, or whether he would grab her in Las Vegas. So much of the plan depended on how close by there were escape routes and hiding places where you could hole up with a screaming kid and not be noticed.

More and more he was leaning in favor of Las Vegas, as the desert was close by and there were huge empty places where no amount of screaming would be noticed.

Places where only the coyotes would give a damn.

13

Aldous Kroc—Badge No. 344536—was middle-aged, paunchy, hated all TV sports, loved *Storage Wars*, and was legally blind, corrected to 20/20 by eyeglasses that made his eyes loom large as hen's eggs.

His skin was like tissue paper, with a bluish tint that turned navy blue at the tip of his lemon-sized nose.

He was exact, he was precise, he thought the Internal Revenue Code one of the books of the Bible, and he studied esoteric topics such as "hobby loss rules" and "net operating loss carryovers" and "like-kind exchanges" at night in bed before falling asleep. It wasn't the best idea for before-sleep reading because the study left him enervated, full of pep, and ready to arrest someone.

Kroc was, by job description, a tax cop, officially known as a Special Agent with the Criminal Investigation Division of the Internal Revenue Service, Treasury Department, United States of America.

He loved his job, he lived for his job, and at age forty-five he was personally responsible for the jailing of over 650 white collar criminals whose key crime was the failure to report income on their income tax returns.

He carried a gun and a badge and rated "expert" every month when he qualified on the ATF shooting range.

Kroc's partner was Mathilde Magence, whom everyone knew as "MM" around the halls of the criminal investigation division in Las Vegas.

Magence hailed from Puerto Rico. She was blessed with dark-skin, which in the blazing sun of Nevada was some protection from the UV rays. Her eyes were hazel and full of good humor—a nice counter-punch to partner Kroc's plodding, dull manner that irritated taxpayers.

Magence was thirty-two years old, a graduate of Princeton on an S.I. Howerton Scholarship, and she had scored the top score on the 2002 CPA exam, Maryland. Which earned her a juicy job with the Service.

She had a warm smile, tiny white teeth, and wore bifocal contacts that caused her blink rate to exceed 175 percent, which was off-putting to some taxpayers. Still, of the team, she was always the first to initiate contact with any subject, since her sweet manner and happy tone were disarming and MM could be counted on to get admissions out of the unwary before Kroc jumped in for the kill.

In short, she was the human being, he was the robot.

They were gathered in his cubicle, pawing over Thaddeus Murfee's personal tax return for the fifteenth time.

The studied grumblings of the IRS computer had flagged Murfee's 1040 return for reasons known only to the computer, as the algorithm that flagged some returns and ignored others was always a secret, like the formula for Coke, and no one, not even the criminal investigators, knew how it worked.

They only knew that when a number came up it was very much worthy of more investigation.

These two confidants worshiped the IRS computers like the Egyptians worshipped the pyramid, the Incas worshipped gold, and the Chinese worshiped petaflops. The fastest American supercomputer in the latest top ten was Titan, the only Opteron-based system to make the top tier. Titan used about half a million main cores and a quarter-million NVIDIA-provided accelerators to produce 17.5 petaflops of computing power to its users at Internal Revenue Service Centers, where terminals were available to a select few, 24/7.

Special Agent Kroc held a passkey and he used it.

He knew more about Thaddeus Murfee than Murfee himself. He told Magence what he had learned.

"This guy owns a casino and he's only twenty-nine?" she said, frustrated and impressed at the same time. "I mean, what the hell!"

Kroc scowled. "He took it away from Bang Bang Moltinari and his son-in-law. I've already reviewed the court records. It was all above-board."

"What's his basis in the casino?"

"Basis" was a term of art in the tax code. It meant, simply, how much the casino cost him. Or how much did he give for the casino—two very different concepts among the Internal Revenue Code enthusiasts.

Kroc hunched his shoulders and flipped through the 1120 corporate return for the Desert Riviera Casino and Hotel, Inc. He thumped the three-inch-thick filing with a pale finger. "Difficult to say. It was valued at one point by a team of experts and it looks like that's the figure used by the corporation's CPAs to formulate the schedules on the 1120 forms."

"Well, casinos are cash businesses. That right there is a red flag. Titan says there's a 99.8899 percent certainty he's skimming cash and there's huge amounts going unreported."

Kroc pursed his lips. "We have the indictments. Let's reconstruct his lifestyle expenses and see if they exceed what he's reporting as income."

"Starting with an inspection of his home, his cars, his bank accounts, his assets—hell, Kroc, I might even let you take a peek up his ass."

He ignored her humor. "And ending with his expenditures. It's going to be a huge job. His personal return is a hundred twenty-five pages long."

"Let's crank out the notice for interview and send it off to him."

Kroc scowled again. "Nix. Let's show up unannounced and flash a badge in his face. Put him back on his heels. Let's arrest him and bring him in for questioning."

"You're the senior officer. Let's do it then."

"Tell you what. We'll bring him in late Friday. That way he can't get bail set until Monday and he'll have to spend the weekend in jail."

"That's brilliant," said Magence. "It'll give him time to think about cheating Uncle Sam out of taxes he damn well owes."

"Friday it is, then."

Kroc felt a chill run down his spine. He totally enjoyed intimidating taxpayers. Sure they paid his salary, ultimately, but, to Aldous Kroc, the truth ran deep. Which was, taxpayers were all guilty of falsifying tax returns, even if the fudge was as minuscule as phony deductions for clothing donations to Catholic Charities.

They were all cheats.

At least that was Kroc's worldview.

Now if he could only nudge Magence further toward that same viewpoint.

She had proved to be a difficult agent to manipulate, he thought, and was all too willing to give the taxpayer the benefit of the doubt.

One day he would permanently disabuse her of that notion.

Then they would make the perfect team.

14

The morning after the shooting dawned hot and clear in Las Vegas, with a chance of intermittent sunshine broken only by sunshine. According to Channel 4 News at Ten.

Thaddeus accompanied PX to the initial appearance of Kiki Murphy.

It was his idea to tag along, as he had realized there might be an issue with bailing her out and he wanted to be there.

As it turned out, the District Attorney had decided to charge the case out as a first-degree murder case and argued violently against bail.

PX argued back just as spiritedly, pointed out the family's (Thaddeus') strong ties to the community, and the judge —who was reminded of his own daughter by Kiki—set bail at $10 million.

Thaddeus called Mickey at the casino. They presented Goodfellas Bail Bond with a check for $1.5 million for the 15 percent fee.

They waited around while Kiki was discharged from

custody and then they gave her a ride back to the Desert Riviera. Her Bug was in the Desert Riviera's valet lot, where it was left the night before.

It was one o'clock by the time they made it back. "Let's get lunch," Thaddeus said to PX. "You too, Kiki, if you have another hour, please."

"Sure."

He had a temporary solution for Kiki. The most important thing was to have her where he could keep an eye on her. He realized at that point that he was thinking like a big brother. Then he realized that maybe it was about time, that her situation was presenting an incredible opportunity to have his sister back in his life. Like him, she had grown up with two strikes against her. Now she was facing a third, and he swore inside that he would do whatever it took to prevent her striking out.

So the first order of business was to offer her hope, some kind of possible solution, even short-term.

Henry Landers down in Navajo-land had taught him about solutions.

They all agreed they were famished.

They ducked into the Floating Gardenia Brunch n' Lunch cafe and ordered salads. Additionally, Kiki ordered coffee—as if she needed the spike, Thaddeus mused—PX ordered Darjeeling tea, and Thaddeus chose Diet Coke.

Of the seven restaurants in the casino, the Gardenia was probably his least favorite, but it was the fastest, and it was pretty clear that Kiki just wanted to get somewhere and get herself cleaned up and gathered together. She had a bad case of the shakes and just kept repeating, "Oh my God, I can't believe I actually shot someone!" Clearly there was still some shock terrorizing her.

PX would pat her arm and encourage her to take deep breaths and slow her pulse.

Thaddeus decided to make his proposition right up front. He wouldn't press her for an answer; she'd definitely need time to get things in perspective and time to think it over.

"So," he began, "how long have you been counting cards?"

"A few months. But I guess that's over, now that I've admitted it and now that I'm going to prison." Her voice was anxious. Her eyes were bloodshot and her lips chapped. Her hair was matted against her head on the side where she had tried to sleep upright against the wall of the cell. When she handled her coffee and creamer her hands shook such that the coffee slopped over.

He gave her a big smile. "Relax, okay? You've got PX in your corner and you're not going to prison. As far as card counting, it's casino policy to plaster your picture on everyone's website so the shift managers and dealers can spot the counters. You're not being singled out and you haven't done anything wrong by counting. It's just that casinos don't like the odds when they favor the customer. Never have and never will."

"I understand."

She stirred half-and-half into her coffee. Hands shaking, she struggled to get the cup up to her lips. She managed a sip and her face relaxed.

"The murder charge is just something you're going to have to go through."

"Which is where I come in," chimed in PX. "You've done the first thing you needed to do, which is hire the best criminal attorney in Vegas. I'm your gal for that."

Kiki nodded. Her lips were tight and her face a white mask.

Thaddeus wanted to reach out and touch her arm, but restrained himself.

Go slow, he thought, go very slow.

"Will I go to prison?" she asked after several moments while the two lawyers let her mull things over. "Is that a certainty? Tell me the truth, I can handle it."

"It's not good, Kiki," said PX. "The video shows the guy starting to retreat from the gun when it went off."

Tears came to the young woman's eyes. "That's just it! It just went off! I swear, I didn't mean to shoot anybody."

Thaddeus reached over and touched her arm. She didn't pull away. "We'll get to how it happened, Kiki. That's something you and PX will discuss when I'm not around. I'm not your attorney and you don't want me to be a witness to anything you say at this point."

"You mean I can't talk about it with you?"

"I mean you should discuss your case with PX and only with PX. Nobody else."

"Do I talk to Dad? I know he'll call."

"Here's what I'd ask you to do," said PX. "This is my card. Have your dad call me if he wants to discuss the case. Let me manage that conversation for you. But please, don't you discuss it with him."

"Because he could be called as a witness in my trial."

PX smiled. "Exactly."

"So what do I do, just go back to my condo and do nothing? Just wait to go to prison or whatever?"

"Maybe I've got an idea about that," said Thaddeus. "I think I just might."

"Will I be card counting?" She meant it as a joke, but no one was amused.

"You seem to be bright and quite good at the whole thing. So maybe I've got a proposition for you."

"I hate it when men say 'proposition' to me. I've turned down some very lucrative offers since I've been here."

Her attempt at humor, thought Thaddeus. At least the kid had guts.

PX laughed. "That's Las Vegas. And you haven't even begun."

Thaddeus plodded ahead. "Hey, it's nothing like that. But I want to offer you a job."

Kiki lifted a hand. "I don't strip and I don't hook."

"C'mon—"

"And I don't want to work in an office. I'll go back to school and get my education hours and teach if I have to. Follow me?"

"I do follow you. But none of that is what I had in mind. I would like to start you out as a spotter."

"What's that?" she asked, hardly intrigued at the title.

"It's kind of a security-management job. Just below shift manager, though."

"What would I do?"

"You would watch players. Nothing else. You would look for card counters."

"That I could do. I've gotten pretty fairly good at it. For example, I know when anyone else at my table is counting too."

"Hey, you told the judge your degree is in math? That sounds like the perfect background to me."

She smiled for the first time that day. "Look, big brother, I didn't get a chance to say thanks for helping me with bail today. And with PX. That was a huge."

He shook his head. "PX will be a huge help. She'll get an investigator on it later today."

PX nodded affirmatively. "Already done. I texted the office on the way back here."

"Will anyone sue me for shooting the guy? Assuming I don't go to prison."

"If there's a widow, she might make noises. But you're probably judgment-proof."

Tears came to her eyes. "I wet my pants, but nobody knew."

"So you probably want to just get home and get cleaned up. Get some sleep. So how about this? How about you think about my offer for a day or two and then we'll talk. Here's my card."

She looked at his card. "You really do own this place."

"I really do. That's another story for another day."

"How much would I be earning?"

"I hadn't got that far," he smiled. "What do you think would be fair?"

"I don't know. Forty thousand? Isn't that about what new grads are getting?"

"How about sixty grand with two weeks paid vacation after twelve months? Plus a matching 401(k) up to eight percent. Plus there's our casino employees credit union, life and health coverage."

"Wow. That's more than fair. I think I want to say yes but I should really talk to Dad. He'll be relieved if I tell him I've got an actual, real job."

"Dad is definitely like that."

She looked at his ring-less hands. "Are you a dad?"

He paled. "Two kids. Sarai and Andromeda. Andromeda is two months older. I'll show you pictures when you come to where I live."

"So you're married?"

"No."

PX smiled. "That's private, right, boss?"

He grimaced. "As private as living in a fish bowl can be around here."

15

The Desert Riviera jet delivered Katy Landers to McCarran International Airport at 7:30 that night.

It was a Friday and she was tired from a long week of med school classes at Stanford. She was wearing jeans, leather sandals, a Hensley shirt, sunglasses perched on her head, and a modern squash blossom necklace. Her black hair was braided and reached below her shoulders. She was 5-7/120 and very fine-boned. It was common for her to look at her hands and remark, "Those look like surgeon's hands. Maybe pediatric surgeon's hands."

Attached to her hip—as she and Thaddeus joked—was the two-year-old Sarai. The little girl was happy and clapped her hands, thought beds were trampolines, and was, according to her parents, brilliant. Her eyes were blue, her fat arms and fat legs were beginning to lengthen—she would be tall, like her parents—and she loved *Sesame Street*.

In addition to a twenty-five-pound baby bag, Katy brought along her book bag, which she usually did when she came down for weekends—which was almost every weekend.

Thaddeus was there to meet her when she plodded down the air-stairs. With her hands full, baby arching her back to be put down, Katy was looking Friday-night-exhausted.

They hugged, kissed, and said their hellos even as Thaddeus was taking his daughter and holding her over his head and making faces, much to the baby's great delight. She liked it so much, in fact, she drooled on her father's face.

Thaddeus turned to Katy and his heart jumped in his chest like it always did when he first saw her after one of these necessary separations. She was a first-year med student. He was a first-year casino owner. The baby was a two year. As they joked, you can't hang with us if you're not in your first couple years of something.

They loaded into the back seat of the black Mercedes. The car seat was already in place; Thaddeus proudly kept it in the car all week even when his daughter was back in Palo Alto with her mother. It represented something incredibly neat to him and he was proud to show it off. There was also a wallet-full of photos always at the ready for anyone who would stand still. One set was of Sarai, the other set was of Andromeda.

Tony Blake was driving. Tony had been with Thaddeus about six months. He was a BAG agent—Beta Armed Guards—and carried a concealed firearm, as he was also Thaddeus' personal bodyguard. If Thaddeus was close by, Tony Blake was close by as well. Thaddeus still didn't trust the mob remnants in Chicago, and Tony had been trained not to trust anyone anyway.

Tony raised the blackout panel between front and back seats, giving the young father a wink in the mirror. They set off along Wayne Newton Boulevard, headed back into town.

"Your stomach is looking very flat, like you've lost all the baby fat," Thaddeus said, which he immediately regretted saying. He always felt shy with her at first, and usually found himself saying dumb things when they were first back together. He was anything but smooth.

"I still hit the gym for at least two hours before classes," she sighed.

She took his hand in hers.

"I don't know if I'm going to make it through the school year or not, not with her. She takes up every minute when I'm home. Actually I shouldn't say it that way. I give her every minute of my time when I'm home. I wouldn't have it any other way. When I study is usually when she's sleeping."

"Does Esme help?" he asked.

"I couldn't do med school without her. She gets up and gets Sarai dressed at six o'clock when my alarm goes off. We all have breakfast together then I spend an hour playing with Sarai. About eight I head off to school. Back home by four—you know my schedule. Thank God it's Friday. I need you to be the chief caregiver with Sarai this weekend. I'm beat."

"I've got it," Thaddeus said, and finger-brushed his daughter's blond hair. "It's coming in."

"It is. Where's she getting blond? I'm brunette, you're brown. She's blond?"

"I was too when I was a baby. I showed you the pictures, didn't I?"

"Yes. I know you were."

"So you were kidding me."

She smiled and laughed. "Had you thinking it was the milkman, didn't I?"

"Hardly. You were a virgin when I met you."

She scowled. "Dream on, buster."

"Hey! Didn't you tell me that?"

She raised her hand. "I'm taking the Fifth. No confessions today. Call my lawyer. His name's Thad."

They laughed and settled back for the ride into town.

After a comfortable silence, Thaddeus asked, "What would you like to do this weekend? I mean besides dump Sarai on her doting father."

"Study. And eat some decent food."

"You're kidding. You're not eating good food at home?"

"Not like I should."

"Do we need to get a dietitian?"

"My doctor has given me an eating guide."

"And you're taking iron? Are you still anemic?"

She punched his arm. "Of course, Thad. What do you take me for?"

He looked out the window. He wanted to say, "I take you for a very stubborn but brilliant woman," which he didn't say. Instead he said, "I'm just double-checking. This is my first time being a dad and—"

"And what?"

"I almost said 'and a husband.'"

She frowned. "There's a topic for you. How is Ilene coming along with Andromeda?"

It was turning into a sore subject, but he couldn't blame Katy. Somehow—as if he didn't know—he had had born to him two children within the span of two months. Ilene Crayton in Illinois was the mother of his son, Andromeda. She was determined to help Thaddeus see his son as much as possible, and Thaddeus was grateful. He was extremely grateful he could provide for both babies—and their mothers—and they both had told him he was an excellent father. He was determined to be the best he could be.

"Ilene is coming along fine. Andromeda talks to me every night on Skype."

"Talks? Serious?"

He shrugged. "You know what I mean. I read him a story every night on Skype."

"Is he talking?"

"He knows my name. 'Da.'"

"So does Sarai."

"Hey, it's not a contest."

"How often do you talk to Ilene?"

"Every night, just like you. She updates me on Drommie's day. And I call her to see that she has everything she needs."

"Does she have anything you need? That's the question of the day."

Her voice had an edge to it that told him she had been thinking about their situation.

Of course.

More and more his marital status was creeping into their conversations. Bottom line, she wanted to get married and he had something blocking him from proposing, though he couldn't say what it was. It just wasn't time yet.

"Will you stop it? Can't you see I've made my choice? You're here with me. She's not. It's that simple."

She sniffed and looked out the window, lost in her own thoughts.

This was an issue that was not improving with time, though he had naively hoped it would. Something more was going to have to be done to cement with his relationship with Katy. Something besides words.

He had a slight shudder and decided to put that on the back burner. For now, they were going to have a fun weekend together.

"So, besides study, what else would you like to do this weekend?"

She shook her head. "Definitely not hang around the casino gambling. That's a total turn-off to me, that whole scene."

"I know that. It's getting that way to me too, truth be told. Anyway, we can swim, we can go hiking, we can take the helicopter over and see Henry, go water-skiing, catch a Broadway show—your call. I just want you to have a great time."

She smiled. "I would love to spend an afternoon with Henry. I miss that old guy."

"That would be perfect. Tomorrow? We could leave around noon and be there by one thirty or so. Do you know if he's up in the cabin or will we catch him at the hogan?"

"We talked last night. He's up at the cabin with his sheep. He's somewhat croupy, with a chest cold. I'd really like to check him out because of that, too."

"You're the doctor."

"Say that in four years. I'm still first year, remember?" She laughed. "But it does sound good. 'Doctor.'"

"So tell me about your project in HumBio."

"For my HumBio internship, I'm working on cardiovascular stem cells, trying to coax them into becoming capillaries that could resuscitate a dying heart. That's it in layman's terms."

"Is it going to work?"

"What do you mean?"

"Will they become capillaries?"

"I'll let you know when the internship ends. But it looks hopeful."

"I'm impressed."

"I know, me too. I hate to leave my stemmies, even for just a weekend."

"You hate to leave your stem cells."

"Yes, wouldn't you?" She was almost defensive.

For a moment he worried that it was too much for her, traveling back and forth on weekends, and he made a mental note to look into changing the routine so he went there. The casino wouldn't dissolve without him. More than anything, he wanted life with Katy and Sarai to work and he wanted her to be happy with their arrangement. But she was an honest lady and she would help him get to wherever it was they were going—he was certain of that. She didn't play games, and that was a must. They would work it out, and they were both comfortably certain about that.

They pulled into the casino's underground parking and headed for the reserved spot, directly in front of the elevator.

Tony helped with her two suitcases, Katy grabbed the book bag and the diaper bag, Thaddeus hefted Sarai onto a hip and up they all went.

16

T hey made it out to Henry's meadow just before two o'clock Saturday afternoon. A crew Thaddeus hired out of Window Rock had cleared a small landing zone and fenced it off from the sheep, so the helicopter had the perfect place to put down.

The sheep were grazing in the meadow, a curl of wood smoke hung in the air over the chimney, and Henry appeared on the front steps to wave enthusiastically at them. Katy had called him on the satellite phone and given him a heads-up, so he was expecting them.

The sun was blinding at that altitude and the air was warm.

A hatch of dragonflies flitted and droned across the knee-high grass in the meadow, along with an Egyptian pharaoh's worth of grasshoppers, crazily jumping on the three visitors as they left the landing zone.

Hiking across the meadow toward the house, Thaddeus could see that Henry was wearing jeans, boots, and a flannel shirt, though it was warm even up at 9,000 feet. He had a checkered bandanna around his neck and new eyeglasses perched on his nose.

He looked to be in bright spirits as he smiled and waved for them to come in.

The men shook hands after Katy had hugged her great-grandfather for nearly a minute.

"C'mon in," he told them. "Don't be strangers. Now let me hold that baby!"

Henry took a seat on the day bed, arms outstretched, and Thaddeus nestled Sarai against his chest. The baby planted her feet against Henry's legs and stood on her tiptoes. She flopped a wet hand against his craggy face. He turned and kissed her cheek.

"This is your solution," he told the young couple. "This is the best it will ever be. Your age, new baby, income, no wars to go to, doting grandfather."

They laughed.

Henry pulled the baby close and inhaled her baby fragrance. Delight came into his eyes and joy lifted his face.

"I've been wanting to catch up with this one," he said. "Now I'm holding her and she's almost a century younger than me. So much I could tell her, so little she cares to hear. But she will. I think I'll stick around for that."

"Of course you will, Grandfather," Katy said. "Here, let me change her diaper before she springs a leak."

Henry returned Sarai to Katy and clasped his hands on his knees, prepared to be the perfect host. "Water?"

"I'm good," Thaddeus replied. "We keep water on the chopper."

Katy immediately went over to the sink and began going through things. "What have you been eating, Grandfather" she asked.

Henry moved across the room and took a seat in the

recliner. "Beef stew. Dinty Moore beef stew. It has every-thing: protein, vegetables, vitamins, gravy—"

"Funny boy," she said. "Beef stew has exactly none of what you need."

Henry shrugged. "It's filling. I need that. And it comes ready to heat."

Thaddeus took the baby from Katy and took the over-stuffed chair with felt fabric. It was springy, but comfortable enough.

The baby began bouncing in his lap and he smiled. He would hold her every minute of every day, were that possible.

Katy stood before Henry. She jammed her hands against her hips, ready to get down to business, the real reason for the visit. "How are you feeling?"

He nodded. "All right. Something in my chest."

"Does it hurt?"

He nodded again. "It does hurt, but only a little."

"Are you coughing up anything?"

"I am."

They discussed his health issues for several minutes. Thaddeus reviewed the cabin. In a flood of memories it all came back—the time he had lived there, the lawsuits he had filed, the woman he met while living in the mountains, the peace and solitude of watching over the grazing sheep, catching fish out of the rushing stream, all of it came back.

For a minute he could feel his eyes moisten as he real-ized just how much he loved the place. He wondered if his own life would ever be this peaceful. Probably not, he decided, and turned his attention back to Sarai.

Katy turned to him. "I think he needs to see a doctor."

"We can make that happen."

"Like stat. Right now, today."

"Well, we've got wings and we've got a house doctor at the casino. Do we fly him back?"

"Absolutely."

"What about the sheep?"

"Now hold on," Henry said. He waved his ninety-eight-year-old hand at his great-granddaughter. "I can't just leave my sheep here unattended. You know I won't do that."

Katy looked at Thaddeus.

He shrugged. "I'll stay with them. You can ride with him back to the casino. Take Sarai in case the sheep need me. Seriously. We've got the helipad on the roof and I can call ahead and make sure Doctor Ralston meets you as soon as you touch down."

She stared at Henry.

He finally nodded and spread his hands. "If you say so. It's not that bad, though. I'll be back tonight, Thad."

"That's fine. Everything's under control back in Vegas. It would do me good to wait around out here while they look you over."

Katy smiled at Thaddeus. She stooped down and gave him a wet kiss. "Thanks, buddy," she said.

He handed her the baby, who took her assigned spot on mom's hip.

"No problem. I'll take care of things. What's on the menu, Henry, in case I get hungry tonight and you don't get back?"

"Two cases of beef stew under the sink."

"Perfect. I'll survive then. Go tell Jackson he's flying you back to the Desert Riviera. I'll call Doctor Ralston as soon as you're gone."

"What about it, Henry?" she said. "You up for this?"

"Do I have any choice?"

"Not really," the couple said, and laughed.

"Let me get my hat then."

Two minutes later they were out the door.

Thaddeus watched them disappear across the meadow and into the landing circle. Minutes later the helicopter fan jet screamed to life and he could hear the rotors begin turning, slowly at first, and then "Whop-whop-whop-whop-whop!"

Minutes later the machine lifted up from the ground, took a nose-down attitude in the air, and went skimming away across the up-stretched arms of the Ponderosa pines.

Thaddeus made the call to the casino on the satellite phone.

Mickey Herkemier came on the line and Thaddeus explained what was needed. Dr. Ralston would hustle Henry down to the hotel clinic and do a head-to-toe examination. The doc would call Thaddeus when he was done making his assessment.

Now what to do? he wondered.

He grabbed a bottle of water. He remembered Henry's words from long ago, and smiled. "Remember, you must hydrate." He decided to take a lawn chair in front of the cabin.

In less than five minutes the sound of the helicopter had faded away and they were gone.

With nothing else to do, Thaddeus started counting sheep.

The Getting Reacquainted Seminar he and Katy had attended last night, in their bedroom at the casino, had continued until half past three. He was exhausted but he'd never let her know that.

She, on the other hand, was amazing. At six a.m., Sarai had started babbling in her crib, walking up and down against the rail. Katy had bounced out of bed, retrieved the baby, and brought her into bed with them. She stuck a bottle in Sarai's mouth and soon father and daughter were fast asleep. Which meant Katy could grab a few hours of study time before her world opened its eyes in the bedroom. She had lugged her book bag into Thaddeus' office and spread her things on his desk.

DR. RALSTON CALLED Thaddeus at four o'clock. He had seen Henry in the casino clinic. He had taken chest x-rays, drawn blood for blood work, put Henry through an extremely thorough physical exam, and talked with Henry—and Katy —at great length.

It was Dr. Ralston's opinion that Henry had an upper respiratory infection, and he had started him on a ten-day course of antibiotics. He was to moderate his activity level, stay dry, and get plenty of sleep. Other than that, he was fit to return to a normal routine. Which for Henry meant up at dawn, work with the sheep all day, and fall asleep when the sun went down. While Thaddeus had outfitted the cabin with generators and electric wiring and outlets two years ago, Henry saw fit to rarely make use of the utility. He thought electricity unnecessary and preferred to cook over an LP burner, use a single lantern until bedtime, and avoid foods that required refrigeration, just as he lived in the hogan when he was back down in the desert.

The helicopter flew overhead and set down in the clearing just after five. Thaddeus was in the process of herding the sheep into the corral for the night.

Katy waved, and Henry bent low under the helicopter prop wash, holding his Stetson on his head. They tramped across the meadow to the cabin.

"Welcome!" Thaddeus cried as he took Sarai and planted a huge kiss on her forehead. "I hear it went well."

"Doctor Ralston called you?" Katy asked.

"He did. He's an internal medicine specialist and I trust him implicitly. The best man in Vegas to see Henry."

"He looked in every nook and cranny," Henry laughed. "And gave me some green pills. Don't know that I'll take them though."

Katy and Thaddeus halted in their tracks. "Yes, you will!" they cried and Henry got a devilish look in his eyes and congratulated himself for scaring them.

The rest of the day passed uneventfully. The pilot wrote emails on his tablet and read eBooks, Thaddeus and Katy fished while the baby took a nap with Henry close by, and seven small trout made it into the frying pan Saturday night.

That night Henry slept in his bed. Thaddeus, Katy, and Sarai slept on the fold-out couch, and the casino pilot slept beside the helicopter in a tent, on the cot and air mattress they had packed. Everyone ate Dinty Moore beef stew and went to bed happy.

They were up when the sun came up and Henry made coffee in the ancient percolator on the LP burner.

The smell of the coffee warmed the place considerably and everyone felt at home. It was going to be a great day and, when he had changed Sarai's diaper, Thaddeus served coffee to all takers.

JUST BEFORE THEY flew out noon Sunday, Katy listened to Henry's chest with her stethoscope.

"He sounds better already," she announced.

At 12:15 they lifted off for the flight back to Las Vegas.

The helicopter took them directly to McCarran Airfield, where Katy and Sarai said their goodbyes and climbed aboard the Learjet for the ride back to Palo Alto and school.

When they were gone, Thaddeus immediately felt alone and became more convinced than ever that it was time to do something about their situation. He had to admit, Katy was his choice, and there was no longer any doubt about that. He just couldn't imagine a life without her. Their original coming together had been almost magical and he felt it was predestined, that in the grand scheme of things he was meant to be with her and she was meant to be with him.

It was time to get married, he finally admitted. And start living together.

Now to figure out how that all would work, with all the commitments they already had.

17

L angster Eugene Moretti was a fourth-generation Nevadan, a graduate of UNLV School of Law (Honors, Law Journal), held a CPA license in Nevada and California, and had worked mergers and acquisitions for four years at Morgan Stanley before returning to Las Vegas to take on the General Counsel role at the Desert Riviera Casino and Hotel.

He was thirty-five, thin and limber, and he preferred cross-country skiing around Reno to golf in Vegas.

He was unmarried but seriously involved with, of all people, his house cleaner, who was an undocumented worker from Ensenada.

His staff included nine attorneys, four of whom were dedicated solely to administrative law—mainly keeping up with the daily onslaught of records demands from the Nevada State Gaming Commission. And lately, of course, responding over and over to IRS requests for financial records. The others were liability lawyers whose sole duty was to handle claims and represent the company against such things as slip and fall cases, allegations of employee theft, workers compensation, claims the games or the slots were a cheat, and a raft of other legal activities that went on around the clock.

Lang Moretti was in his mahogany-paneled office on the seventh floor when Thaddeus called.

Andria buzzed him and said, "It's your boss, Mister Moretti. Your real boss."

His thick black unibrow shot upward in anticipation.

It was immediately worrisome and Moretti took a deep breath as he reached for the blinking button—worrisome because the guy was young, probably still learning to patty cake, and might blindly go around cutting people loose who he didn't like.

Moretti was a good guy and people liked him and he thought he might survive any such general bloodletting, but you could never be sure. Not with someone under thirty who owned a casino, for god's sakes.

"Please come to my office," Thaddeus said. The message was curt and the tone ominous.

Moretti slipped into his coat, told Andria he was meeting with Thaddeus, and hurried to the elevator.

He punched 2 and drew a deep breath. It was always some emergency, he thought. Which in a way turned him on. He had always liked the ebb and flow of the casino's legal affairs, almost like a living organism that attracted feeders and bloodsuckers as it went along day by day.

Moretti entered and took a seat beside Thaddeus' desk.

"You need to be in on this," he told Moretti. "You're not going to believe who wants to talk."

Thaddeus punched his phone and told security to bring up CID agents Kroc and Magence, whose cards had already been hand-delivered by floor security to Thaddeus when they first arrived.

"IRS," he said, and rolled his eyes.

He gave the two cards to Lang Moretti, whose eyes widened.

"This is CID," Moretti said gravely. "Let me do the talking."

"Be my guest," said Thaddeus.

A knock at the door and the two agents were escorted in.

Hands were shaken and cards exchanged, briefcases were opened and plunked down on the slate coffee table, and seating was arranged, the two agents side-by-side on the sofa nearest the door.

Kroc spoke slowly and with studied diction, like one speaking to non-English speakers.

"I'm Special Agent Aldous Kroc and this is Special Agent Mathilde Magence. We're with the criminal investigation division of the IRS, Treasury Department, assigned to Las Vegas. Would you mind speaking with us a few minutes?"

Moretti said, "Who do you want to speak to, exactly? The hotel officials or Mister Murfee personally?"

"Mister Murfee," said Kroc, who wet his lips and whose egg-eyes shone with anticipation.

"I can talk," said Thaddeus. "Mister Moretti is my attorney and represents me both as the owner and person-ally. So what can we do for you?"

Kroc clasped a knee in his hands. "Well—"

Special Agent Magence smiled broadly and said, "We have a couple of questions about how your taxes are prepared. Can you tell us who does your returns?"

"My personal returns?"

"Yes."

"The staff here at the casino. I can't say any one person, exactly."

Special Agent Magence said, "If memory serves, the

returns for the last two years show they were prepared by a Dwayne Willard, CPA. Ring a bell?" She smiled and her eyes twinkled.

Thaddeus heard only bells going off and red flags going up.

Great smile or not, he didn't trust her for a second.

"Dwayne Willard is a staff accountant," Moretti replied.

"Does he still work here?"

"He does."

Kroc broke in, "How are the returns prepared, by his review of your records or from summary sheets you give him?"

Lang Moretti raised a hand. "Hold up, please. This is beginning to sound like a civil tax audit. But you're criminal investigators asking the questions. Is my client under investigation personally?"

Kroc nodded solemnly. "He is. Certain discrepancies have been brought to our attention."

"Discrepancies such as what?"

Kroc shook his head violently. "Oh, we're not at liberty to say. Definitely not at liberty to say. Our investigation is confidential and it is secret."

"Then we're done here," Moretti said. "You can go now."

Kroc looked at Magence, who only continued with the same smile she had worn into the office.

"It would be easier if you just answered some simple questions," she said. "Then the whole thing might just go away."

"I don't think so," said Moretti. "If there's a criminal investigation then you can file charges and we'll respond accordingly. But we're not going to discuss anything further with you today."

At which point Kroc reached inside the CPA briefcase he had lugged in with him.

He happily whipped out a stack of papers.

"Right here we have a criminal indictment for income tax evasion. Guess whose name is on it?"

He held it out and Moretti took it from him.

"When did you indict my client?"

"Friday," Kroc beamed. "Ten o'clock Friday morning."

"And you're here asking questions?"

"Well, we have a warrant for his arrest. That's at the bottom of your stack."

"A warrant!"

Thaddeus felt his heart thump wildly. "What the hell? Are you serious?"

"Why haven't you given us the chance to respond to any questions you might have had?"

Kroc leaned back and smiled, his egg-eyes glistening. "Oh, we have all the documents for that. We're just here to settle a few remaining issues."

"And take your client to jail," said Magence, who had stopped smiling.

"Would you please stand and place your hands behind your back?" said Kroc. His smile said it all: he was enjoying this no end.

Thaddeus looked hard at Moretti, who gave a defeated nod.

The air went out of Thaddeus and he stood up from his desk and turned around.

Kroc boldly approached from behind, produced a silver set of handcuffs as if from thin air, and clamped them hard and tight around the exposed wrists.

"Shit!" said Thad. "Too damn tight."

"It only gets worse," said Kroc.

"Now please come along," said Magence.

He rode along in the back seat of a black Crown Vic, leaning forward in the seat to avoid putting pressure on his hands and arms cuffed behind.

It was uncomfortable and he was breathing shallow, frightened breaths.

Thaddeus had never before been arrested and going handcuffed to a jail was the last thing he ever thought would happen to him.

On the drive to the Las Vegas Detention Center the two agents up front laughed and joked and made reference to the fox they had caught in the hen house.

"Hey, Thad," Kroc shouted into the rearview mirror. "What's six feet, white, and locked up for two days?"

Thaddeus returned the look on the laughing face with a dark glare. He was suddenly furious, even more than he was scared. They had planned it out, coming for him on a Friday so he couldn't make bail and get out right away. He would have to wait until Monday to be taken before a magistrate and have bail set then. Sons of bitches had planned every bit of it, he thought. Then he decided to keep his cool. There would be a time for payback and pay back he would. He'd never run from a fight before and he damn sure wasn't about to start running now.

As they rode along, Moretti back at the casino was working the phones, looking for a tax lawyer with a specialty in tax crime defense. It was late on a Friday and it seemed everyone was gone from the office for a weekend.

He stretched his arms over his head and yawned.

He would keep looking and dialing.

There had to be someone.

18

Tubby Watsonn was a golfer and a tax lawyer who would rather hit a drive 330 yards than take in a $50,000 fee on a new tax case. The one made him feel fabulously virile, the other made him feel that much more indebted to the IRS when his own taxes came due at the end of the year.

He was given to wearing bright colors on the links—coral slacks with canary sweaters, orange-checkered slacks with pink shirts, and a bewildering array of Oakley golf shoes in every conceivable hue—as long as they bore no resemblance of match to either slacks, shirts, or sweater being worn that day.

He kept score down to the stroke, obeyed all rules, and insisted his golfing companions do the same. He invested heavily in lessons twice a week, hit the driving range every night after work, and played eighteen on Wednesday after-noons and Sundays.

Saturdays were reserved for squiring Eryn Watsonn around town in their white Caddy, while she returned items of clothing to the boutiques where she had taken them home on spec during the week. And of course she made payments for those she would be keeping, at the same time. At those shops she required Tubby to accompany her inside the store and pay for the item(s) with the platinum American Express he kept sequestered deep inside his wallet, far away from her no-known-limits spending style. If he was going to devote his life to golf then she, by all that was holy, was going to give her wardrobe the same attention and investment of funds, dollar for dollar.

Tubby Watsonn was a tax lawyer who specialized in tax crimes.

Or it could be said of him that he was a criminal lawyer who specialized in tax cases.

It didn't matter to him how he was touted in the Google paid advertising for which he paid $1,000/day, the clients came rolling in no matter how his expertise was formulated.

The reason for his lucrative tax law practice was twofold.

First, there was an abundance of tax cheats in Vegas—people who won at the tables but who did what they could to avoid paying the tax on their winnings. The IRS office in Las Vegas was double-staffed compared to every other IRS office in the country, all to snare all the cheats they could possibly round up.

The second reason for his lucrative tax practice was that Tubby Watsonn, simply put, had never lost a case.

He knew the tax law better than the IRS, taught state bar seminars to lawyers on tax issues, studied the new laws at least two hours each day, first thing in the morning on coming into the office at seven, and he wrote prodigious articles about tax law issues affecting the gambling industry and the tax treatment of winners and losers. As a result, his name was synonymous with "tax lawyer" in Nevada. He was the first person called when a big name got nailed.

Lang Moretti reached Tubby Watsonn's cell phone that Friday, at the same time Thaddeus was being chauffeured downtown by the two arresting officers, Kroc and Magence.

Watsonn was playing the seventeenth at Winterhaven Short Nine on Friday because the Friday afternoon IRS revenue agent interview was suddenly discontinued by the agent who had unexpectedly eaten a bad fish taco and left the office early.

Tubby took the blank spot on his calendar and immediately penciled in the short nine. He would be home in time for the Sabbath, Friday night.

They weren't Orthodox at his house, but they did observe the Sabbath—at least on Friday at sundown. Saturdays, well—Tubby figured the Lord wouldn't mind him tending to Eryn's impulse-buying on Saturdays and the necessity of running her around town while she returned and purchased her ensembles. So far the Lord had kept His peace about it and Tubby felt they had a good, workable understanding in place. Negotiation—it worked with the IRS and it worked with the Lord, at least as far as Tubby could tell.

He was steering the golf cart down the seventeenth fairway when his cell beeped angrily.

He ignored the call and it went to recording.

Minutes later it beeped again and he again ignored the call.

The third time was the charm, as he whipped it from the zippered pocket on his golf bag and shouted, "What!" so loudly into the phone that the putters on the seventeenth green turned and looked, making shush motions at him.

Tubby saluted them back, in apology.

"This is Tubby Watsonn," he said.

"Mister Watsonn, Lang Moretti here. I'm calling from the Desert Riviera."

"If this is about a transactional tax issue, you've got the wrong guy. My particular milieu is code violations. I leave the transactional stuff to the smart guys. And since you're calling from a casino I can only assume it's transactional tax problems you have on your mind."

"Mister Watsonn, the owner of our casino has been arrested on criminal tax charges."

So quickly did he pull over, Tubby almost steered the cart into a culvert. He smelled a $1 million fee and for that his beloved game could be interrupted. "When arrested?"

"Not thirty minutes ago. Some guy named Aldous Kroc slapped the cuffs on him."

"I know that asshole Kroc," said Tubby, which was true. They had gone toe-to-toe at least a half-dozen times. He knew Kroc to be a vicious attack dog who would let nothing come between him and a conviction. This was going to require money up front—lots of money.

"We should meet now," said Tubby. "Give me one hour."

"I'll be waiting," said Moretti. He slammed down the phone and buzzed downstairs for a whiskey sour. It was going to be a long night and he was going to need a quick drink—in and out—before it got any further underway.

He wasn't a drunk, Lang Moretti, but he was known never to miss a chance for a quickie after five. Italian, of course, he jokingly referred to himself as "Irish about some things—like overindulgence." He was a transplanted New Yorker and old prejudices died hard with him. The micks were never above humiliating, in his worldview.

An hour later the two attorneys were meeting in Moretti's casino office, seventh floor, with a panoramic view of the Strip.

Neons were glaring as the sun dipped lower in the west, and the crowds were picking up as it was Friday night and there were paychecks to be cashed and wagered away.

Moretti, wearing his standard New York pinstripes and wingtips, stood behind his desk when security ushered Tubby Watsonn into his office.

Watsonn was decked out in teal golf slacks from Oakley, white bucks footwear, and a linen navy blazer over a white golf shirt, open at the throat. He clenched a half-burnt cigar in the chubby fingers of his right hand, having stubbed it out when he entered the Desert Riviera. Half-glasses were perched on his forehead and his hawk nose sniffed the air dramatically as he swept into the office.

"You've been drinking," he said to Moretti. "I smell booze a half mile away. How about you order me a single malt Scotch before we get down to it?"

Hands were pumped and seating assumed.

Taken aback but game, Moretti tapped a button on his desk phone and placed the drink order. He covered the mouthpiece with his hand and said, "Anything to eat? Snack? Steak?"

Watsonn raised his hands. "I'm set," he said, "just the Scotch."

They wasted no time after that.

Watsonn absorbed the inch of papers submitted by Aldous Kroc not two hours ago, and read the indictment three times.

"Hmm. Tell me about skimming. And tell me the f-ing truth. We might as well get that up front right away. I get the truth from everyone I speak with or I'm gone, sayonara. How's the skim work?"

Moretti blanched. "There is no skim. At least not that I'm aware of."

Tubby Watsonn pulled a Bic from his jacket and fired up the cigar.

"Ridiculous. This is a casino. Of course there's a skim on. Otherwise we wouldn't be seeing one of these!" he said, smacking the indictment for emphasis. "The Service's DIF algorithm has aimed these people at this casino. Something ain't adding up, you get my drift."

Moretti nodded fluidly. "I do, I do. And we can talk about all that. But for right now, can we get bail set and spring Thaddeus from custody?"

"Hmm. I know a magistrate I can call. He'll sign a bail order for me tonight—but only because it's me. That's if— and it's a big 'if'—I take the case."

"What's it take to get you on board?"

"Simple. I leave here with a check drawn on the casino's general account for one million dollars. Then you've bought my time, my attention, and my drag around town with the powers-that-be."

"Done," said Moretti. He buzzed CEO Mickey Herkemier and placed the order for the check.

"That's Watsonn with two n's?" said Moretti.

Tubby Watsonn blew a thick plume of cigar smoke into the ceiling.

"Exactly two," he said. He was already envisioning the cabin cruiser he would soon be enjoying on Lake Mead. He would leave Eryn at home with a credit card and take the boat out by himself. Maybe with some topless coed from UNLV on board, someone who was pre-law and who needed to make a few dollars on the weekends. The economy was toast—such arrangements were easy anymore.

Best of all, they were tax deductible.

T he sally-port door rolled up and Special Agent Kroc pulled the Ford Crown Vic inside.

The door slowly creaked down and closed behind them.

Both agents exited the vehicle and came around to Thaddeus' door and helped him to his feet.

"Nice," the young lawyer said. "And I'm certain this was all absolutely necessary. There must be some IRS rule in some well-thumbed book somewhere, about arresting citizens on a Friday night so they can't make bail until Monday. Isn't that what we're looking at here?"

Agent Magence eyed him without the hint of a smile.

"Attorney Murfee, you'd do damn well to tell your client —which is you—to shut his damn mouth. He wants to be sure he doesn't say anything that can and will be used against him."

Thaddeus closed his eyes and shook his head.

Nominally she was right.

He was going to have to hold his tongue while they controlled his freedom.

But he swore, right then and there, this would never happen to him again as long as he lived. There would be precautions on top of precautions henceforth. He would insulate and isolate himself from all governmental agencies and entities whether local, state, or federal.

His bodyguards would be traded in for lawyers, a whole cadre of lawyers religiously dedicated to keeping the hounds at bay.

He mentally kicked himself.

How naïve he had been to have trusted the people around him without the safety net of checks and balances and eyes looking over shoulders to make sure everything was being done on the up and up.

Somehow there was money missing from the casino—that much was clear from the indictments. And he would get to the bottom of it and heads would roll.

He was even thinking about burying the guilty party in some faraway hole in the sand out in the middle of the godforsaken Nevada desert.

He was all that furious.

The woman inside at the first desk recognized him from the visit he'd made there a week ago to visit Kiki following her arrest. She couldn't resist burrowing under his skin.

"Well, it's the hotshot lawyer, back again, this time in cuffs. Who are you here to see this time, counsel, yourself?"

Thaddeus gave her his best smile and shook his head. "You've got me there," he said. "Looks like I've screwed the pooch this time, for sure."

"Welcome to the Las Vegas Detention Center. We hope you're stay with us is a pleasant one—isn't that what you tell all the high rollers back at the casino?"

"Something like that. But we don't handcuff them, nobody makes them come there."

"Well, there you are," she said, in her best brush-off voice, already busy with something more important than his own intake.

The Special Agents went through the motions with the woman and soon Thaddeus was being printed and mug shot.

He was then taken into a gang shower where he was told by the jailer to strip and shower, which he did.

The orange jumpsuit came next, while his clothes were taken away in a basket perched on top of a cart.

Then he was led into a large, circular island, where a dozen or more inmates surrounded him, in varying degrees of interest about the new guy.

Most were absorbed in watching *America's Most Wanted* on the center-stage TV, but a couple gave him more than one lookover.

There were jailhouse tats milling around and there were $1,000 tats milling around, which told him the holding cell's clientele came from all walks of life.

He looked for a remote perch to make himself less obvious, saw none, and settled for an orange plastic chair six rows back from the TV screen. Might as well watch, he thought, and try to fit in.

Which wasn't all that hard. In the orange suit of the day, no one stood out and everyone stood out.

They were all equals at being in the wrong place at the wrong time, no matter what kind of name you put on it.

~

SIX FRANTIC CALLS and Tubby Watsonn finally tracked down U.S. Magistrate Peter J. Gladston III as he was in line to board a flight out of McCarran, bound for San Francisco and the 49ers game.

Judge Gladston unhappily agreed to step out of line as Watsonn hailed a passing cart and was rushed to the boarding area, an order for bail in hand. "It's a lawyer, a casino owner," he shouted breathlessly at the impatient, stewing magistrate. "IRS grabbed him on a Friday night so's he'd have to cool his heels in jail over the weekend. I know you always set these things at one million, so that's what this one orders."

A cursory reading of the order, and Judge Gladston signed off with a dignified scrawl that left no doubt it was he who had signed. Wordlessly he turned away and headed through the boarding tunnel.

"Thank you, Your Honor," shouted Tubby at the judge's receding backside. "I won't forget this!"

THE FIRST CONTACT in jail was made at 6:15 by a black man with one eye missing, that same Friday night.

The man was fidgety, walked listed off to one side, and sported a Mohawk cut just like James Harden of the Rockets, his hero.

Unlike Harden, however, he had no job, no place to live, and zero prospects of either. The cot offered him by the jail was the first time he had slept up off the ground since the last time he was incarcerated.

"I seen you before," the man told Thaddeus. "Hey, everyone, I know this dude," he shouted over the TV and general clamor. "This here one's casino something."

Not one head turned to look. Just some old fool babbling on, they thought.

"What can I do for you?" Thaddeus asked the man.

"Desert Riviera casino. I seen you there. I never forgets a face."

"I work there," Thaddeus said. "So you're right. But why do you care?"

"Got any money to loan for bail? I needs outta here yesterday."

"What are you in for?"

"I sold some two-bit narc a zip of weed. Thas all."

"What's your name?"

"Billy A. Tattinger. Most call me Bat for short."

"Well, Bat, selling narcotics is a serious crime in this state. Nevada has tough drug laws."

"How you know that?"

"For one, I'm a lawyer."

And at that exact point Bat leaped to his feet and exclaimed, "Hey, y'all, this one here's a lawyer!"

This time the heads did turn.

Within moments they were surrounded by a ring of onlookers who had questions for this lawyer.

"How much is bail? Ten percent? Will they take plastic?"

"If I lose my job and it was a false arrest can I sue them?"

"My kid went with DES. Can you help me get her back after I'm out?"

"How could a lawyer be in here?"

Thaddeus was barraged with questions and hands reaching for his attention from all sides. He slouched lower in the orange chair, but it was no use. There was no place to run, no chance of making an escape.

He was every bit as stuck as his new acquaintances.

All right," he said. "How about if I take a chair over between those tables and you come visit with me one at a time? Just like a real lawyer."

"That'll work," said Bat. "But I found you so's I'm first."

"Fair enough," said Thaddeus.

He stood and dragged the plastic chair across the room.

Bat followed close behind with another.

Immediately a dozen or so inmates formed a queue of prospective clients jostling to visit with the lawyer.

Why not, he thought, might as well make the best use of my time while I'm here. And who knows, I just might help one or two.

"So you sold a zip to the undercover officer. Did he entice you into making the sale?"

"He offered me fifteen hundred for the bag of weed. That enticed me."

Thaddeus shook his head. "What I'm trying to find out, is whether there was a predisposition toward committing the crime, or whether the police put the idea in your head."

"Oh, it was my idea, all right. I was hongry as hell."

Thaddeus sighed. "All right, let's back up. Where did the weed come from?"

"Stole it out of a BMW where these honkies went inside the Pink Palomino. I knew they was holding in the glove box. Rich honky twenty-somethings on the prowl is always holding. So I smashed the window and made off with their stash."

"How much was there? That makes a difference in Nevada."

"Hell, Thaddeus, I didn't exactly weigh it."

"But if you had to guess. How much did you steal?"

"Probly a half pound."

"Shit! Really?"

"Maybe more. Plus there was an ounce of blow. But I sold that to a brother on the corner so's I could get a steak. Hadn't eaten in seventy-two hours. And they say there's money in Vegas. Not if you're black, busted, and got no gig they ain't."

"I'm sure. So here's the deal. Do you want to work?"

"Damn right."

"How about you come see me once you get out. I'm sure we've got something for you."

"Naw, I got a felony already. No one will hire me."

"We'll give it a whirl. If you don't steal, and show up sober, and put in a solid eight, we'll get along fine."

"What would I do?"

"Got a driver's license?"

"You kidding?"

"How about this. You start out busing tables. We'll make a room available to get you off the street. But no visitors, no girls, no booze, no drugs, no guns. You read me?"

"Hella."

"All right then. How much is your bail?"

"Thirty thousand."

"Then you need forty-five hundred to bail out. You willing to sign a note for that?"

"Say what?"

"If I loan you the money, will you pay me back?"

"Hella."

"Good. Then let's shake on it. You'll get out when I get out."

"You shittin me?"

"Not at all. We need good workers at the Desert Riviera."

"You the manager?"

Thaddeus nodded. "Something like that. You come there and ask for Thaddeus. Tell them I'm expecting you. Because I will be."

Bat jumped to his feet. Exuberance brought him fully

upright, the first time in years. "Hot shit, y'all. We gots a lawyer here!"

Next in line was a man charged with theft of Social Security checks from mailboxes in a senior citizen assisted living venue.

Then came a motorcycle gangbanger whose alleged crime was issuing bad checks to Harley shops for repairs to his "scooter," as he called it.

Another man was facing three years for food stamp fraud. He had learned how to forge the stamps and sell them. "Since they made the hundred-dollar bill impossible to forge, everyone was jumping over to food stamps." Evidently they could be sold for fifty cents on the dollar and they were selling out every time they printed a run.

The line was still five deep when the *Tonight Show* music fired up on the TV.

Thaddeus was exhausted but still listening.

He'd had no idea he would one day open a legal clinic in Las Vegas.

He realized that he was living in a dream world of a money flood and that he was out of touch with real people.

The stories he was hearing in the jail were moving him.

Sure, there were cons, slicks, and thugs, but there was also a huge population whose only crime was being poor and trying to snatch a meal, or a dry bed.

Of those folks, probably nine out of ten of were alcohol or drug related, that much was clear. Addiction, that's what brought the majority of his fellow travelers to this place. He already had one idea in mind about that; maybe this was another.

At midnight, Tubby and Lang Moretti came for him.

The proprietor of Blackjack Bail Bonds was in tow. He

had just earned a quick $150,000 on the bail he was about to post and he was happy to be staying late at work.

Thaddeus had also told him to bring a second set of bail paperwork. They would be bailing out one inmate who went by Bat.

The bail order was presented to the front desk, the bail bond was slid under the glass partition, supervisors were consulted, and phone calls placed.

Finally it was determined that the bail was legitimate, the passport was surrendered as well, and the prisoner who went by Thaddeus Murfee could be released.

Inmate Billy A. Tattinger—Bat—was part of the deal.

They paid his $4,500 bail in cash, and he exultantly followed the three white guys into the cool 1 a.m. air of the Las Vegas morning. Outside on the sidewalk he did a Bojangles click of the heels and started to walk off.

"Bat, where you off to?" Thaddeus called after him.

"Nowhere and everywhere. I got no place."

"You're coming with me. I've got a room for you and you start work first thing in the morning. You ready?"

"Yes sir!" cried Bat, and he slid into the Mercedes seat beside Thaddeus. "Let me shake your hand," he said.

"Not necessary. We'll shake after your first thirty days without drugs and alcohol. Did I also mention that AA meetings are part of the deal?"

"Spare me that God shit and shinola," Bat spat at him.

"Just keep coming back, that's what they tell you," said Tubby from the front seat. "Half my tax clients wind up there. I know all about it."

"You're a lawyer too?" Bat asked, his eyes growing wider.

"I am."

"Shit," said Bat. "Shit."

"Pull over next corner," Thaddeus told the driver. The car edged to the curb and Thaddeus turned to Bat.

"You want to get straight?"

"Yes."

"You'll go to the meetings? Yes or no, because I'll dump your ass right here if I don't like how you answer."

"Mister, I loves me some AA."

"All right," Thaddeus said to the driver. "Let's go home."

20

It was into the Desert Riviera environment that Kiki Murphy walked two days later, to talk to Thaddeus about becoming a spotter.

Thaddeus was meeting with Tubby Watsonn when Kiki arrived.

The two lawyers were poring over a bathtub-size stack of papers spread across the Vermont coffee table in Thaddeus' office. So far, everything had been arranged by year. Now it was time to start categorizing.

Teller tapes, count room records—all paper trails of cash transactions were the first target and it was a moving one. As cash moved from the tellers' cages, the numbers looked fine at first; but then, after processing in the count room, numbers were changing.

Totals weren't adding up.

What was $250,000 in teller tapes at the far end of the graveyard shift turned into $235,000 in count cards in the count room.

Again and again they compared tapes to cards and

always it was the same result—short. The count numbers were always less than the teller tapes. Like Svengali's rabbit in the hat, money was disappearing and it was happening somewhere between the teller cage and the count room. Theft on a large scale was ongoing. Now all they had to do was figure out who and how and they would have the "why" of Thaddeus' arrest and indictment.

Thaddeus left Tubby and his associate alone with the records and took Kiki into his private living quarters just off the office.

The penthouse was gangster glamorous and she took it all in as a smile played across her face.

They talked briefly and got the preliminaries out of the way.

She was elated over finding her brother, she blurted, and she was feeling much better since her last visit to the casino.

Thaddeus wouldn't discuss the criminal charges with her—that was PX's job and it was dangerous for Thaddeus to cross over that line.

So they discussed her role.

She—along with seven other floor walkers on each shift —would be responsible for spotting casino cheats. Her area of expertise would be card counting at blackjack, which was the highest-grossing table game and the reason why the casino dedicated 45 percent of its total floor space to the game.

Kiki was ready to get down to business.

She had selected a nice two-piece gray suit, white button-down shirt, and foulard tie. Italian loafers completed the business look.

Her short hair was still worn in the wedge and Thaddeus noticed an engagement ring on her finger, but he didn't say anything. That could only mean stability—he thought.

"So you met with PX and you're feeling good about that. That's excellent. And now you're ready to earn some money."

She smiled. "Well, my card-counting career is officially over, thanks to your sharp eyes. So I guess I am. In fact, I'm excited about working for you. When would I start?"

"Tomorrow too soon?"

"I'll be here. What shift?"

"Let's start you off evening shift, six to two a.m. Sound okay?"

"That's terrific. It fits right into my schedule. I'm enrolling in school."

"Really, what are you studying?"

"Hotel and resort management. It's a master's program at UNLV. The classes are mostly late morning, so the work hours will be perfect."

"I told you sixty thousand to start."

"That's incredibly generous."

He returned her smile. "Hey, I just want you to be happy. You're going to be a great addition to our team."

"Can you tell me a little about the company?"

"Sure. We feature thirty-five hundred slot machines."

"How much do they hold? I've always wondered."

"Well, it took thirty-five armored cars two days to bring in the $4.5 million in coins needed to fill the slots when I took over and the new bank got installed."

"Holy cow!"

"Each visitor spends about four hours a day gambling in our casino. We have to give them other things to do, too, so we've got an IMAX screen that shows movies twenty-four/seven. Admission is ten dollars regardless of age, popcorn is four dollars for a box, and drinks are three dollars. We also have a ride around the river downstairs.

That costs five bucks a head. Together, the IMAX and the ride bring in about five million dollars a year. Not too shabby. But the important thing is, they really help keep our guests on our premises. Plus we've got seventeen shops, four spas, three eighteen-hole golf courses, four Olympic pools, and WaterWorld for the kids. WaterWorld is free to everyone under twelve and offers CPR-trained lifeguards and stewards, who will keep an eye on the older kids while mom and pop blow their college savings. At least that's the whole idea."

"How do you feel about that?"

"About families losing their savings? Not good. But I didn't design human nature. I just cater to it."

"You sound jaded, Thad."

"Maybe I'm getting that way."

"How many guest rooms?"

"They just finished an expansion when I took over. Today there are three thousand eight hundred nine guest rooms."

"What kind of gambling."

"We emphasize blackjack on the table games. But I've also added a baccarat high-rollers area that's now roped off from the rest of the casino. We get a lot of Europeans and baccarat is their game of choice."

"I didn't know that."

She brushed a wisp of hair from her face and the engagement ring sparkled. Maybe she meant for him to ask about it, but he refrained. He would let her tell him when she was ready, if ever.

While they were talking, security manager Gordon Denton had just finished roll call with his people when the switchboard got its first call for that shift. The claim from the guests was that someone had broken into their room to take a dump in the toilet, as they so descriptively put it.

Gordon Denton interrupted Thaddeus with Kiki, as that scenario was definitely not in the security manual.

"What do you want to do?" he asked Thaddeus.

Gordon was a tall man in a Brooks Brothers suit who had his master's in business administration from USC and who ran the security service at the Desert Riviera like a small business. He had slick gray hair, yellowish tints in his eyeglasses, and perfectly manicured and polished nails. At first appearance, he was a dandy, but he was anything but. He had won Orange County Golden Gloves in the middle-weight class in his teens, and would have gone on with a career in championship boxing if he hadn't suffered a slight neuro-deficit from his first professional fight. The damage jerked his head to the right over and over, maybe every thirty seconds. Which wasn't even noticed in Las Vegas. He waited for the owner's answer.

"Seriously?" Thaddeus said, halfway astonished. "Someone took a dump in their toilet by breaking in? Anything reported missing?"

Gordon smiled. "That's the damned thing. Nothing seems to be missing. They looked."

"So the perp left something instead of taking something?"

"Left a dump."

"We send someone?"

"I sent a security officer up to take their complaint."

"Don't take pictures."

"Agree. Who needs pictures of shit? Excuse me, miss. My language—"

"That's okay," Kiki grinned. "I'm a big girl. I know shit when I see it."

Gordon laughed. "Maybe I shoulda sent you."

They both laughed.

Thaddeus could see that Kiki was going to fit right in with that rough-and-tumble world. Which was probably the understatement of the day, considering she had already shot and killed an attacker and she wasn't even twenty-five years old.

Just then Gordon got a call from the security officer sent to investigate. It seemed the guests had flushed the evidence. Gordon rolled his eyes and told the employee to take their statement nonetheless.

"Did he do a lock interrogation?" Thaddeus asked Gordon.

Every time someone inserted one of the plastic guest room keys the use was recorded in the security system. Each lock recorded the last 500 times keys had been used to open the door. He felt they just couldn't be too careful with thousands of guests and the tens of thousands of problems that were possible in a single night.

"Okay, Gordon," Thaddeus said at last. "Comp them for two nights' stay and deduct room charges. That should put to rest the unknown feces ordeal they've suffered through."

"Got it, Boss."

Gordon hurried out, apologizing for the interruption.

Kiki simply shook her head. "Amazing."

"I know."

"I'm gonna like it here."

"Yes, you are. You'll fit right in to this carnival."

"See you at six in the evening," she said, and offered her hand.

"Welcome aboard, Kiki. I won't be up until about two o'clock, but we'll probably run into each other off and on.

Just call me if you need help with anything. You'll report to Joel Hagen, Director of Gaming. He's on two."

"Thanks again, Thad. Thanks so much."

"De nada."

21

"I want this guy!" grunted H. Mouton Carraway, United States Attorney for Nevada. "He lies, he cheats, he steals, and—"

"And he's great press," said Mitch Dubroff, his public relations head.

"—and he's great press, indeed."

They were in the U.S. Attorney's walnut-paneled office, studying the two-column newspaper spread broadcasting the arrest of local casino owner Thaddeus J. Murfee.

Assistant U.S. Attorney David Fisher, who had obtained the indictment, was waiting for the fireworks, knew they were coming, knew how badly Carraway had wanted to nail a casino bigwig and prove to his constituents that he was doing a bang-up job of protecting them.

Fisher's left leg was crossed over his right at the ankle, and his foot was nonstop movement, jittering. Inside he was irate and put off by the chief. Only late on Friday nights, when he'd had too much to drink and Michelle had put the kids to bed, did his truth come out. He hated the U.S. Attorney and couldn't wait for the Democrats to leave office so there would be a change. Such change never bothered David. He was a career prosecutor.

H. Mouton Carraway slapped the newspaper article with the back of his hand, and scowled, "There you go, son, a bitch slap. This says he's only twenty-nine years old. How the hell does a punk lawyer all of twenty-nine get off owning one of the city's swankiest casinos?"

"Unknown, Mouton," said Mitch Dubroff, whose job it would be to put the desired spin on today's meeting.

"I'll tell you how," said Fisher. "He sued the mob and won. Something this office has never been able to do. No offense, Mouton. No U.S. Attorney in the history of federal asset seizures has ever been able to co-opt anything as spectacular as an entire casino. The kid must have something on the ball."

The U.S. Attorney's eyes narrowed, full of malevolence.

"But I don't suppose you mentioned his legal talent to the grand jury you persuaded to indict him? Am I right? Hell no you didn't. All right, Fish. You contact the IRS idiot, this Aldous Kroc. Tell him I'm ordering surveillance on this tax cheat twenty-four/seven. That's just for openers. Are you hearing me?"

"Will do."

"And I mean surveillance. Dig through his garbage. Get taps on his phones, in his walls, records from his cell provider, downloads and uploads from his office and personal computer. If he 'likes' something on Facebook that better damn well show up in some surveillance log somewhere. We are going to bury this guy or my uncle's name ain't Sam. And you"—pointing at Fisher—"you are going to seize his casino when it's all said and done. The biggest RICO seizure in the history of racketeering seizures. This guy's skimming money out of this casino, we know that. But what else is he into? Drugs? Money laundering for the cartels? You find out and you bring it back here to papa and lay it on my desk, bleeding with its throat slashed open. Am I making myself clear here?"

The jiggling had ceased. "Absolutely."

"Then let's all hop to it. Out of here now, both of you!"

David Fisher stepped into the hall, counted off twenty steps, and disappeared inside his own private office. His was right next to the big guy's, as he was Number Two in the U.S. Attorney's Office, Nevada.

David Fisher was at heart a good man, but he had learned twenty years ago that good men didn't get very far when it came to prosecuting criminals. Sometimes it was necessary to fudge the facts and he was not above doing so.

The FBI agents he worked hand-in-glove with knew him to be a switch-hitter. With Fisher running the show, stories magically changed in mid-stream, prosecutions doubled back without warning, heads rolled when least expected. In short, he was tiptoeing the line between legal and illegal at all times. So what if there was the occasional venture into the illegal? Who really got hurt, the bad guys? Seriously? Sometimes, if you really wanted to put someone away, someone, say, really evil, sometimes it was necessary to cross over that line.

Truth be told, David Fisher was no stranger to operating in the gray zone and sometimes in the darkest zone of all— he would get down on the same level with the criminals he was hunting and play by their rules.

But he was also brilliant, because he always left himself a way back.

He could take any questionable scenario and give it a little spin to make it appear totally legal. His boss, the U.S. Attorney himself, knew this about David Fisher. Which was why Fisher got all the top-drawer assignments and which was why Fisher had remained a Number Two to an ever-changing parade of political hacks, the U.S. Attorneys.

He was reliable.

He could get it done.

And nothing, absolutely nothing, mattered more than results to the men designated U.S. Attorneys by appointment by the President of the United States.

Which was why Fisher drew the short straw on Thaddeus Murfee. It was very clear. The guy was going down.

Fisher dialed the extension of Aldous Kroc at IRS headquarters, four floors below.

"Al? Dave Fisher here."

"Good morning, Mister Fisher. Who is our entrée of the day?"

"Mister Casino."

"Oh goody. That's one of my favorite files."

"What do you have on him so far?"

"Only everything, sir. Enough to put him away for twelve years. Oh, except for one small item, but I'm sure you'll be able to provide that."

"What's that?" probed Fisher. His voice was low and he was feeling conspiratorial, as he knew Aldous Kroc to be one of the IRS Special Agents who felt about criminals just like he did. Put them away no matter what. "What are we missing?"

"I haven't been able to tie Murfee in to the actual taking and removal of the cash from the casino. I need the smoking gun."

"Hell, that's the whole case, isn't it?" Fisher sounded troubled. Things had taken a sudden right turn.

"Not exactly. I think I can prove the connection with a lifestyle audit."

"Meaning what?"

"Mathilde Magence and I are working up a lifestyle profile on this particular tax cheat. We are looking at proving it was costing him more dollars to live than what he was reporting as his taxable income on his tax returns."

"Won't that be like asking the jury to really reach to make the case? I don't like that at all."

Pause at Kroc's end. Then, "What do you suggest?"

"I suggest we find an insider. Someone who's in on the skim with him. Threaten them with prosecution and then cut a deal in return for their testimony."

"I like that. But who do I get?"

"Go back through your notes. Find the people who had access to the visitor log in the count room. Have them say something like—I don't know, something like Murfee came to the count room at times and insisted on being inside alone. That he did this a few times a week, always alone. That that was unusual, that it violated corporate policy. You make it up—you tell me, Kroc. But get it. We need live testimony to nail this guy. And here's one more thing. Don't actually charge this person with conspiracy, just threaten to do it. We don't want them testifying that yes, they're giving testimony against Murfee in return for immunity from prosecution. Get my drift?"

"I do get your drift. Don't charge them with a crime. Just scare hell out of them."

"Right, and here's one more thing," said Fisher. "Use someone close to him. Someone he trusts implicitly. Maybe some gal he's banging."

"He doesn't bang employees."

"Or someone who's seriously unhappy with how they've been treated at work."

"He has employee satisfaction panels in place. People

whose only job it is to give disgruntled workers the chance to be heard and to have wrongs against them corrected."

"He did all that?"

"He did. Has. This kid isn't going to be easy, Mister Fisher. He plays his cards pretty close to the vest, to borrow an expression from his casino."

Fisher sighed. "Well, you know what I want. Now go get it."

"Will do," said Kroc. "I think I already have someone in mind for that."

"Excellent. Get back to me in one week."

"Done."

"Goodbye, Agent Kroc."

"Thank you, sir. I will make you very happy."

"I know that."

22

M ickey Herkemier didn't like the setup, didn't like it at all.

They didn't exactly invite him to come by the office—it was more like a demand.

There was a veiled threat. "We need to discuss a matter with you that could very well touch on someone's freedom."

Brother, he said to himself as he rode the elevator up, when the IRS tells you someone's going to jail and they want to talk to you, you damn well better show up.

For previous accounting clients Mickey had met with the IRS audit arm probably

300 times.

But he rarely met with the CID—the Criminal Investigation Division.

In fact, he couldn't recall that he had ever met with the CID.

Moreover, it was in all the books that CPAs never meet alone with the CID without a lawyer. Except that this Kroc guy had told him to come alone, that his own well-being depended on it. Who was he to argue?

He carried within his chest a flickering hope that the talk had nothing to do with the fact he had been skimming funds out of the casino. It might be about that but it was highly doubtful.

He was a smart guy, and as a CPA he thought he knew how much he could skim without anyone, including the IRS, getting wise.

So far, Thaddeus was clueless. He was certain of that.

The money he was stealing was money that was coming directly from the casino gaming tables. When it arrived in the count room it was in an unknown amount. The bonded employees who worked the count room tallied the dollars and made entries into the cash tracking system so that anyone upstairs could click a mouse and know to the penny how much money was in the count room waiting to be transported to the bank.

But Mickey beat them to it.

Federal law required a foolproof cash accounting system —the IRS required such a system.

And all casinos were meticulously scrutinized by the IRS agents who were always lurking around. But their primary role was gamer oversight. The agents were there to make certain the winners paid their taxes before they could hoof it outside without paying up. It was literally a form of withholding tax, and the revenue officers were planted there for the players, not for the casino.

The casino itself went about its business for the most part unwatched, just so long as it stayed current on its own tax liabilities. But let it get behind, and the IRS swarmed the place like army ants.

The elevator whooshed open on 7 and Mickey got off.

To his left was a bare wall except for the mandatory picture of the President.

To his right was a door knob with a keypad below and a speaker.

He punched in the code for Aldous Kroc and waited.

"Two minutes," a voice announced.

He closed his eyes and tried to think of areas he wouldn't discuss and would never reveal, and areas where it was safe to tread. So much depended on Lady Luck in these inquisitions, he knew, and he prayed that the Lady would be with him that day.

His pulse quickened. He was a lapsed Catholic who hadn't been to confession in twenty years. Maybe that explained the ease with which he stole the casino's money. He didn't have to tell. Of course God knew, but hey. So far not even God was interfering.

In Mickey's present state of mind he had even convinced himself that the heavenly authorities supported what he was doing, given how easy and anonymously it was proceeding. "The Lord helps those who help themselves," he reminded himself.

Then he wondered if the saying was actually from the Bible or if it was something he had read in his grandmother's needlepoint wall-hangings; she had had so many of them.

Steady, he told himself. Shut off the damn thought machine and simmer down. You need your wits now, more than ever before.

The door came crashing open and there stood Aldous Kroc, egg eyes glowing, a slow smile parting his lips, almost drooling over the waiting feast.

"Thanks for coming," he said to his visitor, and offered a damp, cool hand to shake.

They pumped hands like long-lost fraternity brothers whose secret rituals were hidden away in the Internal

Revenue Code. They were insiders to the largest piece of legislation in the history of mankind, the Internal Revenue Code, and there was instant empathy.

"Follow me, please. Miss Magence and I are happy you came."

"Sure, happy to help," Herkemier said, and instantly realized how lame it sounded. Who in their right mind would be happy to help out the IRS? As if they even needed any help.

He was guided into a small, windowless conference room, again accessorized only with the inaugural photo of the President, who, Herkemier decided, seemed to enjoy lurking around the offices of the greatest inquisition since the actual Inquisition.

Never had a government known so much about the personal lives of its people as the U.S. government now knew about its own citizens, thanks to the inquisitors themselves—the IRS agents.

Mickey's hands broke out in a sweat at the notion. He stuffed them inside his trouser pockets and sat back, intent on assuming the air of a citizen with absolutely nothing to hide.

"This is Mathilde Magence. She's working on this matter with me."

"What matter would that be?" Mickey asked with his warmest smile.

Without warning, his hands, stuffed deep in his pockets, began to tremble. He tried not to jiggle the four quarters inside the pocket (he always knew exactly how much change he was carrying, a moving target that his CPA brain kept nicely tallied).

"We're here to talk about the Desert Riviera Casino and Hotel," Kroc said expansively, as if he had a majority stake in the place. "We know a lot about it already, but we need you to fill in some blanks for us."

"Water?" asked Miss Magence, who had seized the gold and black plastic pitcher and upended it to fill the glasses poised on the table. "Anyone?"

"I'm fine," said Mickey in a subdued croak that sounded like anything but how he wanted to sound—strong, assured vibrato, and all that. He thumped a fist against his chest as if to clear his airway and tried it again. "I'm fine. More than fine."

They looked closely at him. He had the feeling he was being examined by artists.

Did they sense his terror?

Did they realize how far up the horror scale they had sent his mind reeling when they mentioned the casino by name?

"Well," she said, "if at any time during our questions you need a drink or need to use the restroom, just speak up and we'll pause."

"While you get your needs met," said Kroc, a distant memory of *How to Win Friends* prompting his determination to be a helpmate to the victim.

"Fair enough," Mickey said.

"Just a couple of introductory questions. First, do you mind if we record our conversation today?"

"I guess not."

Kroc pushed a button on the pad before him.

"When I said record you, I should mention we're also videotaping as we speak. Do we have your permission to videotape?"

"Okay," said Mickey, and he adjusted the necktie knot.

"First off, you are the CEO of the Desert Riviera Casino and Hotel, are you not?"

"I am." Mickey remembered the most basic rule of all depositions: Answer only what is asked, volunteer nothing.

"And as CEO you have access to all security measures taken by the casino?"

"I'm not sure what you mean."

Kroc shot a look at Magence. She smiled soothingly at Mickey.

"For instance, you have access to the casino's video-taping system, correct?"

"I think so. Far as I know."

"Far as you know? You mean there might be security precautions not even you know about?"

"Anything's possible. I guess." Don't guess, his brain warned him. No guessing.

"So there could be casino security measures being taken you don't know about?"

"Possibly. Anything's possible."

"Who would know about such security precautions?"

"I can't answer that. You're asking the name of someone who knows about something I don't know even exists. I can't help you there."

"Fair enough. You would, for example, have access to the security system that oversees the count room?"

"I would. Plus others would too."

"Names of others?"

"I don't have names. I probably don't know who that would be."

"Let me chime in," said Magence. Her eyes arched and she said, "Do you have a master roll of casino security operations and the names of those with access to those systems?"

"I don't think so."

She gave him a quizzical look. "But you are the CEO?"

"I am."

"And you're telling us you don't know what employees have access to what systems?"

He tugged at his shirt collar. "I don't remember ever seeing that list."

Kroc came back, asking, "So there is a list?"

"You're putting words in my mouth. I don't know if there's a list."

"You just said you hadn't seen that list."

"I meant, if there is such a list, then I haven't seen it."

"Thank you for that clarification. Do you need a glass of water? We have an icy pitcher right here."

"Still no thanks on that."

"Let me ask this. Would you, as CEO, have the ability to disable the security system in the count room?"

The question was an arrow straight to the heart. Mickey was certain they had seen the fear flash across his eyes.

He removed his hands from the table and clasped them below, so they wouldn't see him shaking.

"I don't think I could disable the security system," he lied, and mentally entered a "one" in the federal felony column for lying.

"Have you ever tried?"

Again, felony two. "No. Why would I?"

Kroc's egg eyes widened. "I can't answer that. Why would you?"

"That's just it, I wouldn't."

"Never?"

"Never."

"So it's your testimony here today that you've never tried to disable the security system in the count room at the Desert Riviera Casino and Hotel?"

Mickey inhaled mightily, buying precious time to think. "Define what you mean by 'security system.'"

"Sure," Kroc said easily. "I'm asking about the count room videotaping system."

"I don't think it's tape anymore. I think it's digital."

"But you know the system I'm talking about."

"The count room video system?"

"Yes."

"Have I ever tried to disable the count room video system?"

"Yes."

"No." Three felonies. Or is this a repeat of number two?

"Let me ask this. Have you ever been inside the count room when the video system was disabled?"

"No." Four felonies.

Would it be a felony for each time he stole money and lied about it, or would it just be one big felony for the lie?

Now he was becoming confused and he wished he had been able to bring along a lawyer. Even Langston Moretti would be better than this, and he didn't hold Moretti in the highest regard because, well, mainly because Moretti was loyal to the kid—Thaddeus Murfee—and therefore untrustworthy.

"You've never been inside the count room while the video system wasn't working—is that your testimony?"

"Not to my knowledge, I haven't."

"Have you ever removed money from the count room?"

"Myself?"

"Yes."

"No. That's not my job." Six. A huge six. Martha Stewart did twenty months for one miserable little lie that wasn't even a lie. It was something the FBI cooked up.

But his testimony today—it was purely fabricated.

He unknotted his necktie and pulled the collar away from his Adam's apple. Was it steaming in here, or was it just him? "I'll take that water now," he announced hoarsely. "And I'm getting hoarse. Hope we're about done here."

"We're just getting started. But if you need, we can break anytime and pick it up again tomorrow after you've rested your voice. Wouldn't want to do any damage there, would we, Agent Magence?"

She shook her head. No, they wouldn't want to damage his voice. Put him in prison for forty years, maybe, but in good voice. He would need his voice in prison.

She tilted the pitcher and filled the glass he selected.

"Upsy-daisy." She smiled, indicating a drinking motion as one might to a small child.

He obeyed.

The water was cool and soothing. There were even small slivers of ice that he could suck and he was especially glad for that.

It was the little things that counted in this life, he reminded himself, and wondered how he had ever lost that thread and taken to stealing money.

It was the little things, damn it, but oh no, that hadn't been enough for him.

No, he'd had to frost his cake with stolen funds. And now they were within one misstatement by him of sending him away for the rest of his life.

He drew a deep breath and guzzled more water.

"Better?" she asked.

He nodded. "Much. Thanks. And let me rephrase an earlier answer. You asked had I ever been inside the count room while the security system was disabled. Or something like that."

"Close enough," Kroc agreed.

"Well, I meant to say I haven't been in that situation to

my knowledge. It might have happened and I wouldn't know about it."

Kroc looked puzzled. "How would that come to pass?"

"Well—I don't know. You're the one asking the questions."

"But you're the one giving the answers and it's your last answer that has me, frankly, very puzzled. You're telling us that you might have been inside the count room while the security system was disabled but possibly wouldn't have known the system was disabled. Is that it?"

Mickey sat up straight. "Now I feel like you're putting words in my mouth."

"Sorry, but I must disagree. Can we agree to disagree?"

"Yes."

"Let's move along," Magence suggested. "That question seems to have been just about exhausted."

Kroc shot her a terse look. He was the superior. He would decide when a topic was exhausted, not her.

She caught the look and stared down at the table. "Sorry."

"Let me tell you some guesses we've made about the casino's operations. Fair enough?"

"Anyone can guess," said Mickey. "I can't help you with that."

"Hold on. We're guessing that someone is skimming money from the casino. And we're guessing that someone is Thaddeus Murfee."

You could have flown a 777 ten feet overhead and it wouldn't have been any louder coming in his direction than the words, "someone is skimming money from the casino."

But then, when he realized they weren't talking about him, that they were thinking Thaddeus Murfee, a great balloon of joy floated up through his chest, and his head cleared. The thought fugue slowed and slowed and stopped.

"Yes," he said. "I've wondered about that myself."

"You've wondered about Thaddeus skimming cash out of his business?"

"How could he not? It's there, it belongs to him, and maybe he doesn't want to share it with the IRS."

"Do you have any evidence what you're saying might just be right?"

Mickey looked up at the ceiling as if an entire mural of tattletale images floated there where he could pluck and choose at will, for their edification.

"Yes. I believe that the system log for the count room security system would indicate the system is being regularly turned off."

"Have you examined the log for this?"

"Not yet. I'm still pretty new. Regular audits of security system logs were on my to-do list. I expect to have an engineer assigned to that task sometime this quarter. Next quarter, latest."

He had to admit, that certainly had a ring of authenticity to it.

Plus it made him look damn bright and excellent at his job.

The whole notion of examining system logs—auditing logs—was actually brand new to him, but it really, at bottom, was a terrific idea.

"So you don't really know what the logs have to tell us at this point."

"Not wholly, no."

"Well, partially then."

"Still no."

"Can you bring those logs to us so we can review them?"

"I can."

"Will you?"

"I will."

"When can we expect them?"

"Soon."

"Like, first thing in the morning?"

Mickey was sweating again, precipitously, and realized he was about to bolt from the room. Strong self-talk helped him stay put. "First thing in the morning? I can have them here. Ten o'clock good?"

"Excellent. We'll see you then."

Mickey climbed to his feet. "You will see me then. And I'll have the logs."

"What are these system logs, text entries?"

"Yes."

"Excellent."

They walked him to the door with the keypad and saw him through.

He realized he had no idea if the logs were text entries or scribbling on papyrus, but he had immediately confirmed Kroc's guess because he was about to break and run.

He was that close to running from the room.

He felt the sweat trickle down his back as he watched the elevator lights as the car rose to take him aboard.

He felt faint but he was damn sure not going to faint right outside the IRS offices. He was too strong for that.

He wanted to smile but didn't for fear there might be security cameras spying on him.

He had done it, he had held his own.

Damn, he was good.

23

Bat arrived at work just before eight the next morning.

He told security that he had an appointment with Mr. Murfee and security rang Maria Villar, his day secretary.

"No," Maria told the security officer, "there's no meeting on his calendar with anyone named Bat. Does he have another name?"

Silence.

Then the security officer came back. "Billy A. Tattinger. Says Thaddeus will know him as 'Bat.'"

"Wait one. Let me buzz Thad."

Thaddeus was sleeping on his back and his mouth was parched. He swallowed hard and reached for the bedside phone.

"This better be good, Maria."

"I know. I'm sorry. But there's a man here name of Bat. Says you know him and he sounds desperate. Security said he was about to cry, he was so afraid you wouldn't know him."

"Give me thirty minutes then send him on up to my office. You did the right thing, Maria. Offer him coffee downstairs, and breakfast. He's probably starved."

He flossed while the shower head beat a heavy spray on his head and shoulders.

Then he shaved in the shower. Slowly and methodically, a task he hated more than any other of the day.

"Should just let it go," he told himself. "Grow a beard."

But he knew he wouldn't. Katy hated beards. She hated all facial hair. She was quick to point out that Native American men rarely have facial hair. It's cultural, she had told him. She didn't know that she could stand to kiss a beard and so Thaddeus had promised he would never make her try.

So he shaved. Slowly and methodically, and hated it.

Fifteen minutes later he was dressed and breakfast was ordered.

He had missed his daily sprint for Olympic gold on his recumbent bike, but promised himself he would get it in before bedtime.

The king-size desk beckoned and he took his place at the helm of the casino.

At the same time, a thought was forming. Maybe he should help Bat with his little criminal problem, in addition to the job he was giving him. Why not? The guy had no money, which was obvious. And without money he would wind up with a public defender speaking for him, which meant he would do time in prison for the pot sale to the narc.

While he was at it, another thought formed.

The wannabe clients he had talked to at the jail when he was being held, they had turned on a switch in his brain and he couldn't put them out of his mind. They were hurting, those guys, and most of them would never meet with a real attorney, someone who would really get to know them and hear their worries and fears and walk beside them as they went through the hell of facing criminal charges.

Instead they would get a hurried, bitter visit with a court-appointed attorney who was so overwhelmed with cases he or she simply wouldn't have the time to really listen and really help. With a target on his chest, he would be a number; he would appear before some judge and the judge would sight in on him and pull the trigger.

All kinds of bad things would follow and the guy would be hustled off to some insane form of incarceration and left to rot and learn to hate.

Maybe Thaddeus could figure out some way to donate an hour a day of real, thoughtful time to helping one or two of those folks.

Not a lot, just one, maybe two.

He had the office and he had a staff—hell, he had a full-time law firm working for him two floors down, tending to the casino's legal affairs. He might hit up one of them for some help with his one or two pro bono cases. It would be a way for him to pay back to the system that had made him wealthy beyond anyone's dreams, least of all his.

He switched on the laptop and scanned Huff Post, ESPN, his email inbox, and reviewed the weekend special on the front page of the casino website. Looked good there. It should bring them in by the hundreds, and he was glad.

Service arrived with a blueberry bagel and cream cheese, a carafe of Starbucks, and one orange.

He inhaled the food, washed his hands, and buzzed Maria. "Bring Bat in, please."

"They just brought him upstairs. I'll send him on in."

Bat was shown in and the first thing Thaddeus saw was a changed man.

Today he was bright-eyed (one eye), clean shaven, dressed in clean khakis and a spotless white collared shirt with plain black necktie, and was wearing a smile as he confidently thrust out his hand to shake. They shook hands and Thaddeus waved him to a couch. Thaddeus took a seat across the Vermont table and gave his new employee a big smile.

"You just look like a new man," Thaddeus admitted. "I wouldn't have recognized you."

"Hey, little brother, I clean up nice. Mama said 'first day, dress to stay.'"

"Mama's right on. Now my idea for you is to start you off in a restaurant, working tables. I'm thinking you start out as a bus boy and we see where that goes. What do you think?"

Bat grinned. In fact, he hadn't been able to stop grinning since entering the office. "Man, I'm just excited to finally land something. I'm here to please and the job don't matter. I'll do anything you say."

"Great attitude. Tell the truth, when I was eighteen I left home and walked down the street, no car, no money, and found a job. Guess what it was."

"No clue."

"Busing tables. At the Varsity Inn at Arizona State University. Following semester I enrolled in some classes. Made good grades, because the only way I was willing to go in that world was straight up."

"I hear that."

"Ten years later, I earned my undergraduate, finished law school, and now I own this place."

"You own the Desert Riviera?"

"I do. Which means you can't be fired or let go because

of a criminal record. Not as long as I'm around and not as long as you bust your ass to do a great job for me."

"You got no worries about that. I aims to please."

"Coffee? I'm getting a refill."

"Please. Two sugars."

Thaddeus retrieved the carafe and two cups from the serving cart. He made the preparations and handed a cup to Bat. Bat took a deep draw of the liquid and smiled.

"Great coffee. What are we serving?"

"We serve only Starbucks in the restaurant. In the casino we serve some generic brand, something off-label. Because no one notices coffee when they're gambling."

"How about booze?"

"Same thing. Chivas in the restaurants, off-brand on the floor. Every casino in the world operates this way."

"Got you. When do I start?"

"Right now, after I ask you a couple of questions. Do you mind if I go into your pending criminal case just a bit?"

"You're the lawyer, fire away."

"Well, as I recall, you were arrested for selling a significant amount of pot to a narc, correct?"

"Some might say it was a lot. Compared to what I've seen on the streets, it was nothing. Maybe eight ounces."

"And you made the sale because you were enticed by the officer? Or am I thinking of someone else?"

"Must be someone else. I made the sale because I needed the money. Nobody tricked me into doing something I didn't already want to do."

"Afraid of that. So it looks like you're going to need someone to cut the best deal possible for you and try to keep you out of jail. That about right?"

"Whatever you say. I jus don't know."

"What would you think if I acted as your lawyer in the case? Would you have any problem with that?"

"Man, you kidding me? I'd be—privileged."

"I don't think I would have a conflict of interest. The casino is your employer here, not me. I would be acting as private counsel, not on behalf of the casino. I think we could make it work and at the same time keep it ethical so I don't lose my law license."

"Whatever you need to do, Thaddeus, that's fine by me."

"Tell you what. I'm going to file some papers in your case, enter my appearance, and then I'm going to collect the discovery documents from the District Attorney. We'll sit down, look things over, and decide on some steps we can take to give you a hand here. Fair enough?"

"Too fair. Man, you're already giving me a job. You don't have to be my lawyer too."

"De nada. By the way, I charge five thousand for representation in a drug felony case."

For the first time, Bat's smile faded. He looked forlorn. "I don't have that kind of money. Might never will."

"You can make payments. Twenty-five dollars a pay period. Out of your paycheck. Fair enough?"

"Oh, man!"

"Good, then let's shake on it. I'll have Maria draw up an attorney-client agreement, prepare my entry of appearance, and file some generic motions in the case, including a motion to suppress evidence. I've got some friends downstairs who can help. That motion will require a hearing, but you won't need to testify. It'll probably just be the narc testifying and most likely the motion will be denied and the dope will come into evidence."

"It's Greek to me."

"You've been a criminal defendant before. You never went to a motion to suppress?"

"Nobody ever filed that for me before."

"Well, hang on to your ass, because the Murfee Law Group of Nevada is balls-to-the-wall full-on criminal defense."

"I'm liking this."

"Let's shake."

They pumped hands and Thaddeus escorted Bat to the door.

He told the security officer to deliver his new employee/client to the Riviera Steak and Chop House.

He then placed a call to the manager of the restaurant and told him a new employee was on his way.

"He's a bus boy. Minimum wage. Plus a percent of the tips. And dock him twenty-five bucks on each check to a note he owes me. Got it?"

The manager said he understood and that he would take good care of the new man.

Thaddeus grabbed his coffee cup and returned to his desk. He liked the name of his new law firm, Murfee Law Group of Nevada. He would have it incorporated and get some letterhead, some pleading paper, and some cards to pass out. Nothing big. Just one or two clients, that was all.

Then he called the Las Vegas Detention Center.

He told them he wanted access to the booking log for a certain date. Which just so happened to be the date he had been hauled in. He had heard several painful stories that night from cellmates who were going down the pain path. It just might be that one of them might need legal representation. One, that was all.

Two at most.

IN ADDITION to Billy A. Tattinger—Bat—there was one other brand new employee who started work the casino on the same day.

Kiki Murphy's first shift was the six–two—six in the evening until two in the morning. Which were the casino's heaviest gambling hours. Seventy percent of its profit was made during those eight hours. The remaining thirty percent was taken in over the remaining sixteen hours. So it only followed that the heaviest staffing was during Kiki's shift.

She reported a half hour early.

Her direct supervisor was to be Matty Jones, who was the shift manager for the six–two.

Matty was a card counter who had gone straight—as Thaddeus described him—meaning he had come over to the casino side of the street and now employed his prodigious skills at card counting, as a casino shift supervisor.

His job was to locate and eject gambling cheats.

They came to the casino every night from all over the world, a steady stream of self-infatuated, mostly self-taught, gamblers whose goal was to break the house and end up owning the casino where they were playing.

Matty's job was to make sure that never happened.

Matty reported directly to Mickey Herkemier and indirectly to Thaddeus, who still liked to work the floor every chance he got. Which was becoming less and less as he learned more about the casino and took on more of the hands-on management skills he had been lacking when he first assumed ownership of the business.

Kiki found Matty thirty minutes before her shift and reported in.

She had been told to dress so as not to be noticed. She had chosen navy cotton slacks, a white T blouse, and cordovan loafers. She had ditched the engagement ring but was wearing a modest gold chain. The wedge hair cut was recently cut and styled. Extremely attractive but toned way down, that was how she saw herself in the mirror before leaving her condo for the drive downtown.

Several times coming up the Strip she had checked her makeup in the Bug's rearview.

Nothing alarming there; subdued, almost hard to see any lipstick, if at all. No blush.

Matty looked her up and down and nodded.

"You'll do," he said, and sent her off to fill out the usual paperwork for new employees. "Find me when you're done. We'll work the first night or two within arm's length and then we'll branch out. And Kiki, I'm glad you're working for us now. You were very good at counting, last time I watched. Who taught you?"

She smiled with amusement. Such flattery. "Self-taught." She touched the side of her head and said, "Math major."

"Got it. Okay, see you in an hour. You'll have no trouble spotting me—I'll be the one throwing out the cheats."

She tossed her head with laughter and cut across the crowd to the elevators. She climbed aboard and punched 2.

Executive floor, she thought. Ain't I something? Finally got a real job and, surprise, surprise, my brother is my boss! Things were definitely looking up.

She had met with PX twice since the shooting and they had laid their plans.

First, PX had confiscated the purse carrying Kiki's gun when the fatal shot was fired.

She took the purse into custody immediately upon Kiki

receiving her personal effects back from the jailer when she bonded out.

The purse had been missed by the detectives as a vital element in the shooting.

It had been missed because their investigators hadn't realized, from watching the video replays a dozen times, that Kiki hadn't actually withdrawn the gun from the purse when it was fired. They were under the impression she had actually removed it from the purse and was holding it when she pulled the trigger.

The bullet's exit hole in the end of the purse was simply overlooked.

Plus the fabric was pleated and bullet hole concealed.

Because she had refused to make a statement, they never did learn otherwise.

But PX hadn't missed the significance of the purse.

Moreover, PX wanted the purse full of the same exact contents as when the gun went off. So she simply held out her hand the minute they stepped outside the jail, and waited, tapping her foot, until Kiki realized the purse was being confiscated by PX.

The second step PX had taken was when she had purchased the same exact handgun and sent both purse and gun off to an armorer for testing.

She was going to have the armorer attempt to replicate how the gun might have accidentally fired when Kiki reached inside. She had her money riding on the lipstick tube somehow becoming wedged inside the trigger guard and squeezing off the fatal round. But she would wait and see, she had told Kiki. They would wait and see whether the armorer reached the same conclusion. If he did, they were halfway home. They would have the case downsized to a negligent homicide case, nothing more. And Kiki would be eligible for probation on a plea of guilty to negligent homicide.

So Kiki was smiling when she stuck out her hand and greeted the woman from HR who would enroll her as an employee.

And the woman just took it as a friendly smile and thought Matty wise for hiring her.

24

T he IT department at Nevada IRS, Las Vegas, had
had to assign a group of dedicated sysops to its
hack on the network at the Desert Riviera.

Their target: any and all computer activity undertaken
by any user logging in with the credentials of Thaddeus
Murfee.

So far the network traffic had been negligible and the
sysops were all but asleep at the wheel.

Aldous Kroc called down to the chief of IT over
lunchtime.

"How's today shaping up so far on Golden Boy?" he
asked.

The chief of IT, Las Vegas IRS, was a rotund, thickly
bearded sprite of a man named Lamar. Lamar's idea of a
good time was the new issue of *System Admin* magazine and
a Mountain Dew on a Friday night before catching the latest
Wired news on the Facebook algorithm that delivered its
perfect feed.

He hated what little he knew of Aldous Kroc, and found
the insufferable Special Agent abhorrent. Still, he had to

take his calls. His job depended on satisfying the Special Agents and their slogs into third party networks where they were trespassers.

Lamar checked the Golden Boy log.

"Uh, this morning he logged in just after eight, read *Huff Post* for four minutes, *ESPN* front page for seven, then went to his company website, where he spent all of forty-five seconds. The system logged him out as inactive twenty minutes later."

"Why is it always twenty minutes later, Lamar? You're always giving us twenty minutes."

Lamar sighed. He resented these people who refused to learn anything about computer networks. "Because programmers set up systems to log out users after twenty minutes of inactivity online. It saves connections to the server for reuse by someone else without creating a meltdown."

"Which means he left the computer and the system automatically closed out his session."

"Exactly. See, almost painless, Agent Kroc."

"Buzz me if there's anything new. Don't bother me with ESPN or CNN or crap like that. But if he performs any amount of legal research on any site, I need to be advised without delay. And the session needs to be logged so we can retrace his research steps."

"We're coded and ready to go on that. If he hits Westlaw, Lexis-Nexis, or The Law we're ready to track him. Exactly like you ordered."

"Over and out."

"Right."

Lamar sighed, looked around his cubicle, and cracked his knuckles.

It was an earthy, real, human sound.

Which, to a man whose life revolved around 1's and 0's, was almost distasteful.

He popped the tab on his second Mountain Dew of the day and browsed over to StockX, the latest rage in high-frequency equity trading.

Now to make a dollar.

25

T here was something very suspicious going on in Orbit, Illinois, something Ragman had discovered on his second visit there.

The woman, this Ilene Crayton, he had been watching her closely. And she had a boyfriend.

Ragman dug a little deeper and learned the guy's name was Albert something, and that he was the law partner of one Thaddeus Murfee.

It seemed Albert worked the Chicago office while Murfee was out in Vegas, and every weekend Albert headed off to Orbit, where he was hitting that gal pretty regularly. In fact, they were spending weekends together, which complicated any Illinois kidnapping.

All in all, Ragman didn't like the setup.

Town was too small, located too remotely from interstate highways and hiding places, and he had no doubt he would stand out like a sore thumb if he hung out there any longer, as he was already drawing looks from the small towners who had no idea who he was and who wouldn't hesitate to stop and gawk at him. Too much heat, so he crossed the little boy Andromeda off his list and headed back out west.

26

F or his own criminal defense, Thaddeus added the Reno cowboy lawyer Gerald Browne to Tubby Watsonn's team.

Gerald—Gerry, as he preferred—was forty-five, tall, and large-boned, with a strong Western cragginess to his profile that caused his purplish-blue eyes to shine in their wide-spaced sockets.

To those who had gone up against him he was known as the Great One.

He was also known for leather coats, cowboy boots with under-slung heels, snap-front Western shirts with bolo ties clasped by huge turquoise chunks, topped off by black Stetson hats, flat-brimmed, looking exactly like the image of the Old West gunfighter he meant to portray.

But, like the cowboys put it, he wasn't all hat and no cows. Gerry owned 2,500 head of prime Herefords on his 10,000-acre spread twenty miles outside Reno.

He was known for suing large corporations and hacking away giant pieces of their assets for his Everyman clients, and he was known for winning criminal trials that all the trial luminaries deemed unwinnable.

Legend had it he had defended an out-of-office sheriff who shot his replacement between the eyes from the back-seat of a prowl car because, as the shootist put it, "He looked like he was about to draw down on me." Expert testimony had been presented in that case that yes, gunfighters can tell from the look in the eyes of an adversary whether they are about to draw and fire. The ex-cop walked, Gerry made the cover of *Time*, and soon the calls were jangling his phones 24/7.

Thaddeus knew about the lawyer and called him the day he made bail and left the jail behind forever—he hoped.

He flew up to Reno on a Wednesday morning, arriving just before lunch. The cabbie deposited him just outside the trial hound's office, where he paid his fare and found his way inside.

Five minutes later he was shown inside the Great One's law office.

It was neat and functional, nothing ambitious and West-ern-themed like Thaddeus had imagined.

Gerry Browne in full Western regalia stood fully upright behind the clean desk and extended a massive hand. Thad-deus, himself 6-2, was all but overwhelmed with the man's size. He went 6-6 and weighed somewhere in the neighbor-hood of 300 pounds. With the boot heels he was probably even taller, Thaddeus guessed.

"C'mon in," Gerry smiled with his huge, famous, jury-melting smile. "I'd offer you some coffee or water but I figure if you wanted any you'd have stopped before you got here. Am I right?"

"You are exactly right," said Thaddeus. "I'm good."

"So what brings you up our way, Mister Murfee? Or should I call you Thaddeus?"

"Thad is fine. Well, I've been charged with Filing False Tax Returns. And I'm innocent."

"We're all innocent, Thad, especially in the eyes of the Good Lord. Now, proving your innocence, that's my job. The Good Lord just ain't into that. Which is just between me and the jury we're gonna pick for you, when it all shakes out. Now tell me what they got on you."

The Great One sat back and perched readers on his nose. His enormous hands settled like two crows on a small keyboard, probably a tablet, Thaddeus guessed. He drew a deep breath and launched into his story.

"I won a casino in a lawsuit two years ago."

"Saw that. *American Lawyer* magazine had a cover story on you. And nobody's shot you over it yet?"

Thaddeus smiled. "Not yet. But I'm still very careful."

"Bodyguards—all that crap?"

"Exactly. All that crap."

"Got your own jet? You know the mob's bombing private jets now. Seems they've moved from car bombs to airplane bombs."

"No, I didn't know that. But I'll make a note."

The Great One leaned back and squinted at the ceiling. "Let me ask you something right out of the gate. And you tell me the truth when I ask you. Understand that I'm not here to judge you—I'm not some overpaid ethicist, and I'm not here to hear your confession—that's for Father So-and-so down at the church. But what I am here for is to sever any claims on you the American Justice System thinks it might have. And for that, I require your complete and total honesty. So here it is: Are you guilty?"

"No."

"Didn't think so."

"Why's that?"

"You're too young for evil machinations. Evil doesn't settle in on men until they get in their late thirties, early forties, when they first get an inkling that life's maybe not gonna go their way after all. That's when men seem to first take the law in their own hands and begin twisting things around to fit what they believe they deserve. You're too damn young for that. Unless you're a savant. Are you a savant, Thaddeus?"

"Not that I'm aware."

"Oh, you'd know if you were. But here's one thing I can see about you. You're a hell of a smart young guy, anyone who decides to sue the mob and take away some of their toys. You left even me in the dust on that one. Never saw it coming, did they?"

"I guess not. And I had a very friendly judge."

"I know him. Tried cases before him, down in Hard Times."

"Hard Times?"

"Vegas, Thad. It's always hard times—unless you happen to own one of the money machines, like you do."

"Which is another story for another day."

"So tell me why the IRS is fixated on you. How'd you draw their fire?"

Thaddeus shook his head. "That's just it. I'm clueless."

"Doesn't surprise me. Tell me about the management in your place. Who prepares the company tax returns?"

"Staff."

"Who prepares your personal returns?"

"Staff."

"How do you know how much income to report on your personal return?"

"Tell the truth, I don't know."

"Staff again?"

"Afraid so."

"Who counts the money?"

"Staff."

"Who keeps the staff honest?"

"Other staff."

"Any bells going off yet?"

"I'm trusting staff too much?"

Gerry Browne smiled and stretched. "What do you think?"

"I think you must be right,"

"Lemme ask it this way. Has that staff earned your trust? Or have you simply bestowed your trust on them?"

"Bestowed."

"Bottom line, you don't know any of these employees from Adam, do you?"

"Not really."

"So they could be pulling numbers out of their ass and you wouldn't know it, correct?"

"Correct."

"And how do you know they aren't?"

"I guess I don't."

The Great One put his boots up on the desk and shut his eyes for a moment. Then, "We have a lot of work to do with you." He abruptly sat upright. "Did you bring your checkbook?"

"I brought a check."

"What do you think so far? Do you want my help?"

Thaddeus answered without hesitation, "More than ever."

"When you leave here, leave a check for one million dollars with Angelina, up front. She's the nasty-looking

Latino. Heart of gold but always wearing that nasty frown. I can't make her smile. But your check—that will make her smile. Trust me."

"Will do."

"Now I want to take you for a ride in my pickup. We're gonna go out and see some trees, see some water, look across at some mountains, watch some cows eat grass, and we're gonna talk. By sundown I'm gonna know all about you. You'll be my guest tonight. We'll eat steaks and talk until the wee hours. Then we'll hit the hay, get six hours, get up and run—do you run?"

"I do."

"I've got everything you'll need. We'll come back, have a ranch-style breakfast, and you'll go home with a long list in your hands."

"List of what?"

"List of documents I'm gonna need to get you out of your jam."

"Fair enough. When do we start?"

"Right now. I'll have SusieQ call the airport and get rooms for your pilots and arrange transportation for them. They'll stick around town tonight, have a few drinks, and call it a day. All right, let's hit the road."

"Fair enough."

"And Thaddeus. Stop your worrying right now. You ain't guilty and I'm going to dispose a jury to saying the same thing about you."

"Okay."

"There. You got your life back."

He smiled, nodded toward the door, and Thaddeus followed him out.

27

F riday of his first week, Bat was competing like a madman to keep up with the table turnover in the Riviera Steak and Chop House.

There were six other busboys working the same shift, all Latino, all extremely hard workers, like Bat, and they were hitting it off just fine.

Except for the headwaiter, Bat had no complaints. The headwaiter hailed from the Dominican Republic, voted in all local, state, and national elections—he talked politics incessantly—and was trying to enlist his co-workers in a small drug network. He looked nothing like a drug dealer: mid-size, svelte, impeccable manners, perfect English, and the polished air of one who had served diners in the finest capitals of Europe, which he had. His name was Raoul and he was very friendly with Bat, until Bat flatly turned down his overture to become a seller of narcotics for him.

"This job is the perfect place to meet people. And believe me, our patrons make no effort to hide it from us. Many of them want drugs and they aren't afraid to ask. The money is easy, the menu is exclusive enough that cops can't afford to eat here, so it's all very safe to push a dime bag or a little blow when you are asked."

"I don't sell drugs," said Bat.

They were standing just off the kitchen, where the head-waiter kept a hawk eye on the wait staff and where Bat had no business lingering. His job called for constant movement by him, in and out of the kitchen, flying in with heavily loaded bus trays, flying back out with empty trays and going right back to it.

The restaurant tried to maintain a twenty-four-minute window per table, meaning that it expected to serve drinks, salads, entrees, and desserts, and have the diners out and on their way, all within twenty-four minutes. It was impossible, mostly, but that was the goal. The whole idea was turnover.

As Samuel Lidgard, the restaurant manager, said to the staff, "We can only charge a table once. So get them in, get them out, charge them, and move on to the next load. Fast, fast, fast. If you stand around, I'll notice the grass growing under your feet and I'll fire you without another word."

Bat intended to be the best busboy he could be.

He craved good reports from the wait staff about how fast he was helping them keep the tables turning, and, for the most part, he got it.

Like the rest of the staff, he didn't want to offend Raoul, so more and more it was becoming terribly difficult to keep fighting off the drug overtures while still maintaining a good rapport in hopes of good reports to the boss.

But Raoul, if anything, was persistent.

At least once every shift he would get the busboys aside and make plans with them for that evening's inventory of narcotics.

Again and again Bat refused to join in, and more and more he was afraid it would result in his dismissal.

So, out of pure need to avoid the upcoming calamity and likely dismissal from his job, he turned to the only friend he had. He called Thaddeus and asked if he could see him.

"Of course," Thaddeus relied. "Come right on up."

They settled across the Vermont table and Bat spoke first.

"Thanks for the help with the artificial eye, Thad, it's changed my life."

"Glad it works for you. Your health insurance plan covered it, actually."

"Well, now I can stand to look people in the eye again. I'm grateful."

"So what's up? We're still waiting on the DA's discovery on your sale of narcotics case, so nothing new there."

Bat scratched his head. "There's a guy at work."

"Oops. Have you talked to your manager about this? Before you came to me?"

"It didn't feel right. I'm scared to."

"So what gives?"

"It's one of the guys on the staff. He's putting the moves on me to sell drugs."

"Just give me his name," said Thaddeus. His look was grim and he was ready to take immediate action. "Name, please."

"It's Raoul. Normally I wouldn't rat on a guy, but you've been too good to me to just stand by and let it go."

"Any witnesses?"

Bat shrugged. "Unknown. But I know other guys are selling for him."

"Names. Can you give me names?"

"Oh, man, I don't wanna do that. I really like some of those kids."

"We can't have that. I could lose my gaming license. That's how serious this is."

"Oh, man."

"Let me get some help on this."

Thaddeus went to his desk and punched a phone line. "Maria? Get Chuck Berenson in here. I need him, no delays."

They passed a few minutes in idle chatter while waiting for Charles M. Berenson, the Director of Security at the casino.

A knock on the door and Berenson lumbered inside without waiting. He was a large man, built like a brown bear, but richly dressed and at ease around anyone. In a crowd he would go unnoticed and that's exactly the way he wanted it. "What's up, Thad?"

"Grab a seat, Chuck. Meet Bat—Billy Tattinger. Bat buses tables in the Riviera."

"Hey, guy," said Berenson. "Good to meet you."

"Chuck, Bat has come to me with a problem."

"Yes?"

"Seems we've got an employee soliciting other employees to sell drugs in the casino. While they're on duty, no less."

"Okay. You want me to arrest him and take him to the LVPD?"

"I'm thinking so. Yes, what do you think?"

"Boss, you can lose your license over that. Give me the word and he's gone."

Thaddeus nodded. "Word."

"Consider it done. Bat, anyone else selling for him?"

Bat shrugged. "If they are, I don't know names. I keeps to myself 'round here."

"Not a bad idea. Tell you what though, you become

aware of any others who had been dealing for him, you come directly to me. Here's my card."

Bat raised a hand, refusing a card. "I get caught with that, I'm toast. Don't worry, I know who you are. Truth be told, I've seen you around."

Berenson nodded. "Totally understand. Well, whatever you tell me is absolutely confidential. So if you do come up with any names, you let me know. Fair enough?"

"Word," said Bat. He rose to leave, but Thaddeus motioned for him to remain. Bat sat back down on the couch.

"Thanks, Chuck. I'm not quite finished up here with Bat, so if you'll excuse us?"

"Later, gents. I'll give you a heads-up on how the PD handles this Raoul guy."

Thaddeus nodded.

Berenson hurried out, anxious to arrest the employee and hurry him off the premises before the roof caved in on them all.

"I owe you big time," said Thaddeus. "Thanks, Bat."

"No problem. You'd do the same for me. You had my back since I met you. My lucky day."

"Bat, have you thought about working for us as a waiter? It would about double your pay and you'd get a huge increase in the tip jar."

"Wow. It never crossed my mind, truth be told. Would I want the chance? If someone trained me, I'd jump at it. Maybe I could get my own place then."

"Really? Where you staying now?"

"YMCA. Cheap but no food."

"Let me call Mister Lidgard. Come dressed like the wait staff tomorrow. They'll probably have you shadow someone for a week or so until you learn the ropes. Then you can jump right in. I'm going to have Maria cut you a check for two hundred fifty dollars. Get some clothes like the other waiters wear. Nothing expensive, but clean and new. You'll fit right in."

Bat was shaking his head. "Man, oh, man. You don't gotta do that."

"Yeah, I do. You saved my ass when I got tossed in jail."

"I did, how?"

"You talked to me, man. You came over and talked to me when no one else would."

"Oh, hell. You looked like you needed a friend."

"Well, you made a friend, Bat. Okay, off you go. Maria will have a check for you. Cash it downstairs, any teller. Cool?"

"We cool."

"So long, then."

Bat wanted to hug his employer but was embarrassed.

When he was gone, Thaddeus looked down through the one-way glass onto the casino floor.

His look was one of grim determination.

"Son of a bitch," he said. "Gerry's right. I'm going to have to wise up. This place is going to eat me alive if I don't get real smart, real fast."

Maria paged him on the phone and he was interrupted from the plans he was making in his mind, plans to restructure the casino operations so that he was personally more in touch with the daily happenings. Plus he wanted to implement new ideas for employees to voice their grievances to him directly. He wanted to hear from them all—especially those too frightened to report problems to their direct managers.

He picked up on the fourth page.

"Yes, Maria?"

"PX Persons, line seven."

He punched the flashing button. "PX? Thaddeus here."

"Well, this is a call I dreaded having to make."

Thaddeus frowned. "Why, what's up?"

"I've been suspended by the State Bar Association. I need to return your money and withdraw from Kiki's case. I cannot tell you how sorry I am."

"My God, is there anything I can do to help?"

"What it is, Thaddeus, is my number two associate lawyer has embezzled a hundred fifty thousand in client funds from my trust account. The Bar is holding me responsible. They've jerked my license for six months, until I complete a list of several CLE courses."

"What kind of CLE?"

"CLE courses to teach me better law office management skills and better management of my trust account."

"Do you have the funds to reimburse the client?"

"The State Bar has already taken care of that. The Lawyer's Fund, you know."

"Well—I mean, would it help if some of us wrote letters of support for you, anything like that?"

"No, the Supreme Court has already entered the order. It's official, I'm suspended as of the first of the month."

"Damn, I'm sorry to hear that. I know Kiki really likes you. So do I. Well, look, if it's going to put you in a bind, just take your time about returning the fee. You might need that to get by on for a while."

"God, Thad—"

"No, I'm serious. Let's give it twelve months before you repay. Who knows, we might even need to get you back onboard as soon as the suspension period is over. In fact, that's a for sure thing, far as I'm concerned."

"So who will you get to replace me?"

"Unknown. I'm still pretty new around town. Any recommendations?"

"Do it yourself, I'd recommend. Based on your past track record, Kiki would be damn lucky if you took over her representation. She could do a lot worse around this town, believe me."

"Hadn't thought of that. Well, I'll talk to her. And look, if you need anything, please pick up the phone. I'm just seven digits away."

"Thank you. I guess I will take you up on the twelve months thing. That's extremely generous."

"Maybe, but the truth is, I don't want to lose you. If I do take over and if I mess up the case I would definitely want you to handle the appeal. Hopefully that won't be the case. I'll have to talk to her."

"Goodbye, Thad. Thanks again."

He hung up and returned to his window overlooking the casino floor. The place was jammed, shoulder to shoulder, and Kiki would be coming on in two hours. He would talk to her then.

He shook his head.

Should he chance it?

Could he defend his kid sister on a murder charge and do it with a clear head?

Unknown.

28

S pecial Agents Kroc and Magence gathered in the small conference room and closed the door.

It was time to review.

She had brought along a Dr Pepper; he had herbal tea. Each was armed with a yellow legal pad.

Kroc dropped a thick printout containing surveillance updates.

They began pawing through them.

They knew he was twenty-eight, almost twenty-nine, that he was about to get engaged to Katy Landers (he had called a jeweler named Cassie at Jared's and told her he was coming in to pick up the ring they'd been holding for him), that he spent a great deal of time early each morning on the ESPN website, especially the NBA and NCAA hoops pages, and that he ordered a late night pot of coffee every night, with salmon cream cheese and one sesame bagel. He rode his recumbent bike most mornings, jogged along the Strip beginning punctually at seven a.m., and then returned to bed for a few more hours of sleep, as he usually didn't turn in until after three a.m.

The undercover team watched video of him as he studied gamblers and traded notes with the 6–2 shift manager whose name badge said "Matty."

They had bugged his office and hotel condo and had recorded and analyzed over 400 hours of video the past month.

"H. Mouton Carraway wants this guy big time," Kroc muttered, when they had finished up with the pile of reports.

"So do I," said Agent Magence. "And you need him, too. We haven't had a PR arrest in six months. We've got to earn some newspaper ink or Washington will be snooping around, checking up on us. We can't have that. I need this job too bad. We need results."

"Let's review our witnesses."

"Well, right out of the gate we got Mickey Herkemier. He's provided us with count room security logs that prove the video is being shut down every night between two and three in the morning."

"Usually at two a.m. when the shift changes over."

"Exactly. So whoever is shutting it down is someone who knows the heavy gambling is done during the 6–2 shift. They're waiting for the shift to end, waiting for the teller's receipts to flow upstairs to the count room, running everybody out, and then screwing with the surveillance video."

"Or something like that. So far we don't know if it's one guy or twenty."

"We don't even know if it's a guy. Might be female, for all we know."

"So why don't we do this. Why don't we install our own video system in the count room and catch the guy redhanded. See what kind of fish that hauls in."

"Now that's brilliant. Mouton will love us for it."

"Wait up. How do we shut down the video surveillance so we can install video surveillance of our own?"

"Good question."

They sat in silence several minutes, she working on her Dr Pepper, he sipping green tea. She hummed a Beyoncé hit and he drummed his fingers on his saucer. Soon, his drumming was keeping time to her humming, which, when they both realized what they were doing—at the same instant—embarrassed them no end. He looked away; she flipped a page on her yellow pad and began writing furiously.

Finally he said, about her writing, "What do you have?"

"I'm thinking we throw the power on the whole casino, rush in with a battery-operated camera, stick it in place, and run like hell. Power back up, and nobody's the wiser."

"I'll do you one better. How about we bribe the on-duty security officer, throw a switch, install our camera, and leave quietly. Nobody's the wiser."

"I like that," she said. "We'll get a list of security workers from Herkemier. Then we'll figure out the 6–2 shift people, and make a move on one of them—someone who's hurting for money."

"No, no," he said, "this is even better! We'll barge in and badge the guy, tell him it's official government business, and have him shut down the system while we install our camera. We don't have money for bribes anyway."

She sniffed. "Well, I wasn't actually going to pay the bribe, in my plan."

"Of course not. But I like the idea of bluffing them with a badge. That scares the hell out of John Q. Public, when the IRS Special Agents come badging."

"You're right. We always have the fear factor. But how do we keep them quiet?"

"Just like always. Threaten them with a tax audit. That always shuts everyone down."

"I like that. All right, let's get this Mickey guy on the phone and get that employee list. Oh, I've got it even better. We'll make up a search warrant, forge some judge's signature, and wave it under the guy's nose like we've got court authority to snoop. And that they are required by law to keep it confidential, court's order. That way, no one gets tipped off."

"Exactly! But wait, what if the guy we're crashing in on is the same guy who's stealing out of the count room? Then what?"

"Then we don't tell anyone. We've still got Thaddeus Murfee in our cross-hairs at that point."

"Even if it's someone else."

"Exactly. We need the press."

"Perfect. All right, you give Mickey a call."

"I'm on it."

"We'll crash the guy tonight."

"Exactly."

Goose bumps erupted along Kroc's arms. My god he loved this job. Absolutely loved every minute of it. Guns, badges, and scaring hell out of people—what's not to love?

29

L angston Moretti didn't like what he was seeing. As General Counsel of the Desert Riviera it was his job to work with Tubby Watsonn and Gerry Browne in defending Thaddeus Murfee on the income tax indictments.

Gerry Browne had conferenced them and given out his marching orders.

Langston would do the footwork; Tubby would do the legal aspects of the tax crimes alleged; Gerry would oversee it all and put it in trial format.

As General Counsel, Langston was accumulating the documents that Tubby had requested. What he didn't like were the numbers: they were all adding up. Which meant there were no suspicious items in the accounting records.

Moretti knew that the IRS looked for what it called LUQs whenever it was examining taxpayers' records. These were items that were Large, Unexplained, and Questionable. In all of the records he had reviewed, Moretti had found no such LUQs.

First came the video drives from the count room. Nothing there. Check.

Next came the source documents from which the tax returns had been filed. Both personal and corporate. Nothing there. Check and check.

Next came corporate and personal balance sheets for all years. Nothing there. Check and check.

Next came income statements—P&Ls—for the years in question. Nothing there. Check again.

Source documents ran to 500,000 pages. These were the documents that supported the balance sheets and P&Ls: receipts, invoices, checks, itemizations. So far he had stashed on the loading dock no fewer than 130 bankers boxes of documents for Tubby. Floor to ceiling. So much that the shipping department was complaining about the obstruction.

And he had the same documents on disk. They had been scanned and cross-referenced and entered into the casino's litigation software by date, creator, topic, recipient, fact proved/opposed, and a dozen other categories of reference.

With two mouse clicks Tubby could see what documents went with what witness, what documents went with what fact in dispute, what documents were prepared on what date and delivered on what date and received by who and prepared by who. It was a huge job but he had help—four paralegals, three data entry workers, and a database administrator.

The casino—and Thaddeus—was pulling out all stops in the defense of the case.

And so far the numbers all added up.

Balance sheets balanced, income statements reported net incomes that were within projections and created a forecasted rising curve from prior years, but nothing sudden or out of line. Nothing Large, Unexplained, Questionable.

Not one line was listed in any income statement, balance sheet, or P&L that wasn't immediately provable by a single mouse click to view the source document. It was excellent work and Accounting could be proud.

So Moretti called Tubby and Gerry. It was time to talk.

"Tubby Watsonn," said the voice on the other end. "Langston?"

"Gerry Browne. I'm listening."

"Lang here, Tubby and Gerry. We've finished up our first review."

"How's it looking?"

"That's why I'm calling. Everything balances. We don't show one day or even one shift reporting period where income falls below projections compared to prior days, weeks, or months."

Tubby went first. "That's not very helpful—but it does prove there's nothing untoward going on."

"Exactly. If there's cash being skimmed or removed, it can't be proven on paper. At least not on our paper."

"So the IRS is going to have to come up with a different theory of proof. What could that be?" Gerry mused.

"That leaves a pre-count skim. They have to prove that Thaddeus is skimming cash off the tables, out of the slots, before it's even counted."

Gerry spoke up. "The way I understand it, the slots are self-reporting, so it's not there."

"True, the slots cough up electronic reports showing in-going and out-going. No mystery there at all."

"And no room for a skim," Tubby concluded.

Moretti scratched his head. "So the slots business is clean. We can forget that part of it."

Tubby said, "Which leaves roulette, the card games, and craps. We need to focus there and see if we can spot any chance of a skim. How do we do that?"

Moretti field that one. "I've already tipped Berenson that we need extra eyes on those games."

"Berenson?"

"Chief of Security. Highly trusted, passes a lie box test every month."

Gerry sounded surprised. "You make him submit to a lie detector test each month?"

"What can I say? Company policy. Because it's a cash business there are many of us who face the lie box each month."

"Great. Get me those lie detector records, too," Gerry said.

"But lie detector tests aren't admissible in court."

"That's true. But I can use them to influence the judge. If we try to admit them, the judge learns about them, learns all employees are passing the tests with flying colors."

"Even if they aren't allowed into evidence."

"Right. We prejudice the judge; then we can get favorable rulings in other questionable areas where the law isn't so clear. Elementary."

Gerry sounded very certain about the game.

And why shouldn't he, thought Moretti. He had been before more federal judges than half the lawyers in Las Vegas added together.

"Rudimentary," added Tubby.

"Basic."

"Smart. I like your thinking."

"Okay," said Tubby. "Put extra eyes on cards, roulette, and craps. Bring in some outside people. Someone with impeccable credentials."

"Will do."

Gerry had a follow-up. "This leaves the count room. Is there any way someone is skimming out of there?"

"Negative. We video all count room activity."

"Get me those video logs. Let's make sure there are no gaps."

"Good point. That's the next item I'll run down."

"In fact, you know what I'm thinking?"

"What's that?"

"I'm thinking we sneak in and install a backup security system in the count room."

"Cameras to watch the cameras?"

"Cameras to watch the workers. A second set of eyes."

"In case the official cameras and official recordings are going off-line and the logs are forged."

"Exactly. Someone might just be that smart."

"Some insider."

"Insider, plus they have access to the count room. That means someone highly placed."

"That would have to be management level. Or even corporate officer."

Tubby pulled at his chin. "No one is above suspicion. I need a list of all management and corporate employees."

"Done."

Gerry said, "Then I'm going to need you to statementize them all. Get them nailed down."

"Got it," Moretti noted.

"Including you," Tubby laughed.

"Hey, that's fine. No one is above suspicion."

"Not even our CEO Mickey Herkemier."

"Not even Mickey."

They talked on for another ten minutes about logistical matters, and then signed off.

Moretti called Berenson. It was time to get more eyes on the tables. Time to call in the cavalry.

Plus there was the matter of a backup video surveillance system in the count room. Something totally hidden. Somehow foolproof. Something to view all activity, record it, and broadcast it off-premises, so it couldn't be doctored or manipulated.

He knew just the person to call.

"Buddy Bob," he called to his secretary. "Get Henry Frazier over at BAG on the horn. And make sure it's a secure line."

30

T haddeus filed his entry of appearance in Kiki's homicide case.

The State, by District Attorney Imogene Alvarez, immediately responded with a motion to disqualify Thaddeus from serving as attorney for Kiki.

The motion was based on grounds of an alleged conflict of interest and it came on for oral argument on a bright, hot morning in the Clark County Court.

"Oyez, oyez, oyez," cried the bailiff, "the District Court of Clark County is now in session. Let all who have business before this honorable court come forward now and be heard."

Wanda Morales, Chief Judge, entered the courtroom and sailed to her lofty perch overlooking all mere mortals spread below her.

Thaddeus and Kiki were at counsel table farthest from the empty jury box; District Attorney Alvarez was seated one table over, closest to the phantom jury, which was one advantage she would have when the case actually got underway at trial. Thaddeus always resented the fact that the State got to sit closest to the jury, human nature being what it is, but there was nothing any defense attorney in the U.S. could do about it.

Thaddeus came upright, climbed to his feet, motioned Kiki to stand beside him, and was immediately told by Her Honor that all could take their seats.

The judge pushed the onyx eyeglasses up on her nose and squinted at the file.

She was a woman probably mid-fifties, Thaddeus guessed, who had an excellent reputation as a fair-minded, but firm, trial judge. She was also one to follow the law to the letter, he knew, so she would be very interested in the pending allegations of conflict of interest being claimed against Thaddeus.

"Counsel," the judge said to the D.A., "you may be heard."

District Attorney Alvarez leapt to her feet, ready to shoot big game.

"May it please the court. Judge, this is a case where a lawyer who owns a casino is trying to represent a defendant who was followed out of the casino by two men, one of whom she shot and killed minutes later. She has potentially got a civil claim against the casino for failure to provide safe premises upon which to come inside and gamble, or whatever she was there for. Because she might have a claim against the casino, it's the State's position that the owner of the casino would have a conflict of interest and shouldn't be representing the defendant at all in the criminal case. Which is what he's trying to do here."

Eyes rolled to Thaddeus. "Counsel?"

Thaddeus stood and scanned his argument points.

"Thank you, Your Honor. What we have here is a case exactly like the D.A. has framed it, but with one significant fact omitted. Your Honor, the Defendant in this case is my sister. And she won't sue me. It's just that simple. So while counsel is theoretically correct in her allegation of conflict, in reality there's no conflict at all, and there won't be. Kiki Murphy is my sister and we've talked about her legal right to sue the casino. I can avow to the court that that will never happen. Not only that, but Kiki is now an employee of the casino. For what difference that might make."

The judge studied the ceiling, then said, "Counsel, was Miss Murphy a casino employee at the time of the shooting?"

"She was not, Your Honor."

"So there is no issue of pre-emption by the worker's compensation laws of this state?"

The judge was asking whether Kiki was an employee of the Desert Riviera at the time of the shooting because, had she been, then by law she wouldn't have been able to sue the casino.

Thaddeus explained that she was not an employee at that time.

"No, Your Honor, there's no pre-emption by the worker's compensation laws of the State of Nevada."

"Judge," said D.A. Alvarez, "this case has the potential for imposition of the death penalty. The indictment alleges First Degree Murder with malice and premeditation. If Miss Murphy is found guilty, it would place Mister Murfee in the horrendous position of fighting for his own sister's life in this matter. It's probably not in her best interests that she have someone so close to the case representing her in that case."

The judge shook her head. "That may be, counsel, but that's not your argument to make."

"But you want a clean record when it goes up on appeal."

"The Court must weigh what you're saying against the Defendant's right to be represented by counsel of her choosing. That's actually a Constitutional right—or has that flavor—so it's the Court's opinion that far outweighs any potential for anxious feelings Mister Murfee might be facing on down the line."

"Judge, I will probably associate trial counsel on this case. If that helps with your decision. And one other thing. I have thoroughly discussed this issue with Miss Murphy and she knowingly waives any potential conflict. I can avow that to the Court as well."

"Not necessary, Mister Murfee. The Court is going to deny the District Attorney's Motion to Disqualify Thaddeus Murfee as Counsel of Record for Kiki Murphy. It is so ordered. Anything further?" The judge leaned forward and pointed an index finger at each attorney. "Anything?"

"No, Your Honor."

"Thank you, no, Your Honor."

"Then we're adjourned."

All stood and the judge sailed back out the door to her chambers.

District Attorney Alvarez turned to Thaddeus and smiled in a friendly manner. "You sure you want to do this, Mister Murfee?"

He paused packing his briefcase. "I'm sure. Someone has to do it."

"But it could get painfully difficult. Just so there's no misunderstanding, I am aggressively seeking the death penalty in this case. The victim had broken off his attack on your client and was in fact raising his arms to indicate the attack was over."

"I'm aware that's what you think happened," said Thaddeus, "but fortunately that's not the entire story."

Alvarez came nearer. "What else do you have?"

Thaddeus grinned. "You're going to have to wait for trial to find that out. We wouldn't want to spoil the surprise, would we?"

Alvarez jammed a hand against her hip. "You will be required in discovery to reveal your witnesses and your evidence."

"But not my theory. You're not entitled to my thoughts. Which are, in fact, reality."

D.A. Alvarez took a step back. "All right, if that's how you want to do this."

"Hey, what choice have you given me? Miss Alvarez, you're trying to kill my sister. I'm here to tell you, that's not going to happen. By the way, from now on, for future reference when you're speaking to me, let's don't call the dead guy 'the victim.' You know as well as I do that if my sister hadn't shot the guy you'd be in here prosecuting the bastard for assault on my sister. And in front of the jury, if you ever refer to him as 'the victim' you can be sure I'm going to jump up and yell for the court to strike any such reference and I'm going to explain why you shouldn't be able to use that term and make sure the jury hears every word of what I have to say. If he's the victim then I'm Santa Claus, and right now I don't feel very charitable toward anyone, especially the criminal who assaulted my sister. Now, are we done here?"

"We're done here," the D.A. said and petulantly tossed her head. "See you in court."

"You just did."

As they went out into the bright sunlight and set out on the sidewalk to the waiting Mercedes, Thaddeus noticed that Kiki was unusually quiet.

They climbed in the back of the car and Thaddeus gave the driver Kiki's address. He would take her home and drop her off, as it was still morning and her shift at the casino wouldn't begin for another six or so hours.

"So what's going on in your mind?" he finally asked after they had ridden several miles in silence.

She grimaced. "Did you see CNN last night?"

"About?"

"About Oklahoma."

"No, what happened?"

"They executed Mel Robbiny for first degree murder. Lethal injection. Except he didn't die. They gave him the drugs, he went into horrible contortions, and after nine minutes he strained up against the straps and said something like, 'Oh, man, there's something terrible wrong here.'"

"My God."

"Yes, it got so bad they had to close the blinds to the execution chamber as the witnesses were horrified and crying and screaming at the doctors to stop it."

Thaddeus spoke very softly. "I'm sorry that happened. And I'm sorry you had to see it."

She suddenly sobbed. "Thad, for god's sakes don't let them do that to me!"

He took her hand in his own. "Hey," he whispered, "I just got you back in my life. I'm not letting go. That won't happen to you. Nothing like it, I promise."

"Promise?"

"I'm going to walk you out of there, Not Guilty. I promise."

"I thought you told me lawyers can't make promises."

"They can't, unless it's their sister. Then all bets are off."

31

Sunday night, and Thaddeus with Albert had just finished their biweekly file review for their Chicago practice.

They were in Thaddeus' office at the casino, seated across Vermont from one another.

An order was placed to room service for two Diet Cokes and two bagels, as both were famished after the three-hour review.

Albert had flown the Learjet out from Chicago; Thaddeus' own driver had picked him up at McCarran late that afternoon and would take him back out to the airport so he could fly back out that night.

Both men were wearing blue jeans and T-shirts, and Thaddeus was in moccasins while Albert was in his usual Air Jordans.

The food and drinks arrived and they kicked back and were shooting the breeze about everything and nothing when Albert's expression without warning turned serious.

"Thad, there's one more thing I guess I need to bring up," Albert slowly began.

"Uh-oh, this sounds ominous."

"It's about you and Ilene. And her baby, Andromeda."

"Her baby? Don't you mean my baby?"

Thaddeus had abruptly stopped chewing a mouthful of bagel and was waiting, very puzzled at the direction their BS session had suddenly taken.

"Well, that's just it. Turns out Andromeda is not your son."

"Yeah, right. What else you got to say?"

Albert raised a hand. "I'm serious, Thad. We had paternity tests run."

"We did?"

"Ilene and I."

"You and Ilene?"

"Thad, while you had disappeared two years ago, when Bang Bang was after you, you had me go to Ilene and talk to her."

"That happened more than once. So you talked to her, so what?"

"Well. One night—and you're not going to like this. In fact, you might throw me out. But please, for god's sakes stop and think before you say anything radical. One night things got out of control, we had dinner and wine, her little girl went to bed, and it just happened."

"What was that??"

"We slept together."

"Bullshit. Ilene would never do that."

"Excuse me, but she would. And she did. And I'm so sorry about it, it's just been killing me and I've been covering up. You're not Andromeda's father; I am."

Thaddeus stood and walked to the window overlooking the casino floor. He was silent while several minutes dragged by. Then he turned and faced Albert. Tears were in his eyes and close to overflowing.

"You're sure about this?"

"Positive."

"And Ilene has known about this how long and hasn't told me?"

"Don't go there. We both found out Friday. We just had the testing done ten days ago. It was my idea to get the tests. Drommie looks nothing like you and he's beginning to have some of my features."

"What, he can't speak English, only Spanish?"

Albert smiled. "So you're not mad?"

"Hell yes, I'm mad. You screwed my girlfriend, the woman I was in love with. Or thought I was in love with. The first real love in my life. And you screwed her. Now how can I ever trust you again?"

"You can trust me. It had nothing to do with you."

"How can you say that, it has nothing to do with me?"

"It doesn't. What happened was between Ilene and me. It happened without any reference to you at all. She was lonely, I was finding myself more and more attracted to her, and you weren't around and hadn't been for a long time. Plus, there was the wine that night."

"Shit, Albert. Shit."

"I know. I'm very sorry. But I promise you, everything about our law practice is foursquare. We're totally good there. I am one hundred percent loyal."

Thaddeus shook his head. "Well, I'm so buried out here, I don't have time to make any changes in Chicago."

"Besides all that, there's no reason to make changes in Chicago. You know the money's a hundred percent accurate and accounted for, you know I'm the best med mal lawyer in the entire city, and you know I'm taking care of our clients."

"Like you took care of my girlfriend?"

Exasperation crept into Albert's voice. "You can fire me, or give the cases away and close up shop back there, but that really doesn't do anyone any good."

"Least of all you and Ilene. What do you plan to do about all this?"

"This is crazy, but I want to ask you for the right to marry her."

"I can't give you that right. It's not mine to give."

"Still."

"No, I have no right to control who she marries. I've made my choice. I'm with Katy."

"True."

"You're sure Drommie isn't my kid?"

"99.999999 percent sure. One chance out of six billion we're wrong."

"Those are worse odds than the lottery."

"I know. And I love Ilene. I'm mad about her."

"So what is the plan?"

"We're going to keep her place in Orbit and we're going to move her to Chicago."

"Shit, you've talked this all over with her."

"She wanted to call you, but I told her I needed to talk to you first. You and I go back a long ways and the whole thing was my error in judgment for going off the rails. So I felt like I owed it to you. But she begged to let her go first."

Thaddeus sniffed. He took a long draw out of the Coke can. "Does she want to talk to me? Do I just call her up and ask how she is?"

"She wants to talk to you. Just not right now, not tonight."

"That's cool. I don't much want to talk to her right now."

"Don't go there, Thad. You've been running off with Katy

for the last year. It was bound to happen with Ilene sooner or later. If not me, then someone. She's too beautiful and too attractive in so many ways to just walk off and expect her to wait. She waited almost a year, anyway."

"And then you got her in bed."

"It wasn't like that. We fell in love. That's not about you."

"You're right. I'm sorry. And you're right; I have no claim on her, no right to be upset. I had made my choice. I have no right to expect her to be sitting home beside the phone, waiting for my call. That's not Ilene. Damn, I'm going to miss her though."

"I know you are. But that was then and this is now."

"True."

"And now I want to give you some free, unsolicited advice."

"I'm not sure I'm in the mood for your advice, Albert. But go ahead."

"Marry Katy. Now, don't wait. Get her to transfer med school to UNLV and get her the hell out of Palo Alto. She's too dreamy to leave running around alone up there. You're a fairly decent-looking guy, but Brad Pitt you're not. Grab her while you can."

"You know, you're right about that. I think I'm going to do that very thing."

"Like yesterday."

"Like yesterday."

~

At first the U.S. Attorney's office was reluctant to agree to Thaddeus leaving the state of Nevada.

His conditions of release on bail had required that he

surrender his passport, which he did, and that he not leave the state of Nevada.

He was sitting in Tubby's twentieth-floor office suite while Tubby discussed the case with Assistant U.S. Attorney David Fisher.

"What the fug, Fisher, it's only a couple of days. Lighten up, man."

Fisher's voice was tinny over the phone and Tubby wondered whether the line was bugged.

"We don't want him leaving Nevada. Why can't he get married here? Tahoe would be great for it. Especially this time of year."

"Oh, so now the government gets to decide where Mister Murfee gets married? Are you bullshitting me? Are you actually serious, man?"

"Well—"

"Well, nothing. You can shoot me an email that he's leaving with your permission, two days in California, or I'm going to the judge and I'm asking for and getting attorney's fees for having to bring such a ridiculous motion to modify conditions of release."

"Are you threatening me, Tubby?"

"You're damn right I am! Now get that email to me in the next thirty minutes or I'm filing."

"Give me a couple of hours. I need to run it past Mouton."

"You want to run it by the U.S. Attorney himself? Why would he give a shit?"

"It's political too."

"I thought so. This whole chickenshit prosecution is political, isn't it, Mister Fisher. Your asshole boss is going to toss his hat into the senate race, right? Or some such bull-shit. Well you tell H. Mouton that he signs off on this by

noon or I'm going to file in court and I'm going to hold a
press conference and let the people know how the U.S.
attorney is trying to manipulate where Nevadans get
married. Especially Nevadans who haven't been convicted of
anything!"

"Settle down, Mister Watsonn. We'll work it out, I'm
sure."

"Noon, Mister Fisher. Or I press FILE on my computer
and take you guys to court."

He slammed down the phone, pulled a white handker-
chief from his suit pocket, and fiercely wiped his face. "Get
all lathered up over these assholes."

Thaddeus shook his head. "So? Do I get to go to Malibu
or not?"

"I'm sure they'll get onboard. It's just a matter of having
it in writing."

"Is an email good enough? They won't try to claim it's
not from them?"

"Naw, we do this all the time with the feds."

"What about the fools who've been following me? Kroc
and Magence? I get glimpses of them every day. Will they
follow me to Malibu? Will they attend the wedding?"

"Look, I'm sorry about that. But I warned you. These
people will hound you and try to manipulate you into doing
something that can cause your bail to be revoked. It would
be huge if they could take you back into custody, even on
some bogus claim of violation of conditions of release.
That's why I told you to always use your driver. That way,
you can't be pulled over even by the cops. The fastest way
they can get to you, believe it or not, is if you drive. The
second fastest way is if you leave the state and they find out
about it. Let me do my job here and we'll have you off to
Malibu."

"Promise?"

"That I can promise."

"I can go ahead and make reservations in Malibu? Get things set up for the ceremony?"

"What date?"

"One week."

"That wouldn't give me much time if I did have to take it to court."

Thaddeus spread his hands. "Look, expedite it, then. I'll pay what it costs, I don't care. I want this wedding to happen and Katy wants Malibu. I don't know why, I don't care why. She wants Malibu and she wants her great-grandfather there so we have to start making plans for all these logistics like yesterday. Please. Let me know by noon too. Can you do that?"

"Absolutely. Go ahead with your plans. It'll work out."

"Then I will."

32

F irst came the IRS agents, badges on chains around their necks, guns in plain view, storming the security officer's headquarters.

Systems were overrun, cameras shut down, and an incursion made into the count room where employees were chased out and cameras were planted in the HVAC vents.

When they left, no evidence of their appearance could be found.

All systems seemed to be in working order, so Thaddeus and Berenson took no further steps just then.

Four hours later the BAG agents arrived, secured the count room, disabled the security system, and swept the room.

The IRS spy cameras were immediately located and their digital images rerouted through BAG headquarters, where they were looped to play, over and over, twenty-four hours' worth of count room activity. There were twenty-seven days' worth of video feed available for the ruse. So in effect, what the IRS surveillance technicians would be watching—ostensibly from their spy cameras—were randomly selected day after day of prerecorded count room activities. Never would their feed be "live," never would they actually receive a video signal that displayed anything like what was actually going on in the count room.

Following the hack of the IRS video feed, the BAG agents then installed their own hidden video system that would provide a 24/7 live video feed to BAG headquarters where surveillance crews were in place.

All footage would be analyzed. Any theft of money from the count room would then be pinpointed and reported to Thaddeus.

Steps taken by the BAG agents were reported to Thaddeus and Thaddeus alone, orders of Langston Moretti, who had tapped the group for the job.

The information given to Thaddeus was for his eyes only, as all steps were being taken to close any loop where there was the possibility that security measures were being disabled and uncounted money was being removed.

It was a busy day in the count room.

No employees were the wiser.

Not even the CEO.

33

B at reported to Thaddeus' office at noon on Friday.

It had been a stormy day in Vegas, which was very rare, and many gawkers and window-shoppers sought cover inside the casinos, so business was booming. The restaurants were busier than usual and Bat was serving eight tables.

He was now averaging $300 a day on tips alone, not counting his minimum wage hourly.

The job had enabled him to move out of the YMCA into his own one-bedroom apartment, purchase a used Honda with $500 down, and replenish the wardrobe that had been worn out from years of wear on the streets and back alleys of several American cities.

He felt like a new man; he was happy.

He had even gone to the dentist and paid $1,500 for some very basic hygiene and upkeep that was brightening his smile.

To top it off, one of the cooks was making eyes at him and she was probably fifteen years younger and very fit. She looked enticing to him, even in her apron, and she often sought his advice on investments she was making in the stock market. He had no advice for her about such things, but the premise gave them the opportunity twice a shift to sneak off to a table together and have coffee while they discussed. Less and less the talk was about the stock market and more and more the talk was about them getting together for dinner— maybe even that weekend. Her name was Maria Consuelo, she was from Hermosillo, and Bat was head-over-heels.

So it was with a certain amount of fear and trepidation that he reported to Thaddeus' office that afternoon. Things had been going so incredibly well in his life, and he was praying he hadn't done something wrong to put the kibosh on his great good fortune.

"C'mon on, Bat," Thaddeus said, and joined him across Vermont.

The coffee table called Vermont was more and more bothering Thaddeus; it was too big and he was making plans to have it replaced. In fact, he was making plans to have the entire office redone—just as soon as he whipped the IRS' butt.

"Have I done something wrong, Thad? Is that why I'm here?"

"Good grief no. I hear you're doing a great job and everyone loves you. Are you making enough money to survive?"

"More than I ever dreamed. I can't thank you enough."

Thaddeus nodded solemnly, and said, "Actually, you can help me enough. If you will."

"Just say it, Boss. Whatever you want."

"Well, I've been charged with filing false tax returns."

"Who said that?"

"The IRS said it about me. They charged me with a crime for it."

"You ain't going to jail? I'm not about to lose my lawyer and best friend?"

"No, Bat, but as your lawyer I needed to make you aware of my predicament, just so you could find other counsel if you wanted. And if you do want someone else, the casino will loan you the up-front money, just so you know."

"I don't want anybody else. I want you, Boss."

"All right, thanks. Let me tell you what else is going down around here."

"Shoot."

Thaddeus leaned forward and lowered his voice. "Someone is stealing from the casino."

"In my restaurant?"

"No. I need to write this down. My snoops tell me this office is bugged. We don't know how they're getting in here, or when, but it's bugged. So read this."

Thaddeus tapped on his tablet and began writing his instructions for Bat.

Bat sat politely upright, his hands folded in his lap, and waited.

Thaddeus held up the tablet. Now it was Bat's turn to read. As he did, his eyes grew wide as an owl's and he swallowed hard. "You mean this?" he asked.

Thaddeus nodded. "I do. And it's okay for you to do."

"Promise?"

"Bat, you have my solemn word. I will take care of it if anything happens to you."

"I'm—I'm—I don't know what to say."

"Please, don't say anything. Too many ears around this place. Will you help?"

"You know I will."

"All right. Come here when you're done. I'll be waiting."

"It's as good as done, Boss. What time you got?"

"Twelve twenty."

Bat displayed his new gold watch. "Me too. Exactly."

"Then we're synchronized, ready to embark."

"Ready to proceed, Boss."

"Thank you, Bat."

34

At precisely 1:50 a.m. that same Friday night, Thaddeus buzzed security. Berenson picked up.

"Thaddeus calling. I need your entire security crew in my office now."

"Who do I leave here to watch things?"

"No one."

"No, I mean who do I leave down here to watch the count room when the shift changes?"

"No one."

"Come again?"

"Damn it, Berenson. Listen to my damn words. I want every member of count room security in my office. Now!"

"Including me?"

Thaddeus sighed angrily. "Are you a member of security, man?"

"Yes."

"Then come the hell up here, please. All of you now. I'll see you in four minutes."

Four minutes later they piled into his office and he waved them to the couches. There were the two screen men, who did nothing but constantly scan the security screens. These weren't the same men just above the casino watching the tables. These men were watching for people who wanted to do the casino and its occupants harm. The card cheats were watched by an entirely different group.

The system administrator for the entire computer system was there, drinking a Mountain Dew and popping his knuckles.

There were the two uniformed officers who ordinarily were stationed outside the count room. They were looking nervous, their faces twisted and red, extremely fearful that the entire casino would be robbed while they were away. The guns on their hips were loaded and they were ready for any menace. Why they had been called to the owner's office was beyond anyone's comprehension.

"All right," said Thaddeus. "I want this in your logs. Write that you came into my office on this date, one fifty-five a.m. Write down the names of all those present, including me. Write that you stayed with me until two oh-five a.m. and then were dismissed back to your posts. Any questions?"

They all looked at each other. There were no questions. Berenson cracked open his tablet computer and began making his notes. Three others began doing the same thing on their tablets. Everyone looked at his or her watch, noted the time, and did as they were told.

FOUR FLOORS BELOW, the count room was empty.

At exactly 2:03 a.m. the banks from the tellers' cages arrived on twelve carts. It was a huge amount of money, usually $600,000 or more from each shift. Of course part of the money would go right back out, after the count, and right back into the tellers' cages to constitute the casino's bank, a collective fund from all tellers' cages, minus the profit from the shift, which remained in the count room, inside a ten-ton safe and electronic security, awaiting transport to the brick and mortar bank the next day.

The carts were unloaded.

The transport employees followed protocol and immediately left the room without talking. There was never to be any discussion coming or going about the funds being transported or, for that matter, any other topic.

At exactly 2:06 a.m. a figure wearing a black ski mask entered the count room. The room was empty and the video cameras overhead were whirring. The BAG cameras, that is.

The figure was wearing a black turtleneck, black denim pants, and white running shoes, no emblems on the sides.

He walked to the count table and pulled a bank bag from under his arm, placed it on the table, and began stuffing it from the money piles.

The entire process took less than one minute, then he was done, he zipped the bag, disappeared from the room, and the cameras recorded no further movement.

Until the usual security staff, with the count room staff —also part of the security staff—returned to their normal jobs.

Again, there was no discussion while the bills were fed into the count machines. The only sound was the high-pitched clatter of armatures as they riffled through the bills and scored their tallies on electronic displays, in tens, hundreds, and thousands.

The men and women in the room were wondering what they had just been called to the Boss's office for, but they were certain they would never know, except he had made what seemed to be a perfunctory and very general speech about count room security, casino security, the Heimlich maneuver, and other areas totally unrelated to their normal duties. It was almost like he was treading water, they thought.

Which in fact he was. They had returned to their posts at 2:10, leaving him utterly alone.

At exactly 2:30 there was a knock at the door and security stuck his head inside.

"Someone to see you, Boss. Name he gives is Bat."

"Send him right in. And Charlie, send up some bagels and cream cheese. And a pot of coffee, two mugs, cream and sugar. Thank you."

Bat slipped inside. He was wearing white running shoes, black denim pants, and a black turtleneck. He handed a bank bag to his boss, who thanked him.

"Here's your cut, Bat," said Thaddeus, and he counted out fifty $100 bills.

"No, Boss, you don't hafta do that. No way. You've give me enough."

"I owe you. Big time. I want you to have this. Save another five K and you'll have enough for a down payment on an FHA loan. I'll co-sign and you'll have your own place."

"Jesus," said Bat, his eyes tearing up. He folded the $5,000 and tucked it inside a denim pocket. "Jesus."

"Yes," said Thaddeus. "That's always a good prayer."

"I got nothing else to say."

"Hey! We got coffee on the way, and bagels. What do you say we stay up and watch the sun come up?"

"Why the hell not. Yes, Boss, let's do that."

"We'll get some cards and I'll teach you Honeymoon Bridge."

"I don't gamble, Boss."

"It's no gamble, playing against me, Bat. I stink at cards."

"Holy shit."

"I know. That's what they call 'irony,' Bat."

"Let's play, then."

"First the coffee and snacks, then the cards."

"You're on, Boss. You're on."

35

They had the beach house for a week, though Thaddeus wondered if he could actually get away with being out of Nevada for that long.

In the end, the U.S. Attorney's office agreed to his being gone for three days, so he was pushing it, renting the beach property for a full week. But in the end he decided to go ahead and try it, the hell with what the U.S. Attorney thought. If a fracas ensued over his absence he would plead his case to the judge, who thus far had seemed friendly enough.

Henry wouldn't leave his sheep, it turned out, and he hated the ocean anyway. He had worked in Long Beach during the war, at a Naval munitions dump, and he had seen enough of ships and beachcombers to last him a lifetime, he said.

Secretly, Thaddeus was glad he refused. He wanted and needed this time alone with just Katy. And Sarai, of course.

The beach house clung to the seashore in Malibu with the other ten-million-dollar escape pads overlooking the Pacific Ocean.

The ocean seemed to be filling up with surfers, waders, walkers, and sailboats.

It was an extremely busy area. Everyone wanted to get a glimpse of Malibu, if for no other reason than to say they had been there.

Katy had found the retreat in an online listing site of exclusive Malibu rentals. Money wasn't enough to score a rental; you also had to be someone.

Thaddeus' notoriety as the owner of a Las Vegas casino pulled them through and doors magically opened.

The one-week was priced at $12,500, considered a grand bargain by the Realtor they finally had settled on.

It was a fine home, traditional Southern California beach house with fully windowed western exposure, cantilever roof at enough odd angles to please any modern architect, long decks around all sides, and a private drive.

There were too many bedrooms and bathrooms to count, and Sarai immediately invented a game where she would hide from her parents in different rooms and not answer their increasingly frantic calls to her. She would make them find her and broke into peals of delighted laughter when they finally zeroed in on her location.

There was also a chef, two maids, and a personal trainer, as the eastern exposure contained a full weight room and cardio machines.

Thaddeus was grateful for the chance to exercise and run on the beach. Katy complained about ten pounds of baby fat she was still carrying around her middle but said how thrilled she was to have the cardio workout area to try to make a dent. Thaddeus swore up and down that she had no such problem, for which she was grateful and smiled, but she knew better; the scale didn't lie.

Halfway through the week, the Realtor showed up—

unannounced—and dropped hints that the property might be purchased for a very reasonable price. The owner, it seemed, a writer on an HBO Sunday night series, was going through a financially desperate time due to a full-scale divorce war in which she had become embroiled. The beach house had been the writer's second thought. It could probably be picked up for a song. A song in the neighborhood of $8 million, give or take $500,000.

The Realtor said she would even cut her percentage in half, asking only 3.5 percent for her services.

Thaddeus poured her some coffee, listened to her pitch, and sent her on the way.

Katy and Sarai were walking the beach searching for sand dollars, so they missed out on the presentation. For which Thaddeus was very grateful, as Katy was falling in love with the property and the area.

The Realtor was halfway out of town when her cell phone beeped.

It was Thaddeus.

He had changed his mind.

He had decided to give Katy the home as a wedding present.

The Realtor was instructed to wrap the key in a small box with a bow, fax the papers to his Vegas office for signing by Langston Moretti, who would have the power of attorney, and who would wire the funds to the Realtor's escrow account that afternoon.

The Realtor nearly ran her yellow Mercedes off the road as the excitement of the unexpected sale sent her pulse racing and the adrenaline pumped. She would take care of it all, just as he required.

Fine, he said, drop the key by this afternoon, for my eyes only.

He was also calling a local justice of the peace and making arrangements for a quick, quiet marriage ceremony.

The time had come; everyone was ready, especially Thaddeus, who was not only desperately in love with his bride, but who was also heeding Albert's advice when he had run off with Ilene. "Do it now," Albert had said. "She's too special to put it off any longer."

They were married quietly, at home, at dusk, in the huge living room overlooking the Pacific, by the JP.

Of course he would perform the ceremony, his office reported, and would personally officiate right in Thaddeus and Katy's living room.

And thanks for the proffer of the $5,000 stipend for his services. It was a first, he almost said, then thought better of it, gift horses and all that.

The ceremony went off exactly at six p.m. Thursday evening. Thaddeus, Katy, and Sarai were present, along with the JP, and two witnesses. They were the young Hispanic maids who had agreed to sign off on the certificate. It was unknown whether they actually used their real names, but it didn't matter. The marriage license was in accordance with California law, it was legal, and that's all that mattered.

They were each given a $1,000 bonus for their service and attendance at the ceremony.

When it was over, everyone enjoyed an outdoor dinner, grilled over charcoal, of abalone steaks and cheese fries— Sarai's favorite. The little girl had chocolate milk; Thaddeus and Katy toasted with non-alcoholic champagne, the JP told several funny stories of weddings where he had officiated famous movie stars and other Hollywood lights, and it all broke up at around eight o'clock.

They put Sarai to bed and then sat outside, alone, before

retreating to a seaside hammock fastened to the ocean side of the deck, where they kissed, covered with a cozy blanket.

"I'm so grateful you agreed to spend your life with me," he whispered.

"Smart of me, eh?"

She punched his side.

"Yes, smart of both of us."

"And we've got Sarai, too. We're the luckiest people in Malibu."

"In California."

"In the world."

"Thaddeus, will you always tell me the truth about us? That's one thing I must have."

"Sure. You just do the same toward me. And if you do fall in love with someone else—I'll have you both shot. No, just kidding. No, I'm not actually. I couldn't stand to lose you. In fact, I want you to move down to Vegas and live with me. We'll get a place, put down roots, and give Sarai a neighborhood, a community, for her to grow up in."

"That sounds wonderful. I agree."

"You'll do it?"

"Uh-huh. I have to get admitted to UNLV Med, but I think I can. Second year is much easier admission than first year."

"You just made my week."

"I'll see that and raise you one, Mister Gambler. You just made my whole life."

They had fallen fast asleep by the time Jimmy Fallon said "Hello, everyone!"

The remainder of their week was spent enhancing Sarai's seashell collection and dining at a Malibu French bistro Katy had wanted to try. Thaddeus took two surfboarding lessons, swearing after number two that he'd never try that again.

He had seawater plugging one ear and scraped knees from being deposited with a huge crash along the shore in the foam and sand, ripped off the board by the tumultuous waves he had challenged and never subdued.

They climbed aboard the Learjet on Sunday morning and were back at McCarran Field in Las Vegas before one p.m.

After a quick ride back to the hotel and their condo, the newlyweds began making plans for their life together.

By noon Monday, they had some answers. As soon as Katy had finished her first year in medical school she would transfer to UNLV, where she had already been tentatively accepted as a medical student in their second-year enrollment.

Things were finally coming together, compromises were being made, and Katy began the process of locating a home for their small family on the outskirts of the city, which by now was burgeoning with a population in excess of 1 million souls, 95 percent of whom never set foot in a casino. That was the crowd they wished to join.

All except for Thaddeus, who had other plans for his future in Las Vegas.

36

The end began innocently enough, just another day at the office.

The day was bright and sunny, like all Las Vegas days, and as he went for his run along the Strip he saw the same preoccupied looks of people he saw every day when he ran. Except this time the thought made its way deep inside his brain: they were all preoccupied with getting something for nothing, for winning big at the dice, the cards, the wheel—except it wasn't actually going to happen for any of them. It was a ruse, a hoax—a fraud—being perpetrated by him and all the other casino entrepreneurs. Bright lights and dollar signs in the neon.

That morning, in his huge, gaudy office, he listened to complaints and successes, except this time it was just different enough to make a game-changing impression on Thaddeus.

Then came the married couple that would change his life.

The couple managed to get in to see him just after his third coffee.

They were a Midwestern couple, which Thaddeus saw from their muted grays and navy slacks and shirts even before they were introduced. What was surprising, however, was that they hailed from Hickam County, in Illinois, where Thaddeus had begun the practice of law some years earlier. Incredibly, their small soybean farm—eighty acres, been in the family 200 years—was just four miles up the road from the city of Orbit, Thaddeus' jumping-off point.

Her name was Bobbie and she was fifty-five, a thick, stout woman of German descent, whose hands fluttered between them like starlings when she spoke. She appeared fearless as she told Thaddeus why they had needed to see him, and several times he saw that her pale blue eyes were about to overflow with tears as she told the story of Theodore—Theo—her husband of thirty-five years.

Theo was ten years older, sixty-five, and stricken with terminal pancreatic cancer. Which of course always comes at the wrong time, but in the case of Bobbie and Theo it had come at a really bad time. Reason was—as Bobbie explained, with Theo jumping in with the details—they had just refinanced the farm after two disastrous growing seasons in which local drought had killed off 95 percent of the harvest.

For two years in a row they had bet on the weather favoring them; for two years they had lost that bet. It cost $3,500 in soybean seed for eighty acres, $11,500 in fertilizer to put in one crop, another $15,500 for pesticides and herbicides during the growing season, $6,500 in tractor fuel and maintenance, and $1,500 for general equipment repair and sundries, as the seed was planted and the crop cultivated, fertilized, and watched over.

The money was spent on the come, a wager, and they

had lost it all two years running. This didn't include normal living expenses, and electricity and propane gas (country living), as well as gas for the car, insurance, medical care, dental health, and groceries, although Bobbie also planted and maintained a vegetable garden, which was watered with well water and thus thrived even when the field crops turned brown, withered up, and died unproductively.

Theo's life expectancy was six months.

At first they had tried prayer and lottery tickets to dig themselves out of the deep hole dug by the refinance commitment and living costs. The note was $250,000 and it was secured by the eighty acres plus the home. They also had a CD at the bank worth another $65,000 but it had also been put up as collateral on the note. In short, every penny they had was tied up and dependent on five good years of crops and the ability of Theo to work and make it all happen until he was seventy. At seventy they had planned to sell out, take their $350,000 net worth, and move to Florida for the good life. Except Theo didn't have five years. He had only five months and sixteen days, and counting.

When they hadn't won the lottery, they decided to take the $15,000 bankroll that all farmers keep buried in the barn, and journey to Las Vegas for a chance at making a fortune. Their game was roulette. They had tried betting only black. After two hours they were up $3,500. Then the roof caved in. After their first night in the Desert Riviera they were down $6,500. By the end of day two they had lost it all.

"Now we don't even have the money to get back home," Bobbie cried, and the tears finally overflowed and bathed her cheeks.

"We don't mean to whine," said Theo.

Thaddeus looked him over. The man was obviously down to about 120 and fading.

"And what do you want from me?" asked Thaddeus. He felt a huge amount of sympathy for these people, but their story wasn't all that different from the others he heard every day, except for the six-month life expectancy of the man who had lost everything on Thaddeus' roulette wheel.

That was a deep thorn in Thaddeus' side.

He felt nothing but sympathy and sorrow for Bobbie and Theo.

Then Bobbie sealed the deal. "He's going to die and I'm going to get his insurance policy," she cried, "but that's only fifty thousand dollars. The bank will get it all. And I'll be alone, unemployable, with no place to live and no family to go to. We never could have kids, though Lord knows we tried. I have a sister in Moline but we haven't spoken to each other in thirty years. She's very hateful, was always jealous of me growing up, and will have nothing to do with me. We have nothing."

Thaddeus spread his hands and asked again. "And what do you want from me?"

"We want our money back," said Bobbie. "Just give us our money back so we can make it home and have six months of groceries while we wait for the end."

"Fifteen thousand will get us through. We'll play like we were when we were first married, broke but in love. Except the 'in love' part ain't make-believe. We really are," Theo added. His voice was desperate but he was too proud to beg and too strong to whine. Besides, Thaddeus could see the man was resigned to his fate. There was nothing left for him but to wait.

A knot in Thaddeus' chest then unraveled and his own

feelings broke loose. "I'm going to do that. I'm going to give your money back."

"Praise Jesus!" Bobbie erupted. "Oh, my God!"

"You'll never know what you just did," Theo said, and Thaddeus could have sworn that even this tough, proud man had a well of tears in his eyes too. As did Thaddeus.

"Excuse me," he said, and he went out of the office to speak with Maria. She nodded and lifted her phone and called for a check to be made out.

Theo and Bobbie were downstairs twenty minutes later, prepared to cash their check at the first teller's cage they came to, when she opened the envelope they had been given.

Slowly the words formed on her lips when she saw the check. "Sweet Jesus," she exhaled in one long breath.

"Lemme see," said Theo, and she turned the check to him.

"Don't make a ruckus," she warned, glancing about to see whether they were being watched by anyone. There was no one within twenty feet. It was safe to whisper.

"That ain't right," the man said.

She nodded solemnly.

Theo read it again. The check read: "Pay to the order of...the sum of $250,000," and it was signed by M.M. Herkemier, President.

"It ain't right but we taking it," she said, and set off for the entrance, Theo firmly in tow. They did not stop at the roulette wheel on their way out; they did not drop a quarter in the last slot before they reached the real world.

It was a beeline and there was no looking back.

～

THAT NIGHT, Thaddeus told Katy, "I can't do it anymore. I'm taking money from people who don't have it to lose. I'm putting the casino up for sale."

She smiled and continued dishing up vegetable soup from the crockpot.

"I've been wondering how long it would take," she said. "Dinner's in five. Round up Sarai."

37

S ale of the casino was easy. The money angle was difficult.

The primary mover in American business deals, bottom line, was always taxes. What would be the tax consequences of an out-and-out cash deal? What would be the tax consequences of cash plus property? What would be the tax consequences of an installment sale? Should the purchase be made in the names of partners, an LLC, a corporation, or a single individual? What were the tax consequences? What were they!

Tubby Watsonn steered Thaddeus to a local group of transactional tax lawyers and they took him under their wing.

The buyers—a Silicon Valley group heavily invested in social media startups—were from California and Washington. One of them owned 3 percent of outstanding shares of Microsoft—an oil sheik's treasury.

California's tax laws are very different from Nevada's tax laws. For example, where California has state income tax,

Nevada does not. So the origination and execution of the sale would take place in Nevada—Las Vegas, to be exact.

Because Nevada was a community property state and because Thaddeus was married but the casino was what was known as separate property, the proceeds of the sale were taken solely in Thaddeus' name, except for 10 percent, which went into Katy's name and which was memorialized in writing as her share of the community increase in asset value that accrued post-marriage to Thaddeus.

Which meant, bottom line, that he had made a gift to Katy of $75 million, from the gross proceeds of the sale of $750 million. Minus the $250 million he still owed, his bank account was suddenly on FULL. It now contained $435 million, he no longer owned a casino, and he was looking for office space for the law practice he planned for downtown Las Vegas.

He said goodbye to the office he had never had time to refurnish.

He held a staff meeting and said goodbye to the staff. He gave all employees a thank-you bonus of 2 percent. Then he left. In his own car, no driver. The black Mercedes and driver stayed with the casino. The BAG agents were portable, however, and they went with him. Thanks to the Chicago mob, he was thinking he would always need to have BAG covering his back. Even, sometimes, his front.

He was always the optimist. On the day he went shopping for office space, his new practice boasted all of two Nevada clients, one of whom was his sister and unable to pay, the other of whom was Bat, also unable to pay, except for a small amount every two weeks.

Nevertheless, Thaddeus was encouraged.

More than once he had been enormously successful in helping people overcome their legal difficulties by the mere act of taking them by the hand and walking with them through the problem until it was resolved. He had no doubt that would once again be the case.

Yet there was a serious problem overlaying his new direction, a problem he'd never faced before. These two clients—his sister and Bat—were people he cared deeply about. The one he loved because she was his sister and because, well, he just found her adorable. For the other, he —he wouldn't call it love (or would he?)—felt genuine caring. A great compassion. Like Bat, Thaddeus had been way down before and no one had extended him a hand. When he really needed a hand up, there wasn't one. He'd had to fight every step to get to where he was. In fact, he'd even had to kill—not once but twice. He had loathed himself both times for days after pulling the trigger. But he had also learned something in the process: there would be times when he would find himself pushed in a corner not of his own making and the only way out would be past some very strong, even evil, people. At those moments, he had learned, you did whatever it took to get out of that corner. In other words, you did whatever it took to keep breathing, heart beating, to stay alive.

Now he knew his sister was at that point. She was in a corner, put there by a system she didn't understand, and he was going to have go in there after her. Already the State of Nevada had told him that it planned on killing her.

Taking her life.

For what she did. Rather, for what they were *claiming* she did.

And he knew how Bat had lived before—on the street, feeding out of Dumpsters on good days, going without on the bad days, with no hand, no help, and so he had sold marijuana to an undercover officer, a narc, all because he was hungry and wanted money to buy a meal. That was the sum total of what they had on him, and for that they were going to send him to prison, which meant that ultimately he would be released and would find himself exactly where he had started out, on the street.

Thaddeus wanted nothing more than to save his sister and save Bat from the system.

With these strong feelings pumping adrenaline through his body, he left home one Monday morning to find office space where he could begin. Nothing extravagant, nothing so flashy it would exclude people. Rather, it had to be simple yet attractive enough to include people. He wanted them to come there and know they were among professionals. And he wanted them to know when they walked in that they were among people who actually cared. He was setting the bar high for new employees. They would have to care, to work there. Care more about other people than about themselves. There was always a risk in such caring, and it took strong people to plunge ahead in spite of that risk.

As he pulled away—driving his own American car—he realized how completely he had downgraded his life. He no longer lived in a castle. Katy had been adamant. She didn't want Sarai growing up privileged. She wanted "adequate" for their child, not "perfect." Katy had grown up knowing need and she had grown up to learn that the best way to get her needs met was to meet them herself.

Which was exactly what she wanted for their daughter.

So they didn't live in a sixteen-room home on twenty beautiful acres looking down on Las Vegas. Their home was secure, first of all, because Thaddeus still required BAG protection from the old Chicago crowd. Hence, there was a guest cottage out back. Men with guns lived there. And there was a small barn and tack room where the family could house and care for their several horses, along with a corral for working them. But the million-dollar horse barn Thaddeus had enjoyed in Illinois—that was a thing in the past.

Their home looked like any other of the three-acre tracts where they bought. There was a street out front where the kids could ride their bikes. There was a school two blocks away where Sarai would attend first grade. There was a park four blocks away. And there were children Sarai's age in the neighborhood. Some of those would stay around and they would grow up together. Thaddeus had grown up in a neighborhood full of kids and this same community of possible playmates was something he wanted for Sarai.

So they hadn't gone isolationist, which was a dangerous place where great wealth could have misled them. They had decided they were a family and they were going to live as much like their neighbors lived as possible. "There's even a mailbox out front," he had wryly observed to Katy. "For the first time in my adult life I have my own street with my own mailbox out front. Welcome home, Thad. Welcome home, Katy. Welcome home, Sarai."

38

L incoln "Mask" Mascari was in a rage. He had read in the *Chicago Tribune* that Thaddeus Murfee of Chicago had sold the Desert Riviera Casino and Hotel for $750 million. To a group of Dot-Commers out of Silicon Valley. Cash. No carryback, no installment, no down payment + pay later. None of that. He had the bucks and he was rolling in them.

Why was Mask's blood pressure up ten points? Why had the runs returned, committing larger parts of his waking hours to the bathroom?

Because half that money was his. He and Bang Bang had owned the Desert Riviera together. And Murfee had ripped it out of their hands with his bogus lawsuit. The deck had been stacked against him, he believed. The judge had been in bed with Murfee. That's why he got the amount of money he got. Because the judge got his on the back end. Mask was certain of it.

He wanted revenge, to be sure. But more than that, he wanted his money back. He wanted his money plus Bang Bang's share. After all, he was married to Bang Bang's daughter, the one who hadn't gone into Witness Protection, and she should have inherited Bang Bang's share. All he was looking for was what was rightfully his. And what was rightfully hers.

The time to move was now, while Murfee had the cash in the States, before it went overseas. He put in a call to Johnnie Getti in New York.

Tell Ragman the time is now.

THE OFFICE BUILDING contained the one feature for his new firm that was a must-have. Within the underground parking garage there were twelve charging stations for electric cars. His Tesla would never be without juice.

The building's features read like a list from a law firm's episode of *Lifestyles of the Rich and Famous*: electric-car charging stations in a 75,000-square-foot parking space; a full gym with showers; four conference rooms on each floor; and a mock courtroom on the third floor "built for students at William S. Boyd School of Law to practice and host mock trials."

Thaddeus was impressed and he signed a five-year lease for 15,000 square feet. The per-foot charge was mid/high-range, but that was all right.

The building was within a stone's throw of the George Federal Building and that was perfect.

Black and white marble floors and original paintings distinguished the interior, with the reception area having the feel of a foyer in Louis XIV's Versailles Palace.

A young lawyer whose star was in its ascendancy owned the building, and Thaddeus took to him immediately. At the end of the day, Thaddeus was impressed with his new surroundings and he was also comfortable—a major requirement.

By the end of the week the office was furnished, phones were installed, the main number was listed with directory service, high-speed Internet was serving web pages, and the kitchen was fully stocked.

Within two more days he had hired a receptionist for the phones and a paralegal to help with the legal research and writing, as well as brainstorming. The receptionist was Terey Hatcher and she had a history in the District Attorney's office and was on the cutting edge of criminal law and procedure in Nevada. She would do double duty at first, answering the phones and drafting pleadings. So far his two clients were both criminal defendants, and Thaddeus had a feeling that the thrust of his new firm was headed in that direction.

MONDAY HE HAD his first two clients appear in the office.

Kiki Murphy walked in at 10:00 a.m., right on schedule. After a brief tour they settled in Thaddeus' new office and Kiki sat there blinking, astonished how quickly Thaddeus had created his new firm.

"It's the third time I've opened an office," he said with a smile. "I'm very experienced at this part of it. But now we need to focus on you."

She brushed a wisp of blond hair from her face. "Things are good at work, but that's about it. Every night I have dreams about shooting that guy. I wake up all sweaty and cannot go back to sleep. So I get up, make some tea, and listen to rap on my iPod. Rap is the only thing that stops the images of the gun going off and a man crumbling to the ground."

"Are you getting any help for that? Seeing a professional?"

"Dr. Gouda, you told me about her. I've seen her five times now."

"Is that helping?"

"I cry every time we talk about it. It's still too fresh. I would do anything to change that night, Thad. Anything."

"That's how it is. I've been in very similar circumstances and had to do violent things. Want to know the truth?"

"What?"

"It never goes away. Your job now is to learn to live with what you've done."

She groaned. "That's going to be extremely difficult."

"But not impossible. It will happen—you'll see. Now let's talk about your case."

"Let's do. That's another reason I can't sleep."

"Well, the indictment charges you with first-degree murder. There are allegations of malice and premeditation. I dispute both of those, of course. Not only that, there's the question of self-defense. If you pulled the trigger on purpose, it was because you were in reasonable apprehension of immediate great bodily harm or death. If you didn't pull it on purpose, but if the gun just went off, then there's the element of negligence. Either way, I don't believe they can convict you of first-degree murder."

"What can they convict me of?"

He smiled grimly. "That's the problem. Maybe negligent homicide."

"Oh, God."

"Wait, pump the brakes. I have a report from Dr. Gunnar

Andersen, an armorer out of Seattle. The report helps you immensely."

"What does he say?"

"Well, PX got your purse and found a gun just like you had in the purse that night. She sent the purse and the gun to Dr. Andersen. He spent a month performing tests. Last Friday we received his written report. It is his opinion that the gun was discharged accidentally, and that the mechanism that caused the firing pin to come down and cause a bullet to be expelled from the muzzle was the lipstick you were carrying in your purse."

"What?"

"I know. It's very simple, according to Dr. Andersen. The lipstick became wedged inside the trigger guard, you went to remove the gun from your purse, the lipstick pulled against the trigger and caused the pistol to fire. The firing was purely accidental. He will testify to that in front of a jury."

"Does that mean I didn't do it on purpose?"

"That's exactly what it means. It was purely an accident."

"Oh, Thad!" She tossed her head back and tears of joy rolled down her cheeks. "I can't tell you how that makes me feel. It was an accident!"

"Not so fast. There's more, and this is even better."

"Okay."

"Dr. Andersen goes on to say that the interior of the purse contains powder burns where the muzzle was against the purse when it fired. The powder burns, the pattern, and the hole in the purse all prove that the gun couldn't have been aimed. Which brings us to intent. If there was no aiming of the gun, there was no intent to shoot anyone. If there was no intent, there was no first-degree murder, there was no second-degree murder, and there was no homicide by intent. Which leaves manslaughter. Either intentional—heat of the moment, or unintentional—accidental. It's my opinion that yours is the negligent type. You were carrying a gun, you attempted to seize it, and you were negligent in how you tried to seize it. Because of that the gun went off, killing your attacker. That is an offense for which the court is required to sentence you to one year, in Nevada. Which I'm not willing to see you do. So we're looking for something less."

"What's that mean?"

"I'm meeting with Doctor Andersen. He says you're not guilty of anything."

"Doctor Andersen said that?"

"He did."

"Does this mean I can stop having bad dreams?"

"You got it, Kiki. You can stop now."

They went on to talk for another thirty minutes. They discussed her job at the casino. Thaddeus, in the sale of the casino, had secured a one-year employment contract for her. If they fired her within that first year they owed her $50,000. No ifs, ands, or buts. He got the same deal for Bat. You can only control things so far, he told her. He had done for her and Bat what he could. Now he wanted to give them back their freedom. For once and for all.

Bat arrived at one o'clock. He looked healthy and happy, and was seeing Thaddeus on his own day off. He told Thaddeus he had a car, $7,000 saved toward a down payment on his own place, and a girlfriend he was seeing every night, with a four-year-old son who evidently idolized Bat and was intrigued that Bat's eye actually came out. "He laughs like a hyena when I take it out and scare him with it. That's just too cool!"

"Let me ask you a couple questions, just for my file,"

Thaddeus said. "I need to know a little more about you on the day you sold the dope."

"Fair enough. That's what I'm here for."

"First, you weren't working then and you had no income, correct?"

"Correct."

"Where were you living?"

"In the winter I was at the library all day, usually sleeping in the reading area. Staying warm and dozing off where it was safe. The library makes for great temporary lodging when you're on the street. Nights I stayed in mission. If there was a bed. If no bed, I hit the cardboard."

"Cardboard?"

"Find a box, flatten it out. It puts a layer of air between you and the sidewalk. A little warmer."

"So there were nights you were sleeping outside on the sidewalk?"

"Oh, plenty. Usually."

"How did you put food in your mouth?"

"Hung in the alleys."

"Meaning?"

"I'd hang out around loading docks downtown. Truck pulls in, the driver's tired and worn out, coming in from Phoenix or LA, he sees me hanging around. Before you know it I'm helping him unload and he's paying me twenty bucks. That's enough for me to eat on for three days."

"Seriously?"

"I've got one of those Swiss Army knives. Can opener. I take my twenty dollars, hit the Quik Stop. Get me a can of hash, pop the lid, nuke it, and I'm getting full in three minutes. Knock it down with a thirty-two-ounce soda, and I'm good to go. Total cost under three bucks."

"I'll remember that."

"It's the way of the street, brother. You pick up here and there, you hustle. Sometimes you shoplift. You gotta eat, man. Everybody gotta eat."

"I get that. So what happened with the dope? Where'd it come from?"

"Two white kids head into a club late at night. Leave their ride parked on the street. I know they're holding. So I jimmy the window, pry open the glove box, and there's my zip. Probably eight ounces of weed. And I'm gone, down the alley, around the block, dope in my shorts. Cops say they look in your shorts, but they don't. Not if they know you're from the streets."

"Why not?"

"Smell too bad. They don't even like to touch you, much less look inside your shorts."

"So what happened next?"

"Guy takes me down an alley. Wants to buy some of my weed. I say okay. We no sooner get down there but he stabs me. Cuts my arm. I can't get the blood to stop, so cops call the EMTs. Long story short, I get a ride to the ER, stitches, they do tests. My eyes look wrong. So I go back in three days. Guess what? I'm HIV. Got it from all those needles before I got dried out at the Sallie."

"Sallie?"

"Salvation Army. They took me in, dried me out, three hots and a cot. I get off the needle but I'm still holding, still got that weed. Doc says I need to go on this drug regimen. So I don't come down with AIDS. Fine, but it costs money. So I decide to sell my weed. That's when I sold to the narc. Guy drives up in a black car. Can I get him something? It smelled wrong, felt wrong. Yes, I hop in, money and weed hand-to-hand. Next thing I know I'm riding down to jail. That's when I met you. Best night of my life, that was."

"So let me understand. You sold the marijuana because you needed money to buy your HIV drugs?"

"I couldn't get no work. They say I gonna come down with AIDS if I don't. What would you do?"

Thaddeus shook his head. "Probably the same thing. Or worse. Okay, that's good for now."

They shook hands and, when he was leaving, Bat was suddenly overcome. He hugged Thaddeus. And while he was hugging him he said, faintly, "Thanks, man."

Thaddeus could only nod. He turned away and took the pocket square from his jacket. He dabbed his eyes and wished he had a tissue. He'd have to remember to order tissues. That was the thing about having your own business: everything came back on you. You need ink pens? Better order them because no one else is going to. Tissues? Same thing.

He walked back to his computer and made a paragraph worth of entries in Bat's file. When he was done he was smiling. Now he knew how he was going to spring him free of the trap. Right now his paw was caught and the hunters were coming, but Thaddeus was about to change all that.

He was going to see him free.

39

T
he IRS, meanwhile, wasn't standing around taking patty-cake lessons. The Special Agents summonsed his bank accounts.

Bank of America coughed up two years of Thaddeus' bank statements, with checks and deposit slips.

Far West National contributed eighteen months' worth of savings account records.

Fidelity Investments came across with 350 pages of investment records, everything from 401(k)s to investment accounts to SEP-IRAs.

Chicago wasn't overlooked in the mix; Fifth Third Bank turned over five years of records, business and personal.

Then they went after the credit cards.

Agent Kroc was in charge of the living expense reconstruction; Agent Magence oversaw the bank deposit analysis. In the end they would know just about everything there was to know about the money passing through Thaddeus' hands for the last several years.

During this hunting-gathering process, Thaddeus was copied on each summons that went to the institutions. The documents the banks sent back, however, he wasn't copied on. So, while Thaddeus looked over his shoulder, Tubby Watsonn was accumulating the same documents. Then he was performing the exact same analyses they knew the feds would perform.

THE SPECIAL AGENTS met in the windowless conference room consisting of a table, four chairs, and the President of the United States.

"Okay, here's what I got," said Kroc. "Adding the cost of living where he's living, to the food it takes, plus car payments, plus all the rest of his monthly nut, it's costing him $150,000 a year to accommodate his lifestyle."

"But that could come entirely from the cash at his disposal in the bank accounts and investment accounts. He can live like that for the rest of his life and never earn another penny."

Kroc looked thoughtful. "I thought of that. So I traced every dime that came out of any savings or investments."

"And?"

"And he's living totally off earnings during those years."

She nodded. "Good. Now let me tell you about his bank deposits. Let me tell you the full skinny on those earnings you're talking about. This will blow your mind."

"Go ahead."

Her workup was thorough. As always. "He deposited three hundred fifty thousand the first year. On his tax return he reported two hundred twenty-five K."

"So he failed to report a hundred twenty-five grand."

"Exactly. Which is a crime."

"Did any of that hundred twenty-five come from savings

or investments? That wouldn't be unreported income if it did."

She shook her head fiercely. "Zero. None of it can be traced back to savings, loans, or investment accounts."

"That does it. He failed to report income."

She smiled. "So he's guilty."

Kroc shrugged. "Unless he can make money out of thin air, he's guilty. What about succeeding years?"

"Following year he failed to report a hundred fifty thou. Year after, two twenty-five K. We've got him by the short ones."

He shivered. "I love this. I love it when a big dog goes down like this."

"Which proves that he's taking unreported income out of the casino to live on. In other words, he's stealing from himself."

"Which is legal. But failing to report the money he took, that's a crime."

"I rest my case."

"We're all but ready for trial."

"We're ready."

She high-fived her partner, who, for a moment, wasn't sure why she was raising her hand, and he flinched.

"High five, Kroc. We're gonna put one Thaddeus Murfee behind bars. Let's get a drink."

"Can't. Henry's expecting me."

"Tomorrow then. We'll take early lunch and celebrate, one martini each."

"We'll see."

"Jeez, Kroc."

40

H e went by Sparky, last name Burgess, and he had
a paralegal certificate from the Worldwide Institute of Legal Training.

When Thaddeus asked where the hell that was, Sparky
couldn't say. It was some school he had discovered online.
He had paid them $6,500 and it had taken six months. He
had enrolled in property, civil procedure, criminal law, criminal procedure, bankruptcy, legal research and writing, and
contracts. Plus an entire week had been devoted to nothing
but torts. They sent him a diploma—which he brought to
show Thaddeus—and he kept it in a fluted silver frame.

Sparky was tall and lanky, with a shock of red hair that he
kept combed straight back from a widow's peak. He wore wire
eyeglasses with a bifocal line, spoke with just the hint of a lisp,
and physically looked ready to rumble on a moment's notice.

In a prior life he had worked for Panhandle Western
Pipeline as a welder's helper, moving with a maintenance
crew through Texas, Oklahoma, Colorado, and Nevada,
where he had decided he'd had it with traveling, sublet a

studio apartment, and found Worldwide Institute of Legal Training online.

He had been turned down for eleven paralegal jobs, he admitted to Thaddeus, because he had no experience. But he had gumption, as he put it, and he would promise to always have Thaddeus' back. All he wanted was a chance.

Thaddeus had résumés of better-qualified candidates on his desk, seven of them. But Sparky reminded him of himself when he was just starting out and no one would give him a chance.

"I shouldn't do this," Thaddeus scowled, "because I doubt if you really know shit, but I'm going to roll the dice with you. You've got six weeks on a trial basis. You're not an employee during that time; you're an independent contractor. Reason for that is I don't want you suing me for wrongful termination at the end of six weeks if it doesn't work out. Fair enough?"

"Hell, Thaddeus, you just made a bud. I'm here to give it everything I've got. When do I start?"

"Right now too soon?"

"Son, right now suits me just fine."

"Good. Take the office next to mine. There's a desk, a chair, and a computer. You've got access to Westlaw and Lexis. I want an analysis of all Nevada self-defense cases in the last ten years. Due tomorrow at noon."

"I'm on it, son."

"Knock yourself out. And quit calling me 'son.'"

"Yes, sir. What should I call you?"

"Thad. I like Thad."

"You got it. One other thing. Do I get paid?"

"Hadn't thought of that. How much you need?"

"I can live on twelve an hour."

"Then let's make it fifteen. That way you can buy me a Christmas present."

"You got it, son."

Thaddeus gave him a long, hard look. "Get in your own office," he growled. "I've got work to do here."

"I'm already gone."

He told Terey, the new receptionist, that he was headed to Tubby Watsonn's office. Call and let him know he was running about thirty behind. Terey, who was fielding a call, nodded and kept talking into the headset. Thaddeus rode the elevator down to the parking garage and unplugged the Tesla. Coming up out of the parking, he floored it and fishtailed into traffic.

"Tesla," he smiled, "there is no other."

TUBBY WATSONN THOUGHT himself fabulous in canary golf slacks, $2,000 Gucci's, and a linen navy blazer over a canary golf shirt, open at the throat.

He clenched a half-burnt cigar in the short, fat fingers of his right hand and poked it between his lips. He gave it a chew, inhaled, and blew a plume of swirling smoke across the desk.

Thaddeus leaned back and fought the smoke. "Jesus, Tubby, is the smokescreen part of what I'm paying for?"

"Naw," said Tubby in his most accommodating voice, "smoke is free. Brain is seven hundred fifty an hour."

"I thought it was five hundred."

"That's for people who can't afford my true value. You, sir, can afford to pay for my very best and that's what you're going to get."

~

SPARKY WANTED TO TALK. He had a few questions about Nevada criminal law. Thaddeus told him to come right on in. It was the second day of Sparky's employment as an independent contractor and he was anxious to please. Plus, he thought he might have an idea for the Tattinger case.

"Billy A. Tattinger—"

"Bat," Thaddeus said.

"This Bat guy presents an interesting case for us."

Thaddeus shook his head. "Hold on, Sparky. I thought I told you I wanted a memo analyzing all Nevada self-defense cases. Why are we jumping over to the Tattinger case? I didn't assign that case to you."

"That self-defense memo is in your inbox, son. I sent it two hours ago."

Thaddeus blushed. "I should check my email. Sorry. Now proceed with what you were saying."

"Right. Well, I read through the Tattinger—Bat—file. And I've got a few observations. For example, the statute reads, 'To constitute crime there must be unity of act and intent. In every crime or public offense there must exist a union of act and intention.' Do they have that in Bat's case? I mean, is there intention? Please allow me to continue. The next portion of the law says, 'Intention is manifested by the circumstances connected with the perpetration of the offense, and the sound mind and discretion of the person accused.' It just seems to me, since Bat had to have those meds to survive, he had no discretion. His physical need for medication for his body removed all discretion from his mind. And let me point out, the 'and' in that sentence is conjunctive. Which means there must exist both sound mind and discretion. If they ain't got discretion on our guy, they ain't got intent."

Thaddeus grinned. "Now we're getting somewhere. I love it."

Sparky shrugged. "Stick with me, son, and we'll make this work."

"So I'm beginning to see. What else you got on this?"

"You put the defendant on the stand and you go into his state of mind. I believe you walk him out. There won't be a dry eye on that jury when they hear about his predicament."

"While you were looking over the file, did you review the police reports?"

"I did."

Thad thought about this. "And did you read that the transfer of pot for money took place in the front seat of the narc's car?"

Sparky nodded. "I did. So why was Bat in that car? Did the cop entice him? Was it entrapment? Or was Bat predisposed toward committing a crime, no matter who it was with?"

"Exactly. Now I'd like that officer's statement."

"You want to take his statement and set him up for trial?"

"I do," said Thaddeus. "At the very least, the state owes us discovery on the case. The cop's case statement should already be in that package."

"Let me get to work on that. Nevada doesn't give the defendant the right to take the cop's statement. But maybe I can sweet-talk the D.A."

"Now that would be something."

"I'm pretty smooth, son."

"So I'm noticing. So I'm noticing. Anyway, at the very least, get the discovery package. Then we can talk again.

And Sparky. You're very close to hanging on to this job full time."

"We can talk, son, but I'm gonna need more money."

"Really? I thought you said twelve an hour was enough to live on and I said I'd pay fifteen. What's changed?"

Sparky looked at the desktop. "I met someone."

"Oh?"

"She's about my age and doesn't have anything either. Just like me. We're talking about getting a place together. She makes more than me and I don't know that I can afford half."

"How about seventeen an hour. Does that get it done?"

"Absolutely! So I get a raise?"

Thaddeus shook his head. "You don't even get the job—yet. You're still on probation, remember?"

"Oh, you're not gonna want to let me go. I always give my jobs a hundred fifty percent."

"I'm beginning to see that."

Thaddeus went for the coffee thermos on the desk. "Want some?"

"I'm good."

"All right, then. Beat it. I'll read your self-defense workup and we'll talk again."

"Right."

"And Sparky, excellent work on Bat's case. I really appreciate that."

"I figured he might be a favorite of yours."

"He is."

"With his priors, he'll go to prison if you don't walk him out of this one."

"I know. We'll do our best to get that done for him."

Sparky excused himself and Thaddeus took his coffee mug to the window.

He looked across at the George Federal Court.

He could only imagine the wheels of justice grinding away inside, slowly, inexorably intent on putting citizens inside prison walls and early graves.

He envisioned Kiki strapped to the death gurney, and shuddered.

"Over my dead body," he muttered. "We're coming after you, Bat. Kiki. Just try to hold on a little while longer."

41

I t was the first time entertaining for Katy and Thaddeus. Kiki was invited, and they had told her to bring a friend, if she wanted.

She pulled the Bug in their circular drive at 6:15 and exited. With Matty Jones, floor supervisor at the Desert Riviera. He was also Kiki's floor supervisor, last Thaddeus had known.

Kiki was in her early twenties. Matty had to be forty-something, Thaddeus thought as they walked up and rang the bell. Forget it, he had told her to bring a friend and she had brought a friend. Try to stop being the big brother for ten minutes and give her a little space. She had a good head on her shoulders and would do things her way, not necessarily his.

He opened the door and hugged his sister, shaking Matty's hand over her shoulder.

"Welcome!"

"Thanks for having us, boss," said Matty. "What a spread you got here!"

"Hello, big brother," Kiki smiled. "You've done a ton with the place since last time."

"Katy takes the credit. Here, let's let her show you around while I work on the barbecue."

"What's cooking?"

"I know you won't eat meat," he said to Kiki, "so I'm fixing a tofu burger for you. I've also got salmon steaks, if you would prefer."

"Meat," she said. "Salmon is still meat."

"Right. And for you, Matty, I've got a porterhouse. Memory serves, you're medium-rare. Correct?"

"You've got it. Hey, you mind if I smoke out on the deck?"

"That's no problem. Just get an ashtray from Katy."

"Hello!" Kiki cried as Sarai toddled into the room to view the commotion. Seeing Kiki, she held up her arms and allowed herself to be hoisted up and kissed. "She really loves me!"

"You're very lovable," said Matty. "It's no wonder."

They adjourned to the kitchen, took seats at the round maple table, and said hello to Katy. "Morel mushrooms," said Katy. "Help yourselves." She put a plate of breaded and fried morels on the table.

"What are they?" Kiki asked.

"Just taste them," said Katy. "I wouldn't lead you wrong. They're fresh, by the way, flown in from our farm today. Albert sent them."

Kiki and Matty chomped mushrooms and their eyes smiled as they swallowed and reached for another.

"Incredible, boss."

"Oh my God," Kiki exclaimed.

"I know," said Katy. "And all it took was two thousand dollars in J2 fuel for the jet. Men."

Thaddeus stepped up to the Jenn-Air range and moved

tofu and beef around. He checked his watch. "What can we get you to drink? We have sodas, coffee, beer, and iced tea. Sun tea, made by Katy and ol' sol."

"Got any Coors?"

"We do," said Thaddeus. "And Kiki?"

"Just Diet Pepsi or Diet Coke is fine."

"I'm having the same," said Thaddeus.

"Crack me a root beer, please," Katy said to her husband.

Sarai peered out from under the table. "What are you doing under there, sweetheart?" her mother asked. "I was wondering where you'd disappeared to."

Sarai took a quick look and disappeared again.

AFTER SUPPER they went for a walk around the neighborhood. They discussed the casino and its new owners, the law practice, and caught up on the latest gossip about mutual friends. At one point Thaddeus noticed Matty was holding Kiki's hand, but he looked away, determined to mind his own business and keep his mouth shut.

After returning to the house, they settled into the family room for a movie.

"Up here," Kiki said to Sarai, and patted the couch beside her. Just at her other side was Matty, as close as he could get. Obviously smitten, Thaddeus thought, and looked away, trying to ignore the closeness.

THEY WERE deep into the movie when the brown Suburban pulled slowly past the house, down to the end of the block, and came back around. Behind the wheel was the Ragman, newly in town.

He had timed his appearance so the security agents disappeared for five minutes inside the guest house, debriefing and the new shift arming themselves. It was just a temporary lapse in security, but for the Ragman it was enough.

He paused in front, shifting into park so the brake lights remained off, and watched the windows. Without breaking his gaze, he lifted a camera with telephoto lens and snapped a dozen pictures of the keypad over the door. He would find out everything there was to know about that keypad and its vulnerabilities.

Then it would be a matter of choice. It was his choice to make, the when and the how.

Mascari wanted the kid now. He couldn't forget that.

Mascari was paying the bill.

42

Bat's opening day of trial was Cinco de Mayo.

The city of Las Vegas had a large and politically potent Hispanic community, and spirits were high and smiling faces evident as Thaddeus and Bat made their way inside the doors of the courtroom and through the throng. At security, people waited to pass through the magic arch and off to the elevators and their courtrooms.

Outside it was warm—nearly hot—eighty-eight degrees, and inside it was a comfortable seventy-seven. Thaddeus was wearing a lightweight gray suit, heavily starched white shirt, and foulard tie. Shoes were plain black Allen-Edmonds lace-ups. Bat was wearing black slacks, a yellow button-down shirt, and brown striped tie. He looked appropriate for his role as defendant, dressed just like Thaddeus had asked, but not over-dressed, as some attorneys required. Both men were clean-shaven and neatly groomed.

Bat had the entire week off from work. Thaddeus had set aside three days on his calendar for the trial. He guessed it might take two full days, but three, max.

They rode the elevator up in silence. All passengers fastened eyes on the flickering floor numbers, as was mandatory. Thaddeus almost had to laugh. From casino owner to defender of citizens charged with sale of narcotics, controlled substances, in this case, marijuana. How far the mighty have fallen, he mused. Or is it that I've actually arisen? Which is better for my life, screwing people out of their money, or depriving the state of Nevada of new inmates for its Department of Corrections system? That was a no-brainer, he decided.

They stepped off the elevator and hurried into the courtroom.

No sooner had the twosome taken their seats at defense table than Bat leaned over to Thaddeus and whispered, "I'm thinking of going to law school. Is that possible for me?"

Thaddeus was jolted out of his self-calming pre-trial reverie. "Law school?"

"Maria Consuelo says I should set my sights high."

"Look, can we talk about this later? I'm a little busy at the moment." Trying to keep your dumb ass out of prison, he thought, but didn't say. He brushed the thought away. "Get enrolled. Get a year of A's under your belt, and then we'll talk."

"I'm already signed up for Bonehead English starting late this month."

"Who called it that?"

"My advisor."

"God."

At which point the judge entered the courtroom. There was an animated mix of people in the room. Prospective jurors, court personnel, and members of the D.A.'s staff huddled and whispered, but when the judge enthroned himself all conversations broke off. Many began to disperse.

Thaddeus thought him a bland-looking little man; sunshine-deprived pasty, bald with gold-rimmed glasses and blue eyes busily scanning the file he would preside over at trial that day. Probably the first time he's seen it, Thaddeus thought, and he was actually right.

"My name is Richard Martini, and I'll be your judge today," the man began in a huge voice that belied his diminutive stature. "So I'm going to ask those of you who are here today pursuant to a summons for jury service to please say 'here' when the clerk calls your name. Don't try to go into the reasons why you shouldn't have to be here, not at this time. We'll take that up later, once we have our panel drawn. Madam Clerk, please proceed with the roll call."

It droned on for a good ten minutes, A to Z, most of whom answered "here." The clerk then drew a group of names at random, and those called immediately took a seat in the jury box.

Bat leaned close to Thaddeus and whispered. "I don't like any of them."

Thaddeus nodded but shushed him, as the judge continued.

"Ladies and gentlemen, I'm now going to ask you a series of questions, and if your answer is 'yes' to any of what I ask, please raise your hand and I'll come back to you. All right."

He then buzzed through the usual litany of knowledge about the case, opinions about guilt or innocence of the defendant "as he sits here before you today," relationship to anyone in the courtroom, anyone in the D.A.'s office, anyone in law enforcement, anyone in the probation department's office, the DOC, and on and on.

A few raised their hands and the judge made a note to get back to them, which he later did.

On and on the questions went.

Then it was time to take up the half dozen requests to be excused from jury service, for reasons ranging from a sick child at home to extraordinary busy season at work. Some just didn't want to be there, but they were forced to stay anyway.

Thaddeus took notes. He would get rid of those who wanted nothing to do with it, whom the judge wouldn't outright excuse. If they didn't want to be there then Thaddeus didn't want them on his jury. They would be angry and unforgiving toward the defendant who, as they would see it, was the root cause for their discomfort and displacement from home and their customary daytime game shows, soaps, and Drs. Oz, Drew, and Phil. Who knew what illnesses and social problems would go unsolved without the complaining juror there at home in front of the flat-screen, to observe? How could Wolf be expected to explain missing aircraft, Russian incursions, and the latest school shooting without a full viewing audience?

Thaddeus said nothing and kept his head down, occasionally making notes but mostly working on a doodle of a horse in full gallop. Which was where his heart really was, he decided at that moment. What the hell was he doing here, in a courtroom, no view of the mountains and green pastures, scared half to death by what he was facing on his client's behalf? Why wasn't he out at some ranch on some beautiful stallion, maybe seventeen hands, chuffing at the ready to go poking around in a Ponderosa stand? He sighed and poured two glasses of water. It was actually iced and, for that, he was momentarily grateful.

At least they had a good bailiff.

Over the next hour the attorneys were allowed to question the jurors.

First the D.A. went to the podium and tried to work

some magic and make herself and her case sound irresistible to the panel, while playing like she was in good faith only trying to discern their fitness to serve.

Then it was Thaddeus' turn, and he more or less played the same game, trying to ingratiate himself and his client with the jury, looking for people who would be slow to convict and quick to forgive, while at once seeming only to be interested in winnowing out those jurors fit to serve on the jury.

It was a game of words, a game of strategy, and lawyers all over America were playing the exact same game at the same moment, all in the fictional pursuit of seeing justice done.

Early on, in the Ermeline Ransom trial, Thaddeus had been so nervous addressing a jury for the first time that he had found himself gasping for air.

This time, he was slow, steady, and came across as accessible to the jury amidst their desire to find a lawyer they could believe in. He was understated, nothing approaching flamboyant, and came across as truly interested in each juror—because he actually was. The true mark of a successful trial lawyer. Someone whom the jury perceives as caring, because caring equals honest. At least that's how Thaddeus had found it to be.

An hour and half into jury selection he had the names of the panel memorized.

"Mister Youngman," he said, and made eye contact with the juror. "You previously told the District Attorney that you had no compassion for those who would sell drugs. But you're not saying your mind is already made up about this case without hearing the evidence, are you? Because I don't think that's what you're saying at all."

"I can listen."

"Exactly. You're of the same frame of mind you would want a juror to be in if they were sitting in judgment of you, aren't you, Mister Youngman?"

"I am."

"Meaning, you have absolutely no bias as you sit there today, against my client, who has only been charged with the sale of marijuana. As far you know, he might be guilty and he might be innocent. Your mind just isn't made up yet, is it sir?"

"No, I have an open mind."

"So you'll wait to hear the evidence before you decide, correct, Mister Youngman?"

"Correct."

When Thaddeus had finished and returned to his seat, the first thing Bat did was slide him a note. "Get rid of Mister Youngman," it said.

"I plan to," whispered Thaddeus.

The exercise had been nothing more than a teaching moment. He had planned on kicking Youngman off the jury before he had even asked him the first question, based on answers he had given the D.A., and based on how he had immediately warmed up to the D.A. when she started asking him questions.

"He's adios, bye-bye, gone," said Thaddeus under his breath. Bat nodded.

By noon they had their jury and it was time for the lunch break. Back at 1:30 sharp.

THEY STROLLED leisurely down the street, ordered burgers and malts, and started going over the list of jurors.

They were looking for minorities. They were looking for the poor. They were looking for those with teenage sons— the theory being their kids would likely be in trouble or just getting out of trouble. They were looking for employees rather than employers. They wanted college educated, non-farm-owning although farm-working was acceptable. They wanted union members, younger women and younger men, people who wanted to see justice done but who wanted to give a defendant a fair break if he deserved one. They were striking business owners. They were striking the elderly. They were striking engineers (too literal). They were striking all government workers. They were striking WASPs and they were striking the sick, lame, and halt, mainly because such people would argue that they were getting by without the need to sell drugs.

After lunch the attorneys exercised their peremptory (no reason needed) strikes, made their objections to those who plain old shouldn't be on the panel, and accepted the remaining.

It was true that day as it was always true in American courtrooms. The game wasn't about whom you kept, the game was about whom you got rid of.

The state got rid of the poor, disaffected, and minorities, and the defense got rid of the rich, ruling class. If you held a position of authority you weren't going to serve on Thaddeus' jury, all else being equal.

So, in the end, the parties were left with twelve jurors and two alternates. Neither state nor defense strongly wanted what was left behind to serve on the jury; neither state nor defense violently objected to the remaining fourteen. Both sides had gone to great pains to get rid of the jurors the other side would like; so the potential jury foreperson, the person with the alpha dog personality, had been shown the door by one side or the other. The potential jury foreperson was, thus, at that moment anyone's guess.

Opening statements followed.

For the most part they were a drowse, as both parties told the jury what they expected the evidence to show.

In opening statement, Thaddeus knew he couldn't argue the case, he could only describe testimony. Closing argument was where the family's dinner table argumentative child would make his or her money.

But to lead things off, opening statements were pretty much met with glassy-eyed stares from a jury that had zero idea what in the world the lawyers were talking about. Both attorneys spoke and abruptly sat down. When they were finished, Thaddeus put the score at 1-1.

The state's first witness was the arresting officer, the narc who had made the buy from Bat. Much blood was let, as he described how Bat, without any encouragement from the officer, had aggressively wanted to sell dope and how he had aggressively pursued the sale. To hear him tell it, there wasn't a hint of entrapment. No effort by the state to go out and procure the sale from an unwilling seller. Rather, the Bat he described was all but beating on garbage cans and windows trying to get someone to buy his product.

The detective, Angelo Z. Banter, LVPD, was a Marine Corps–looking type, with shaved head, all but the very top, no sideburns, no facial hair, no rings, no necklaces, no jewelry, no tattoos, nothing distinguishing about him at all, which made him all but indescribable by one criminal victimized by his undercover purchase to another criminal who was yet to be victimized by an undercover purchase. And that was just how Detective Banter wanted it. Ambiguous.

When it was Thaddeus' turn to cross-examine, he stood up but remained standing at counsel table. "Mister Banter," he began—

"That's Detective, sir."

"Your mother named you 'Detective'?"

"I am a detective."

"I didn't ask you about your occupation, did I?"

"Objection, Your Honor," said the D.A. "This is already irrelevant. If counsel really does need the detective to recite back to him what he was asked, counsel's best resource is the court reporter, who took it down verbatim."

Thaddeus tossed her a nice smile and told the court that he would withdraw the question.

He began again. "Mister Banter," he said, and paused. This time the police officer didn't challenge him on his rank in the LVPD. The point had been made. Or so he thought.

"Mister Banter, when Mister Tattinger entered your automobile that night, July twentieth, I believe you said he smelled funny?"

"Yes."

"Funny as in 'ha-ha' or funny as in 'too bad, he probably can't afford shelter with a shower.'"

"I don't follow you."

"I'm asking whether he smelled because you saw something funny about his body odor, or did he smell because he was broke, living on the street, and had nowhere to bathe?"

"Probably living on the street. I don't know the guy so I had no way of knowing he kept up with good hygiene or not."

"Let's talk about what else you didn't know about him

"All right."

Thaddeus looked at his notes. The roll was beginnin, just about to launch. "For example, you didn't know that h(

didn't have enough money in the world to even buy a cup of coffee, did you?"

"No."

"And you didn't know he didn't have the money to pay first and last on an apartment, did you?"

"No."

"And you didn't know that the reason he was selling you marijuana was because he had no other way to get money, did you?"

"Objection!" shouted the D.A. "Counsel is testifying to facts that aren't in evidence."

"Let me rephrase, judge," said Thaddeus. "Let's try it this way. You didn't know he was selling you marijuana because he just found out he was HIV-positive and didn't have the money to buy the drugs that would keep him from getting AIDS—did you know that?"

"No, I didn't know that. In fact—"

Then the police officer broke off. Thaddeus narrowed his eyes at him, watching the jury out the corner. "In fact, what? What were you about to say?"

"I was going to say that in fact if I had known he was HIV-positive I probably wouldn't have let him in my car."

"Yes, which was exactly his problem that night, wasn't it?"

"How so?"

"Well, no one would have anything to do with him for no other reason than he smelled bad, would they?"

"Probably not. Most normal people would be offended by how bad he smelled."

Thaddeus looked sadly at the jury. "Most normal people? Did that include you?"

"Yes."

"Were you offended by him?"

"Yes."

"But not so offended you didn't allow him to sell you drugs, were you?"

"No. Someone wants to sell me drugs, I don't care what they smell like."

"Even if they're someone like Mister Tattinger, who can't afford to eat, bathe, or sleep warm. You let none of that stop you from making a miserable little buy and putting them in jail, do you?"

"Objection!"

The tiny, pallid judge, whom Thaddeus had found to be easily troubled, called the afternoon recess. "Fifteen minutes. Then we'll start up again."

AFTER THE BREAK, Thaddeus surrendered the witness back to the D.A.

She navigated here and there with him, but the bell had been rung and couldn't be un-rung. Thaddeus had established that Bat was very sick, absolutely penniless, needed medications to stay alive, and had no hope of obtaining medicine except by the sale of the marijuana to the officer. That was the sum and substance of the case and, when the D.A. was finished with her redirect, Thaddeus could tell by a swift eyeball poll of the jury that she had won over some of them and that he had won over some of them. There was no way she was going to get a unanimous vote; there was probably no way he was going to get a unanimous vote. More than likely there would be a hung jury, followed by the state deciding it was a waste of time to retry the case for such a small amount of dope by a guy sentenced to eventual death by his own blood, and thus a plea would be offered, to a misdemeanor, no jail, and Thaddeus would allow his client to accept.

Which was exactly what happened.

At the end of the state's case, Thaddeus made his motion for a directed verdict; it was denied, as usual, and the prosecutor asked for a recess.

She wanted to talk, and she pulled Thaddeus inside the attorney conference room.

They sat on opposite sides of the conference table; she removed a high heel and began massaging her foot. "I'm twenty-eight and I have bunions," she announced.

"Sorry," said Thad. "Never been down that road myself."

"Look. Your guy will eventually die of AIDS. That much is known. He sold a small amount, you've made your point that he lacked the discretion to sell, under the statute. It's a point well taken but you're not going to get a not-guilty for your efforts."

"Agree," he said.

"So let's split the difference. Your guy pleads to a misdemeanor, simple possession, no jail, one year probation, and we all go home and soak our feet."

"Sounds good. Let's do it."

And just like that—poof!—it was over.

They entered the plea of guilty to a simple possession, waived pre-trial investigation, the judge approved the oral plea but wanted one in writing for the file, Bat was put on one year probation, ordered to pay $350 to the Victims Fund, and told to never come back in that same court.

Bat said he had learned his lesson.

Everyone headed for the door. It was 3:20 in the afternoon, first day of trial.

Bat had the rest of the week off. Thaddeus had two more days off.

THE SUN WAS OUT, not a cloud, and people were dressed in shorts, sandals, and tees, life was a lark and a dream. Bat had escaped with his life.

"Let's find a Starbucks where we can sit outside," Thaddeus suggested.

"I see the green and white sign on the opposite corner."

They purchased their drinks and took their seats outside, on the sidewalk, behind a low white fence, beneath a red and blue umbrella. Life was glorious and they tasted their iced drinks. Life was magnificent and everlasting, they agreed.

"So what's this about college?"

Bat's eyes got wide and a smile took over his face. He cheerfully explained how his girlfriend Maria Consuelo didn't want him to settle for being a waiter the rest of his life. She had asked him what he really loved to do. He had said he wanted to be like Thaddeus. He wanted to wear suit clothes, work in an office, and save people from the cops.

"That's it? You want to like me?"

"I could do worse," Bat observed.

"So you really, really want to do this."

"More than anything. Except I want to marry Maria, too. If she'll have me."

"She'll have you. I've got a feeling about that."

"Hope so."

"So look, Bat, let's do this. You come to work for me as an investigator. You don't need a license to work for me privately. I'll pay you forty thousand a year, and you'll have two hours every afternoon for studies. We do this while you take your classes and decide if this is what you really want. You've been away from school since forever and it might turn out you hate it. Or maybe you'll love it. No one really knows right now. When you start law school you'll get a raise on the condition that you come to work for me for three years when you graduate law school. How am I doing so far?"

Bat's eyes clouded with tears. "No shit? You'd do that for me?"

"Hey, I need an investigator, someone with street smarts. There isn't anyone can outdo you in that department. It makes perfect sense."

"Would I have to carry a gun?"

"Why, you want to carry a gun?"

"Hell no."

"No guns. We're not out to shoot anybody."

"I just know about those BAG guys following you all over. They're carrying."

"That's a whole different job. No, you would wear a suit and tie every day, dress the part, have your own office, set your own hours, and pretty much figure out how to get your assignments done. Come work for me. You know me, you know it's a win-win."

Bat took a long drink of the iced latte and nodded. "Done. When do I start?"

"You've got to give the casino a week's notice. Call them today and you can start next Monday."

"But I'm off all week. They don't expect me anyway."

"Call them anyway. It's good business. Might as well get you used to that."

"Hey, they love me over there."

"I'm sure they do, Bat, I'm sure they do."

Whereupon Bat removed his glass eye, polished it with a napkin, and squeezed it back in its socket.

"There are a few refinements we'll have to make in your style," Thaddeus said. "But they'll come, they'll come."

They shook on the deal and went back to sipping and enjoying the day and the beautiful Las Vegas women leisurely strolling by.

43

B at reviewed the Kiki Murphy police report the first day in his new office.

He was dressed in a brand new seersucker summer suit, pale blue shirt, and yellow tie, and had washed and rebraided his hair. He looked like a million bucks. Thaddeus told him so, and Sparky agreed.

Sparky was glad to have another "working stiff" around, like him, someone he could BS with and have lunch with and bounce things off.

Bat got his new network name and password, and signed up for the courses on Internet and Word that Thaddeus had located for him. Soon he was surfing the web and his world was suddenly three universes larger. He loved Google, loved Angry Birds, and found artwork for his own Facebook page. He invited Katy to join him on Facebook and she accepted. He now had one friend. But there would be more, he knew, lots more.

Finishing up his computer course work for novice computer users, he spread open the Kiki Murphy police report on his desk. Thaddeus wanted the statement of the surviving attacker. The guy's address was Ohio and Bat had to look Ohio up on MapQuest to even figure out where it was. Toledo, he found right away. He sent Thaddeus an email. "Attacker #2 lives Toledo. Do I go there to statementize him?"

Thaddeus emailed back. "See how far you can get with him on a phone call. Don't forget, he's been charged with misdemeanor assault on Kiki, so he won't be friendly."

"Got it," Bat emailed back.

Now to find the guy's phone number.

The Internet found a white pages listing for the witness-defendant. Trouble was, it cost $19.95 on *People Finder* to get the creep's number.

"I need a credit card," he emailed Thaddeus.

Who emailed back, "Use your debit card."

"I don't have a bank account, no debit card."

"Go open one. Get a debit card."

Bat did as he was told. He was back in the office in time to take his afternoon break with Sparky.

It was a warm, early-summer day, temperature reaching the nineties, and they decided to walk.

They hit Panera's, inhaled soup and sandwiches, and then went for a march around the downtown. They talked and exchanged ideas and lies, and Sparky suggested the type of questions Bat would want to ask Linden Morrow, the witness in Toledo.

They ended up buying iced drinks to take back to work, and returned to their offices.

Bat used his temporary debit card online. It produced a phone number and address for Linden Morrow. The address matched the one on the police report. So far, so good, he told himself. He sat down and began writing the questions he would ask, on a yellow pad. Then he dialed the number and waited.

The voice sounded sleepy. "'Lo."

"Linden Morrow?"

"Who wants to know?"

"Billy Tattinger. I'm calling from the Murfee Law Group in Las Vegas."

"I already have a lawyer."

"We don't want to be your lawyer. We're already the lawyer for Kiki Murphy."

"Kiki? You're her lawyer?"

"My boss is. Uh—do you know her?"

"I do. We did."

"So how come you attacked her?"

"Nobody was attacking nobody. We run up to her to catch up. We run up and each of us grabbed an arm to walk with her. We was friends."

"I didn't know that."

"Man, what you trying to pull? It's those goddamn cops out there. They're trying to make me look some kind of pervert, attacking Kiki. She was married to my cousin. Don't that make her family to me?"

"I don't know about that. Look, I'm brand new here. I'm just a poor guy trying to do my job."

"I was gonna say. You don't sound very bright. Like someone only turned on one switch."

"Thanks. Look, would you mind if I recorded your statement about what happened?"

"Yep, I mind. I already gave my statement. To the cops. Night Lamont got shot."

"I don't have that. How about if I just go over some things and switch the recorder on while we're talking. It don't sound to me like you've got anything to worry about.

Being it was family."

"I guess. Turn it on, if it gets you wet."

"It does. It does get me wet."

Bat attached the phone pickup to the earpiece and switched on the recorder. "Okay," he said, "I've got the recorder turned on."

"Knock yourself out. What'd you say your name was?"

"Billy Tattinger. Everyone calls me Bat."

"Okay, Bat. How can I help you?"

"Let me ask. You know I'm recording this?"

"I do now."

"And I'm recording with your permission?"

"Hey, I got nothing to hide. Record away."

"About the night Lamont got shot. That was your cousin, Lamont Alexandr?"

"It was. Married to one Kiki Murphy. She shot him down in cold blood."

"All right. What were you doing there that night?"

"Doing where?"

"Well—the casino. What were you there for?"

"Shit, that's a no-brainer. We was there to gamble."

"And you two were playing cards?"

"Blackjack."

"Were you playing with Kiki?"

"No. No way. She and Lamont was separated. She didn't even see us at first. Then we caught up with her at the high-rollers table. She was pissed but she did ask Lamont if he was getting on all right."

"Why would she ask him that?"

"He was moved back to Ohio. For drug rehab."

"But he was married to Kiki?"

"Well, that's what he told me."

Bat frowned, his mahogany forehead pressed hard

against his hand while he talked into the receiver. "Lamont told you he was married to Kiki?"

"He told me. 'Course I never seen a license or nothing. How was I to know? He was my cousin, I believed him."

"But he definitely knew her?"

"He played football at UCLA. She knew him there. They dated and then she started fooling around with some other guy. But they was married. At least he said so."

"Do you know why she shot him?"

"She was pissed at him showing up there, I guess."

"Did she tell you that?"

"No, I'm just guessing now. Is the recorder still on?"

"Yes. With your permission."

"I want it off now."

"Why? You want me to turn it off?"

"I feel like I'm just saying stuff that was told to me. I don't really know much that was for sure. But when she pulled that gun out, I stopped right there and raised my hands. She didn't look happy and I wasn't about to come any closer."

"You actually saw the gun?"

"Well—actually I heard the gun. I guess you could say. Did I ever actually see it? Probably not. But I saw the smoke come out and saw my cousin get shot. After that, I wasn't looking."

"What were you looking at instead?"

"Man, I had my eyes closed hard. Figured the next shot was for me and I didn't want to see it."

"Fair enough. So you never actually saw the gun?"

"Like I said, I saw the fire come out the barrel. It was night and the barrel just kind of exploded. Next thing I know, Lamont goes down to his knees and then topples to his side. I open my eyes and seen that part of it."

"I'm still recording, is that all right?"

"I guess. I'm done anyway. I ain't got nothing more to say."

"What happened after your cousin was shot?"

"Nothing. I mean we just stood there looking at each other. Then she started crying. She dropped her purse, put her face in her hands, and started crying."

"Did she say anything?"

"She said 'No, no, no, no' about two hundred times. And sobbing. Like hard. You know how women can cry."

"I know how men can cry too. Did you cry?"

"I was too scared. I just didn't move. I didn't want her shooting me."

"Did you see where the gun was when she was crying with her face in her hands?"

"No. But I wasn't looking for the gun. I was hoping the cops got there. Just waiting and praying for the cops to show."

"Did they?"

"In less than three minutes. First two young Mexican cops, then the place was swarming. EMTs showed up and wanted to know was I okay. Cops took me and put me in a squad. Asked me an hour's worth of questions."

"Did you go to jail?"

"No, they gave me a citation to appear in Justice Court."

"Did you appear?"

"I did. I paid a three-hundred-dollar fine and it was dropped to disturbing the peace. I'm done with out there, man. I ain't never coming back to Vegas. I'll go to Atlantic City or one of them Indian joints, but no more Vegas. Not for this boy."

"Okay, well, I think that's all my questions. Anything else you want to add?"

"Yeah, I hope they throw the switch on that crazy broad. She deserves to go down for this. Killing my cousin and all."

"All right. I'm turning the machine off now. And this was done with your permission?"

"Like I said, I got nothing to hide. Didn't do nothing wrong except get the hell scared out of me."

"Okay. We're done then."

"Goodbye then."

"Goodbye."

Bat stirred his iced drink with the straw. He realized he'd been sweating in the interview and his underarms were soaked. But none of that stuff mattered anymore. He had taken a statement and he knew it was an important one. He wanted to immediately play it back for Thaddeus.

But first he would play it for Sparky. He would see if Sparky thought he left anything out, in case he needed to call the guy back, before going to Thaddeus.

But wasn't it remarkable? he thought. The guy never saw the gun. And hadn't Thaddeus said something about the gun being in the purse when it went off?

It was important, what he had.

He was certain of it.

He took another drink and leaned back in his brand new leather chair.

This was going to be a barrel of monkeys. Plus, he was earning $40K a year. Much more than he would ever make waiting tables or selling drugs. The best part? Nobody was waiting to throw your ass in jail for doing what you were doing to survive.

There just might be something to this walking straight.

44

K aty was strolling the aisles at the Safeway store and Ragman was two steps behind.

She hadn't noticed him, of course. He was too slick for that.

Sarai was riding in the cart, reaching for every box of cereal they passed, and crying real tears each time her mother told her no.

"It's past your naptime, young lady," her mother said.

Ragman was at her elbow, looking at a box of corn flakes, reading the ingredients, to all outward appearances making up his mind about a possible purchase.

She never noticed him.

She turned in her coupons—a college habit that was slow to die and maybe never would—then handed over her debit card. The purchase was rung up and she headed for the door.

When she passed through the pneumatic door into the Las Vegas summer time heat, she didn't notice the man outside, smoking, minding his own business.

Nor did she suspect anything when he followed her to

the Escalade. She was putting the groceries in the back, and he was standing across the parking lane, smoking. His back was to her, but he was watching every move out of his mirrored sunglasses. He now knew her car, the license number, where she shopped, and how far from home she was.

He followed her home and would watch as she unloaded the car. He would pay particular attention to what she first took inside: little girl or groceries. Just as she was about to open her own door and get out, the garage door closed behind her.

"Damn," Ragman muttered.

He decided to give it two hours and then return. In another vehicle, of course, something they'd never seen in their neighborhood before.

Sooner or later, someone would walk up to the front door and punch the code into the keypad.

He wanted to be there for that.

45

Kroc and Magence were working late. Again.
It was the third night in a row, and they were
carefully reviewing and re-reviewing the video
records of the casino count room. It was beginning to look
like they had been made fools of.

"They're running over and over, aren't they," said
Magence. It wasn't a question.

"I think so. I think someone has intercepted our feed
and they're showing us like a month at a time of the same
videos. The same recordings."

"We've been had."

"How did they know?" he said.

"Duh. Maybe it was the badges and guns when we went
in and took over and installed the cameras. Someone just
might have gotten suspicious."

"How would you have done it any differently?" he said,
challenging her.

"Hey, don't get your feathers ruffled. I'm not saying I
would have done it any differently. We didn't really have any

other way. They guard that room twenty-four/seven/three-sixty-five. We did what we could."

"But we're not going to catch anyone removing money."

She laughed. "Damn sure not going to with this video feed."

"I know."

"So where does that leave us?"

He turned his chair away from the monitor and faced her across the office.

"Well," he began, "we will have the documents. The returns, the P&Ls, the lifestyle analysis. The bank deposit analysis."

"There's still that discrepancy between what he deposited and what he reported on his tax returns."

"Is it enough to convict him?"

"Hmm. We'd best talk to the lawyers. See what they think so far."

"I'll call them. Want to see them tomorrow?"

"I think so. ASAP."

"I'll call David Fisher first thing in the morning. I'm outta here now."

"Same here. See you in the a.m."

"Adios."

46

T haddeus knew what he wanted to do about the IRS, but he just wasn't certain how to go about it.

He knew that in criminal proceedings brought by the United States against him, he wasn't allowed to take the deposition of the witnesses against him. Which meant he couldn't take the statements of either Aldous Kroc or Mathilde Magence in order to learn about the case against him.

Which was a show-stopper.

How, he wondered, could he ever defend himself in a criminal case if he didn't know what the witnesses against him were going to say at trial? He thought it very unfair. In a civil case, of course, he could take the deposition of any witness, and discover the adverse party's case. But not so in criminal. Which was the most important kind of case that one would ever face.

So he did the next best thing; he called attorney Gerry Browne in Reno.

Gerry called him back a day later.

"Hey, Thad," said Gerry, "what's cookin' down there in LV?"

"I'm trying to wrap my head around this criminal case, Gerry. Something I don't like about it."

Gerry snorted. "I thought we were gonna let me worry about that case. I remember you paying me something like a million bucks to take the worry off your plate. Am I wrong about that?"

"What I don't understand is how to get to the testimony of Kroc and Magence. They just can't have that much against me, because I didn't do anything wrong. But the rules of criminal procedure in the federal courts don't allow me to take their depositions."

"Exactly. One of the worst articulations of Constitutional rights in the law."

"How's that Constitutional?" asked Thaddeus.

"Well, the Sixth Amendment to the U.S. Constitution gives you the right to confront and cross-examine the witnesses against you."

"Right."

"But how can you effectively do that if you don't know ahead of time what their testimony will be? It looks to me like the Constitution gives you the right, but then the Congress pulls it back, out of your reach, by implementing rules of procedure that don't allow you to take depositions."

"Totally agree."

"Well, I'm glad you do."

"So here's what I'm thinking," Thaddeus said. "I'm thinking of suing the feds for malicious prosecution and then taking their depositions in the civil suit."

There was a long silence.

"You know, you just might be on to something there."

"I know. With your blessing, I'm going to get it on file and see where it goes."

"My blessing's all over you, Thaddeus."

They traded information for another ten minutes and then said their goodbyes. Gerry said he would like to attend the depositions of the IRS agents, when the civil case got to that point. Thaddeus agreed and said he would give him plenty of notice.

Thaddeus called Sparky into his office.

The paralegal hustled in and Thaddeus noticed that the shock of red hair had been allowed to grow out and was now covering his ears. He looked several years older, in a Willie Nelson kind of way, but he kept extremely busy around the office and Thaddeus had long ago told him he had earned the job as a full-time employee. Sparky spoke very little of his life outside the office, and he had twice refused Thaddeus' invitations to lunch, telling Thaddeus he preferred not to mix business with pleasure. Whatever that meant, Thaddeus had thought, but he let it go. Strictly business was how it was going to be between them and that was fine.

"Sit," Thaddeus said.

"What's up?"

"I want you to prepare a suit for malicious prosecution against the IRS. That's about all I know right now."

"Fine. What's malicious about what they did?"

"They came into my casino with a search warrant and went way beyond its limits."

"How so?"

"Well, the search warrant gave them the right to search. Fair enough. But they then went into the count room at the casino and installed video gear. That was far beyond the scope of the search warrant they served on my guys. It was illegal and I believe I have the right to name the employees who did it, in the suit against the IRS."

"You're talking Kroc and Magence?"

"I'm talking Kroc and Magence. I want the IRS named as a party defendant, sure. But I want Kroc and Magence named as well. At the same time you prepare the lawsuit, also prepare a notice of deposition for Kroc and Magence, for thirty-five days after the filing of the lawsuit, both deps on the same day, four hours apart."

"Well, I know where I'll be for the next week."

"Huh-uh. Ready to file by noon tomorrow. No ifs, ands, or buts."

"I'll be here all night."

"Time and half, Mister Union Man."

"I wasn't going to ask."

"But you are a member of the pipefitters union?"

"I am."

"And I honor all Union rules and abide by them. Time and a half."

"Actually it would be double-time."

"Double-time then."

"I'll have it by noon tomorrow. Ready for your signature. Then I'll walk it across the street, file it in the George Building, and secure service of process. Hopefully we can get it served on the two little bastards tomorrow afternoon."

"Yes, yes, and yes, they are little bastards," said Thaddeus with a grin. "I like your style, dude."

"I told you you'd like my style. I got your back, son."

"No 'son' shit, okay?"

"Okay."

"Tomorrow then."

❧

ONE WEEK LATER, five days after being served with the lawsuit for malicious prosecution, the IRS dragged Thaddeus into court. They wanted a protective order.

They were falling all over themselves with righteous indignation. How could a criminal defendant even think he had the right to file a lawsuit for malicious prosecution and then take depositions? they cried. He would be gaining an unfair advantage if allowed to proceed. He would be skirting the rules!

The judge was Phineas Y. Barberow, a seventy-five-year-young jurist who had himself twice sued the IRS while a private attorney. He knew all about them and their methods, knew they were almost totally impervious to assault by citizens, and knew they had thousands of lawyers to come in and cry "Foul!" Trouble was, they could only talk one at a time, as Judge Barberow was fond of saying. And that day, their spokesman's words were falling on deaf ears.

"Counsel, are you telling me that Mister Murfee can't take these depositions because they might provide some advantage to him?"

"That's a shorthand way of saying it, but yes."

"Weren't you looking for an advantage when you illegally installed cameras on his business premises?"

"Your Honor, nobody has yet found the Service acted illegally."

"Well, write this down. Write down that I am very close to making that exact finding, understand me?"

Thaddeus had earlier recited to the judge the famous— or infamous—facts of the case of *Morris v. United States*, 521 F.2d 872, 873-74 (9th Cir. 1975). In that case, Melvin Morris, a plumber and contractor, bought eighteen substandard buildings in San Francisco to renovate and sell. Morris relied on credit from lenders, subcontractors, and suppliers to finance the building projects. After Morris began refurbishing investment properties, a union representative told Morris that since Morris did not employ union labor he should expect to hear from the Internal Revenue Service (IRS). Shortly thereafter, the IRS investigated and audited Morris and his wife. The IRS concluded that the couple owed back taxes for excess depreciation deductions taken on the buildings. While investigating Morris, the IRS informed Morris's creditors of his tax liability and told creditors that Morris would become insolvent. Creditors refused to further support the venture, and Morris lost his business.

During their investigation, IRS agents harassed and intimidated Morris and his wife. To collect amounts owed for back taxes, the IRS unlawfully seized and levied upon the Morrises' property. After investigating and auditing the Morrises for several years and collecting part of the alleged deficiency, the IRS realized that the Morrises had properly computed and paid their taxes. The IRS conceded that the deficiency determination was an error and returned the wrongfully seized property. The Morrises sued for, among other things, lost business opportunity, but their claims failed because of sovereign immunity.

Thaddeus had concluded, "This fact pattern is the *modus operandi* of the IRS, as evidenced by its agents in *Morris v. United States.* In other words, they do terrible, illegal things, and then come crying to the court that they didn't mean it. Just like here today. They have rights, they say their rights are being violated, with total disregard for the rights of citizens who have been violated. This must stop and the court should turn a deaf ear to their whining!"

Which is exactly what the judge did.

"Gentlemen—and ladies—" the judge said, deferentially referring to the two female attorneys with the other three

IRS attorneys bringing the motion, "the depositions are going to be held in seven days. And I think we're going to hold them in my chambers, so we can get all objections the IRS always has, ruled on immediately. Does anyone have any questions?"

The IRS attorneys were already packing.

They had no questions.

SEVEN DAYS later they were one big happy family. Plus Thaddeus himself, in attendance were Judge Barberow, three IRS attorneys and one U.S. Attorney, and Aldous Kroc and Mathilde Magence.

The government lawyers took control of the judge's long red leather couch. Thaddeus helped himself to a patterned wingback chair; the judge would maintain law and order from behind his monolithic desk, and to his right was the witness chair, just waiting. The court reporter sat to the judge's left. She extended the tripod stand under her machine, fed a foot of paper though its maw, and announced she was ready.

"We're on the record," said the judge. "Let the record show it's July seventh and all parties and counsel are present. Witness Aldous Kroc has been sworn by me. You may proceed, Mr. Murfee."

Thaddeus watched the witness take the witness chair, settle himself in, and try to smile as if comfortable and carefree. It didn't work quite as planned; within minutes he was tugging at his collar and shuffling his feet as if he were kicking rats.

Thaddeus began. "I just have one question today for you, Mister Kroc. And here is my question. Please tell us by what authority you installed the hidden video camera inside my count room at the casino."

"Objection," said the U.S. Attorney, "assumes facts not in evidence."

"You're objecting to the foundation?" the judge immediately shot back.

"I am."

"Overruled. The witness will please answer the question."

Kroc craned to look at the judge. "What was the question?"

The judge motioned to the court reporter. She read the question once again.

"Please tell us by what authority you installed the hidden video camera inside my count room at the casino."

Kroc stared dumbly at the far wall. He rubbed his hands together as if expecting a treat. "I made the decision to install the camera. It was on my authority."

Thaddeus immediately followed up. "Did any court give you authority to install the cameras by virtue of a search warrant?"

"No."

"By virtue of a wiretap?"

"No."

"Did your supervisor give you authority to install the surveillance equipment?"

"No."

"And at the time you installed the video equipment you were acting as an agent of the United States?"

"It was my job."

"You were doing your job?"

"Yes."

"So you were acting as an agent of the United States?"

"I thought so."

"Yes or no."

"Yes, I was acting as an agent."

Thaddeus bore in on the agent. "Do you know what a search and seizure is?"

"Yes. I think so."

"Well, you're a criminal investigator, correct?"

"Yes."

"So you surely know what search and seizure is?"

"Yes."

"Do you know what an illegal search and seizure is?"

"Yes."

"Tell us in your own words."

"An illegal search and seizure is one that violates the Fourth Amendment to the Constitution."

"And as a matter of law in this country, how do we protect citizens against unreasonable searches and seizures."

"By suppressing evidence."

"How else?"

"By requiring a search warrant."

"Or a wiretap warrant?"

"Yes."

"Did you have any such warrant when you installed eavesdropping equipment in my casino?"

"No."

Thaddeus paused. He studied his notes momentarily, intending for it all to sink in with the judge. Which it had.

"Mister Murfee," said Judge Barberow, "may I ask a question or two?"

"Please do."

"Mister Kroc, was there anyone else acting with you

when you illegally planted the eavesdropping equipment in Mister Murfee's casino?"

"Only Agent Magence. Plus some technicians."

"Well," said the judge, slowly, "I'm not so much concerned about the technicians. They weren't law enforcement officers, were they?"

"No. Just techs."

"Exactly. So you and Special Agent Magence were the only criminal investigators involved in the illegal installation?"

"Yes."

"You were the only sworn officers?"

"Yes."

"For the record, the court is going to give the U.S. Attorney's Office the opportunity to convene a grand jury to investigate the illegal actions of Agents Kroc and Magence. Failing to do so will result in the court appointing a special prosecutor to convene a grand jury and review these illegal activities. Have I made myself clear?"

The government attorneys all answered affirmatively, that the judge had made himself clear. Faces were white, hands shook as folders were fumbled into and out from bags, as if a good answer were about to be produced.

"Very well. Mister Murfee, do you have any other questions for this witness?"

"No sir."

"Miss Magence, your deposition is also noticed for today. Before testifying, however, it is incumbent on the court to warn you that you should seek the advice of counsel and consider interposing the Fifth Amendment rule against self-incrimination. Long story short, your own criminal attorney is going to tell you to keep your mouth shut and refuse to testify. My advice is that you follow his or her advice. Anything else today?"

"No, Your Honor," said Thaddeus.

Within two hours the U.S. Attorney H. Mouton Carraway himself called Thaddeus and advised him the criminal indictments pending against him were being dismissed. With prejudice, meaning they could never be filed again.

Thaddeus thanked him and hung up the phone.

That night the firm, and dates, ate lobster with Thaddeus and Katy and Sarai at Red Lobster. Drinks were ordered, toasts were made, and the meal was a smashing success.

"Thank you all," Thaddeus said to his staff. "Particularly you, Sparky. Thank you for a job well done."

"It's okay, son. Just covering your back, is all."

Thaddeus only gave him a long, studied stare, before breaking into laughter and ordering coffee with dessert.

47

He had been to LA for more cash out of the safe deposit box, and this time Ragman rode the bus into Las Vegas.

He was coming from Bank of America, where he had ratholed $1 million cash for the job. So he could have chartered his own jet had he wanted.

But he didn't.

Instead he was opting for anonymity. The bus lines had no such thing as passenger lists. If a hit man needed to move around without leaving a roadmap of breadcrumbs, Greyhound was the only way to go.

He needed a prison for the tiny girl. He needed sustenance to keep her alive until she was no longer necessary. He needed a bed for himself. And he needed painkiller.

Or what he called painkiller.

What he really meant was speed. He rode the pipe, the magic pipe.

When he was speeding he was untouchable. Feelings blotted out, forgotten, best of all, unfelt. No guilt, no remorse, no hesitation to disfigure and mutilate. Enough slicing and dicing and the money would be surrendered, Murfee to Mascari. He would then ride the bus around while they mourned and swore revenge.

He smiled. Bottom line, he would get the money returned.

"There's this guy with this kid," Mascari had said.

"I'm your man."

That hadn't changed.

Nor would it.

Fifteen hundred dollars cash for a beige Camry. False name, don't need insurance just now, thanks. The salesman scratched his head. That was an odd duck, he told himself. But hey, he kept $500 commission. He turned away and went back to pushing used steel and rubber.

RAGMAN RETURNED TO THEIR HOUSE, but this time he wasn't alone.

It was easy to follow the young lawyer home, always easy to follow a Tesla. They stood out like a rose in a weed garden. He had to admire the kid's taste. Truth be told, the guy wouldn't be able to afford the cost of a battery jump by the time Ragman had finished with him. It would all be gone. Along with his firstborn.

From the ambiguity of a million beige Camrys just like it, Ragman sat low in the seat and watched. He was disappointed when the Tesla pulled into the garage and the door articulated down. The outside keypad wasn't touched.

HE WATCHED the house for hours at night. From a distance,

outside the view of the security agents who roamed the premises at all hours. Different vehicle each time he came; he figured they would notice nothing unusual.

He didn't know yet if it would happen at night, in the morning, at noon, or in the evening. He would find the crack in the armor and slide in and be gone like a whisper.

Next day, he abandoned the Camry and went to a different lot. Twenty-five hundred bucks cash for a used Impala. Pale blue, a million just like them on the road. He was down the street from their house by ten o'clock in the morning, and he watched until the kid came home again in his Tesla. This time they went out.

He followed them to Chuck E. Cheese. He went inside and took the table next to him. They noticed nothing, of course. They were there with the little girl and were seeing the world through her eyes instead of through their own. Had they been alert, they might have noticed his glassy eyes, his salacious gaze at the little girl.

But they didn't.

They prayed before eating, ate and drank and laughed, and carried the little girl, who had fallen asleep in the booster chair, to the car. She was tucked inside, fastened carefully in the car seat, where she awoke briefly and cried because it was past her bedtime. He watched this in pantomime two rows over in the parking lot. Then he broke off the chase and drove away.

On the third night his suspicions were confirmed. The BAG agents didn't spend the night inside the house, which was interesting. Now he needed fifteen minutes alone with the security panel.

That came at 2:30 p.m. when Katy left the house with the little girl and walked her over to the park. The dark-skinned mother wore a T-shirt that confirmed she was enrolled at

UNLV med school, and white shorts. The little girl wore blue jeans, tennies with sparkling soles, and a T-shirt featuring Elmo.

"Perfect," Ragman said to no one, as a single BAG agent fell in behind, walking a deferential half-block behind the mother and daughter.

From his previous observations, Ragman knew the house was empty and the security was off making rounds. They would just be arriving at the rear lot boundary.

He scurried across the street and walked boldly up to the front door and punched rapidly at the keypad. The numbers were memorized from the day before, when the mother had walked the little girl to the park, returned, and used the keypad to gain entry through the front door. The 300mm Nikon lens had blown it up in the video such that a blind man could have read it: 0-3-7-7. Obviously someone's birthday, probably the woman's.

The security panel was just inside and he popped the cover. It took all of twenty-five seconds to disable the alarm between three and four a.m., and he was back outside, gliding like a ghost into his Nissan Altima ($2,200 cash), and was gone. He rolled the latex glove from his right hand and tucked it in his jeans pocket. The left hand had gone in and out ungloved, as it touched nothing.

It didn't matter what night. He would only come when he was fully prepared.

First he had to make a nest for the little girl. It had to be remote, quiet, and invisible.

He knew just the place.

48

Kiki's trial was underway and Thaddeus had called his first witness. His name was Gunner Andersen and he was an armorer from San Diego.

"And are you able to give an opinion whether the gun was discharged accidentally by Kiki Murphy?"

"I am."

Thaddeus paused to allow the suspense to build. The jury—five women and seven men—had their eyes glued to the witness.

Gunner Andersen was polished and perfect. Plus, he was accessible, a real person, someone with whom the jury could connect. His specialty was police shootings and the use of deadly force. He had testified in over 5,000 shooting cases, exonerating nearly 4,900 cops who were under investigation. When a cop shot someone, it was usually Andersen who was called.

He had testified in Kiki's trial that he held a bachelor's in mechanical engineering from Caltech, a master's from Caltech, and a Ph.D. from Stanford. There was also a master's degree in human factors from a school in Florida. Together, the formal education qualified him to testify on matters such as the human element in firearms cleaning, shooting, and examination post-shooting.

He had testified in federal court in all but four states, and had been accepted as a weapons expert in courts in all states.

He was seventy-two years old, had his first great-grand-child, and refused to retire, despite his family's protestations.

As of the date of Kiki's trial, Gunner Andersen had written over 1,200 published articles on firearms and firearm safety and the use of deadly force in police shootings. But he didn't come cheap. In private shooting cases, such as Kiki's, the retainer was $25,000, which Thaddeus had gladly paid. It couldn't be overstated, the importance of using the best armorer in the nation in such a case as hers.

Thaddeus' use of Dr. Andersen had two goals.

One, he wanted to cloak the actual shooting with an air of responsibility. He wanted the jury to see that Kiki's carrying and handling of the weapon was done in accord with accepted firearms safety and techniques.

Second, he wanted to prove to the jury that the shooting was purely accidental, that it was completely unforeseeable by her—at the time and place of the shooting—that the firearm would accidentally discharge.

Andersen testified that, according to the videotapes the prosecution had shown the jury during its case, when the two men ran up to Kiki and grabbed her arms it was totally foreseeable that she would wrest her way free and go for the gun to threaten them. She was a single female, alone at night, in an unfamiliar place, there was no one around to lend assistance, and she had only herself to rely on when the attack came. He used the word "attack" repeatedly and it was effective. At this point in his examination he had succeeded in portraying her as a victim of an assault that must have "scared her to death." He had managed to frame it as a justified shooting even if it hadn't been accidental, which was pure icing on the cake.

The jury was furiously making notes of everything Gunner Andersen had to say. The state's case provided no comparable witness and certainly no such testimony. Moreover, for its rebuttal Thaddeus knew the state had no witness who could even begin to refute what Dr. Andersen was telling the jury.

So Thaddeus repeated the question, just for the effect, and just to make sure every member of the jury heard it.

"Are you able to give an opinion whether the gun was discharged accidentally by Kiki Murphy?"

"I am." The white-haired, blue-eyed, professorial witness looked directly at the jury when he spoke. He was educator and advocate, emphasis on the educator part.

"And what is your opinion?"

"Objection, the witness hasn't been qualified as an expert."

The judge looked down at the District Attorney and shook her head. "Seriously?" her face said. "Counsel, the court finds that the doctor is qualified to render the opinion he has been asked to render. Please proceed."

Thaddeus turned to the court reporter. "Please read back the question."

"Question: 'Are you able to give an opinion whether the gun was discharged accidentally by Kiki Murphy?'"

"I am."

Thaddeus: "And what is that opinion."

"It is my professional opinion that the gun discharged

accidentally due to the lipstick tube in the purse catching inside the trigger guard and pulling the trigger."

"Objection!" cried the D.A., who had jumped to her feet and whose face was contorted with rage. "There's been nothing about a tube of lipstick and a purse until now. We don't know anything about a purse, Your Honor!"

"Judge, if I may?" Thaddeus said, holding aloft the purse that Kiki was carrying that night. "May I have this marked as Defendant's Exhibit Thirty-three?"

"You may."

Thaddeus had the clerk mark the purse, and then handed it to the witness.

"Doctor Andersen, I'm handing you what has been marked as Defendant's Exhibit Thirty-three. Would you identify that for the record?"

"It's a woman's handbag. It's made by a company known as Gucci."

The women on the jury all nodded. All had heard of Gucci bags.

"Have you had the opportunity to study that bag while forming your opinion in this case?"

"I have."

"Please tell the jury how and when and what your conclusions were."

"Objection, multiple."

Thaddeus nodded. "Fine. Let me rephrase. How did you first come into possession of that bag?"

"You sent it to me. At least the first lawyer, Priscilla X. Persons, sent it."

"When was that?"

"I received the purse three days after the incident."

"What if anything did you do with regard to the purse?"

"I first logged it into my laboratory. I inventoried its

contents. Then I did a visual examination. Then I performed a microscopic examination and a chemical examination."

The doctor then went on to recite the handbag's contents when he received it, and went on from there to describe the tests he had run on the purse and its contents.

Thaddeus then asked, "And do you have an opinion how the firearm came to be discharged on the night in question?"

This time there was no objection. Foundation had been laid beyond anyone's doubt.

"I do have such an opinion."

"Please tell us that opinion."

"It is my opinion that the tube of lipstick had become lodged inside the trigger guard of the gun and caused it to discharge when Miss Murphy went to retrieve it from the bag. It was a pure accident and I see no intention on her part to shoot the decedent. If there was such an intention, then it would have to be in the form of intending to have the lipstick get caught, intending to have the lipstick pull the trigger, intending to have the bullet pass through the purse and into the decedent's heart, a series of events which I find not only unlikely but impossible beyond all doubt. It just couldn't have happened with intent on her part. That would be impossible. In my professional opinion."

Objections were made, motions to strike interposed, but the judge allowed it all in. It was true that it somewhat invaded the province of the jury, as the D.A. was complaining, but the judge allowed it anyway. "The jury is entitled to hear the entire opinion," she said, and overruled the objections.

Andersen offered the jury a small smile and they returned it. All men and all women on the jury smiled back and nodded. Now their hands were still, there was no writing; they had clearly made up their minds about the night in question. Thaddeus was about to walk his sister out the door, a free woman.

The state's attempts to cross-examine the doctor were grossly unsuccessful. He was abjectly polite to the prosecutor, seemed to seriously consider all of her alternative theories on how the shooting might have happened and how the requisite intent to shoot might have been formed, and then he slowly built a case against each and every suggestion a pebble at a time, totally dismantling the state's efforts to make its case through the defendant's expert witness.

When she was done, the District Attorney sat down with a blank look on her face. The investigating detective, who had sat beside her all through the case, whispered heatedly in her ear. But she only shook her head. Shook her head and stared at the table. She refused to make eye contact with him and in fact was leaning away from him. It was clear he had missed the handbag, had failed to notice the bullet hole in the fold, and had returned the bag to the defendant when she was released from jail. A key piece of evidence had been overlooked and, as Thaddeus told the jury during closing argument, "this case probably wouldn't even have been filed had the District Attorney been told about the purse. But the police missed it and so we had to have this trial. My client had to wait all these months, in terror, while the State of Nevada sought to execute her. Your job now is to return her to life. Thank you."

They were out fifteen minutes before coming back with a verdict of Not Guilty.

There were tears, hugs, and huge thank yous to Dr. Andersen, who shyly retreated and headed for the elevator to make his escape.

The District Attorney was gracious and for just a moment Thaddeus thought she might even apologize to Kiki for putting her through the hell of the trial, but she turned away at the last instant and said nothing more. The point was made; the prosecution had been ill advised and the case never should have been filed. Now the State could only stand helplessly by and hope Kiki didn't file a lawsuit for malicious prosecution.

Which, she decided, she just might do.

49

He found the perfect holding unit in North Las Vegas. It was located three miles off the 15 Freeway, east on 147, then dirt roads.

The building was a small, abandoned office with two outbuildings where munitions were once made during World War II. It could not be seen from any paved road; no one would ever spot a vehicle parked there unless they drove into the desert 3.4 miles and knew what they were looking for.

He knocked down the wasp nests and forced open the door on his first visit.

It was dark, extremely dry, and maddeningly hot, as it was without electricity and without any form of cooling. It was outfitted with cupboards, up and down, and he made a mental note to pick up a bike lock to keep her safe inside.

Outside at night he could look west and see the moonlit peak of Harris Mountain, Red Rock Canyon National Conservation Area. The mountains reminded him of whales swimming through the earth. He wondered what they would remind her of. Probably very little, he laughed.

~

HE VISITED a local Kmart that was running a sale on prepaid cell phones. He paid cash for ten. They would either have the money wired to them in less than ten calls or that would be the end of it. He would simply drive away and leave her locked in the cupboard. She might last a morning locked inside there without water. But she wouldn't make it through an afternoon, not in that heat. It wouldn't even be necessary to worry about bloodstains or fingerprints on the body. Simply drive off and let the desert do the rest.

He drove back into Las Vegas and traded cars. The final solution was a black GMC that he'd had his eye on. A used car dealer was only too happy to get rid of it as it was an eight cylinder and those were very hard to move. Cash deal, no paperwork except the title and bill of sale. Both fictitious, of course.

He drove off the lot and found his way to Mel's Auto Body, where, for $250 cash, they painted over the black and he now had a beige van. People noticed black; they never noticed beige. It's just how it was, and it was a lesson he had learned and never forgotten, early on.

Ragman rented a cheap room off the Strip and scored a glassine bag of meth crystals. He lay back on the bed and fired up. Within seconds he was floating, then racing, then all pain soared away like a blackbird off Harris Peak.

Then he had no feeling inside and his soul turned black.

Now he could do the job.

50

I t was the second day after Kiki's trial ended and Thaddeus had the afternoon totally free. Which was a minor miracle in itself.

He called Sparky and Bat into his office, got their tasks lined out, and told them not to call him again that day—no matter what.

Then he called Albert in Chicago and checked things there. Every case was smoothly perking along; Albert had it all under control, plus. Thaddeus told Albert he was off the rest of the day and that was understood as a Do Not Disturb.

He flew home in the Tesla.

It was a sunny Nevada day, hot on the desert, and the air-conditioned home welcomed him. He called to Katy when he walked through the door but there was no answer. "Out back, I'll bet anything," he muttered. So he climbed the stairs and changed clothes. He selected his Orchid pattern swimming trunks because, unless he missed his guess, Sarai would want to romp in the wading pool.

The house came with a swimming pool with a deep end and a shallow end. Of course. But Thaddeus and Katy were so concerned for the safety of Sarai and the neighborhood kids that, rather than trust the kids' lives to the mandatory security fence, they had had the pool rebuilt. First it had been broken up and hauled away. Then came a dirt fill that mostly filled the yawning hole where the pool had been. They had the pool builders back at that point, and put a wading pool in the ground where the swimming pool had been. It was cement, it was surrounded by skid-proof Cool Deck, and it was no deeper than twelve inches at its deepest point, three inches at its shallowest. Now Sarai had her own pool. Her parents could easily sit waist deep in the water and play with her, splashing and tossing beach balls, lying down and kicking legs, until the child was exhausted. Sarai loved it. She had a pink two-piece, sand buckets for the sand pile at one end of the pool, and there was a low slide at the deep end. A child's dream.

Which was where Thaddeus found mother and child, just as he'd predicted. Katy was in her two-piece and Thaddeus was immediately aroused, feelings which he stuffed for later. They were both lying prone in the deep end, kicking legs while they swam. Swimming consisted of kicking legs, basically. The whole idea was to get the little girl accustomed to lying flat in the water and moving her legs up and down. Sarai had quickly taken to it and loved the romp.

"Hey!" he called, and they turned.

"Daddy!" cried the little girl. "Daddy, home!"

"How was work?" Katy called.

"Fine. How was your cadaver you're slicing up?"

"Fine. His name is Wanda and Wanda says hello."

"Male or female?"

"At this point, it's impossible to tell."

"You could have gone all day without telling me that."

"You asked," she smiled, and splashed water up at him.

Thaddeus took his place beside them in the pool and Sarai immediately grabbed around his neck and cried, "Alligator River!"

Which was a game they played, where Thaddeus would walk on hands and knees Sarai on his back, and they would navigate around the pool, shouting and screaming at the imaginary alligators that would suddenly launch at them and snap at Sarai's feet and legs.

Ten minutes later and they were ready for a break. Thaddeus and Katy chose lounges while Sarai headed for the sand box.

"She needs a dog," Thaddeus said.

"Uh-uh. She needs a cat. Start them with a cat."

"Why?"

She shrugged. "My cat always let me dress her up. That's what little girls are good at, dressing up their dolls. And their cats."

"So she would need a very patient cat."

"We'll look at the shelter. Shelter cats can be the very best."

"This weekend let's take her. She can pick one out."

"You hungry?"

"Only for you, baby."

She sighed and scowled. "God forbid. It's daylight. We no longer get to sexy-sexy when the sun's up. That's the price of having your heir."

"What else did you have in mind?"

"I made your favorite."

"Deviled eggs?"

"Yep. And you can have root beer with it."

"You got more."

"Sure."

"You do listen to me."

"Course I do. You're my guy."

"Still? Even after you're rubbing elbows with those wannabe surgeons all day at med school?"

"Even after. Besides, you gave me Sarai."

"We gave us Sarai."

"Best thing we ever did."

"Absolutely."

RAGMAN WOKE WITH A START. The pipe was clutched in his gaunt fingers and his eyes were scratchy. He stretched luxuriously and yawned.

The yellow pages were full of outcall.

He selected Feline Fur Fantasy and ordered something Asian. Japanese, he told them. He preferred the youngest Japanese girl they could send. Fourteen, if possible; no older than eighteen, max.

He ran an icy shower. Drying off, he removed the switchblade knife from his suit coat and slipped it under the pillow where he'd been sleeping. He lit up and took two hits off the pipe. Completely nude, he danced in front of the dresser mirror. He admired his circumcised penis. He pulled his testicles to the side and studied them. All the while his mind was flying supersonic and his muscles were twitching for release. Why wasn't she here yet?

He slipped a towel around his waist and lay back on the bed.

"Come to me, my beauty," he muttered.

Fifteen minutes later, there was a subdued knock at the door. Almost an apologetic knock. He peeped through the security lens and saw a very young girl. She was pulling at a braid and looking to the side. He devoured her through the optics.

He flung the door open and waved her inside.

"Enter," he hissed. "And I shall enter you."

"Three hundred first. That's what they told me."

"First show me your breasts. Are they small and firm?"

She sighed and looked off to the side. The shirt was mid-torso. She flipped it up and revealed her naked breasts. He inhaled deeply and came to her. He gathered her hair in his hand and inhaled. "Now your breath," he whispered.

"What?"

"Your breath. Let me smell your breath."

She pushed away and then leaned her head to him. She exhaled toward his face. Inhaling, a smile crossed his face. "No cigarettes. That's worth a hundred too. I told them I wouldn't accept a smoker, no matter how young."

"Haven't you heard? Smoking is bad for your health."

"So is unprotected sex, but that's our burden to bear."

"What?"

"Strip."

She stubbornly held out a hand. "Hundreds. Three. In the hand."

"How old are you?" he asked.

"How old do you want me to be?"

"Eleven."

"Fine. I'm eleven."

He pulled three one hundred dollar bills from his wallet. Passing the money to her, he seized her hand and studied her arm.

"No needles?" he asked, studying her forearm.

"No, I told you I'm only eleven. So no needles."

"Perfect."

"Drugs?"

"E and pot. Nothing else."

"I have no ecstasy. And I have no pot. But I have meth and a pipe. Do you want a couple of hits before we begin?"

"No. I told you. E and pot."

"But meth makes the heart pump faster. I want your heart to pump fast."

She recoiled then, having just pulled off her shirt. "What the hell, you want my heart fast? What's that supposed to mean?"

"You're more responsive when your heart pumps fast. And when I slice open your carotid, I've literally seen the blood hit the wall."

She began turning her shirt, intent on putting it right back on. "No way am I doing this. I told them I don't like men who ask for young. Screw this. Here's your money back."

Whereupon he seized her by the shoulders and flung her onto the bed like a limp rag.

Ragman. It had to mean something.

The way he left his victims when he was finished. Sublimely limp, like rag dolls. So the cops had said. And the name had stuck.

Then he was on her. She struggled, so he choked her until she was white. Then he released her and she took a huge gasp. The color returned.

"Please don't struggle," he said softly. "You struggle, there's no payment."

"Please. Just. Let me go. I don't want the money."

He stretched on top of her and whispered hard into her ear. "Whoever said this was about money? Did I say that?"

"Please, oh God. Please let me up. I won't tell anyone."

"Of course not. You're my child, my little girl, and you know how to keep a secret."

"I do, I promise. Daddy."

"Daddy says do, Daddy says don't. Now which is it?"

She relaxed beneath him. Struggling was futile. "Which is what?"

"Daddy do, Daddy don't. One lives, one says goodbye. Which one are you?"

"Daddy don't! I'm Daddy don't."

He extracted the knife from beneath the pillow. The flashing blade cut the air between them. Then he was astraddle her torso, and pressing the blade against her carotid. "Now how does it feel, knowing you're about to die? Tell me, please."

"Oh God," she sobbed. "Please please please please."

He sat upright and stared down at her. "How old are you really?"

"Nineteen."

"Too bad. I told them not over eighteen. Now I won't pay."

"You don't owe anything. Let me do you and leave. You'll love what I can do."

"Daddy," he intoned.

"Daddy."

With a flick of his wrist, he drew the blade across her carotid, reversed movement, and cut the other on his back swing. Her arms flailed the bed, fluttered overhead like angry branches, searching out the pumping wounds on either side of her throat and settling there, hopeless, but applying pressure. Her eyes rolled back in her head and lodged there.

He sat fully upright and dismounted.

"Nineteen."

He shut his eyes, thinking.

"Or is that twenty?"

He retreated to the shower where he turned the cold tap and washed the blood from his abdomen and chest. Pink rivulets spun into the drain.

Then he dressed, arranged her head so the eye sockets were staring at the door, and was gone.

51

F riday night they hit the family room and watched *No Country for Old Men*. Katy had a secret crush on Javier Bardem, and Thaddeus suspected just as much.

She was lying with her head in his lap as the antagonist walked away with his broken arm in a sling. "Dream on, dreamer," Thaddeus said, "he's married to Penelope Cruz, for god's sakes."

"Wait. Did you just hear Sarai cry?"

Thaddeus hit mute. They listened. They'd last seen their little girl upstairs in her room, door opened, banished to bed at seven. They looked at each other and finally Katy shrugged. "Guess not."

Thaddeus pushed up from the couch and wandered into the kitchen. He opened the refrigerator and began assembling a snack.

"Got any popcorn?" he called to her.

"There's bags in the cereal cupboard. Top shelf."

"Microwave?"

She rubbed her belly. She couldn't be pregnant again. But why this swelling?

"Is there any other kind?" she called back.

The front door bell chimed.

"Probably Bat," Thaddeus shouted. "I got it."

He threw open the door and there stood Bat with a much younger woman than Bat's forty years. She was Hispanic and wearing white shorts, a pressed orange blouse, and sandals. She extended her hand. "Maria Consuelo. You must be Thad."

"Hey, nice to finally meet you. Come on in."

Bat followed. He was wearing the uniform of the day— shorts with cargo pockets, sandals, a black LA Clippers tee, and beret. "Who was the dude in the van?" he asked, coming inside behind Maria.

Thaddeus peered outside. "What van?"

"Tan van. It was parked in front. Did you have someone else over? Are we that late?"

Thaddeus looked back down the street toward the secondary surface street that connected their street to the freeway. "No one else was here. I don't know what you're talking about. But hey, come on in and let me get you a drink. Maria, what would you like? We have Mountain Dew, Coke, Diet Pepsi, and OJ. There's also Coors."

"Diet Pepsi for me."

"I'll have the same," said Bat.

"Go on in the family room. Katy's already in there. I'll just be a second with your drinks."

Bat followed Maria into the family room and Thaddeus could hear introductions again going around. He hummed while he poured the drinks over ice and reached in and cut a slice off the summer sausage. "Delicious," he muttered. "Rattinger's sausage."

Taking their drinks into the family room, Thaddeus called to Katy. "Honey, have you checked on Sarai since we heard her?"

"I'm sure she's asleep. She would be talking to herself or screaming bloody murder if she was awake."

"Should I go look?"

"No, come on in and sit down and join us. We were just talking about how hot it was today."

"Summer is definitely upon us," said Bat.

Maria pointed at a small painting on the wall, above the TV. "Is that a Picasso? Is that a print?"

Katy looked at Thaddeus and shook her head. "No, that's an original. Thanks to Mister Art Fan here."

Thaddeus smiled sheepishly. "At one point I was going to collect original art. Until I found out how freaking expensive it is. That's our only original."

"What's it called?' asked Maria.

Katy snorted. "Thad's Folly."

"Ha-ha," said Thaddeus. "That thing will only go up in value."

"It better," said his wife.

"So you get to choose the movie. We've got De Niro, we've got Pacino."

"Oh, how about the new Matthew McConaughey? The Academy Award one?"

"Let me see if we've got that."

Katy stood. "How about some chips and guacamole? Did you guys eat yet?"

"We had Mickey D's tonight. Big night out on the town."

"I love Big Macs. But my waistline loves them even more."

"I hear that. We were thinking Subway, but we figured we'd lose too much weight if we went there."

Katy laughed and went to fetch snacks.

Thaddeus had located the movie on On-Demand. "Here we go. Katy, I'm starting!"

"Stop at the end of the credits!" she called. "I'll be two seconds. As soon as I find the guacamole in this refrigerator."

"I ate it," Thaddeus whispered. "I didn't want to tell her."

She reappeared moments later. "Did you eat it?"

He grinned guiltily. "I did."

"All of it?"

"Uh-huh."

"For god's sakes. Okay, guys, French onion dip okay?"

"Sure."

"Sure."

"Hurry back. We're ready to watch Matthew wow us all in this great flick. It got prodigious reviews."

Katy called in again. "I'm just going to run up and check on Sarai. Don't start without me!"

"We won't."

She screamed minutes later.

Thaddeus could hear her thumping back downstairs.

"I've looked everywhere! She's not upstairs!"

"Okay," said Thaddeus calmly, "let's settle down. We'll spread out. I'll take the backyard, Katy, you hit the panic button for the BAG guys, Bat, you and Maria go back upstairs and look again in all rooms, under beds, inside closets. Sometimes she hides in the shower with the door closed too, so don't miss that."

"Got it," said Bat. The twosome headed for the stairs.

Thaddeus tore through the sliding doors, across the deck, and began scouring the backyard. Nothing in the wading pool. Playhouse—empty. He looked behind shrubs, walked the fence line and saw nothing. By now three BAG

agents had materialized, guns drawn, fashioning a cordon
around the house. "It's Sarai. She's gone!" Thaddeus cried to
them. His own blood pressure had skyrocketed as the adrenaline began pumping. "You guys start going door to door up
and down the block. Make sure they search their houses
and backyards. Look in all swimming pools, especially on
the bottom."

"We're on our way," shouted Maxwell, the lead agent for
the shift. "I've got more guys on the way."

Thaddeus ran around and opened the garage door with
his key chain clicker. He searched the three cars parked
inside. He looked beneath them. He even opened the trunk
on the Lexus and looked inside. Same thing with the Tesla.
The Escalade turned up nothing. Now he was in full panic
mode. He ran back inside the house.

"Nothing up there," said Bat, who had reappeared downstairs. "But we found a letter."

"Where!"

"It was under the blanket in her crib. I didn't open it and
I've only held it by the edge. Fingerprints."

"Smart man. Let's get a knife."

He slid the knife under the envelope flap and pulled out
the letter and unfolded it. He scanned it along with Bat.

"Everything?" said Bat. "The guy wants everything?"

"He's demanding all sale-of-casino proceeds. And don't
call the cops or we never see her again."

"Better not call the cops."

Katy came into the family room, choking back sobs. "I
called 911."

"Okay," said Thaddeus. "Look."

He handed her the letter, which she examined. "He
wants you to wire the casino money to that bank? Then we
get her back?"

"So he says."

"You got no choice," said Bat. "Do it now."

"You're right." Thaddeus nodded fiercely. "I'll get the bank manager on the phone and we'll make it happen."

"Where's the money?"

"Spread all over. Mutual funds, money markets, investment firms. Let's see, there's Fidelity and—"

"Raymond James," added Katy.

"Right, Raymond James. And lots more. So this guy thinks I'm sitting on the casino money in one cash account and I can just wave my magic wand? This is crazy!"

"Calm down," said Katy. "Calm down. He says he'll send proof of life. What's that mean?"

"He's going to send us proof that Sarai's still alive."

"How do they do that?"

"I don't know," Thaddeus lied. What he did know—what he dreaded to even think about—was how sometimes a finger of the victim was sent. So a print could be taken and matched. BAG had taken everyone's prints two years earlier, so matching prints would be doable. But what he didn't want was a finger. He shuddered at the thought and sweat broke out down his back. "We need help with this."

"Who?" Katy cried. "Who!"

"Let me call Pauline Pepper at the FBI. She'll know what to do."

"Huh-un, Boss. They said no cops."

"Bat's right. We shouldn't get the FBI or the cops involved."

"But you already called 911."

They heard sirens approaching at that moment. "Bat, get out there and make them shut those damn sirens off!"

Bat broke for the front door. Maria came downstairs.

"Honestly, I even opened drawers in your furniture. She's just not up there."

"Okay. Thanks."

"Let me make some coffee," said Maria. "It's going to be a long night."

52

W hen he had opened the front door he froze and listened. Sound coming from the rear of the house. He moved half his body inside and listened again. Then he had waited several minutes. He guessed the little girl was upstairs, as it was after seven.

If nothing else, Ragman was bold.

He had planned to wait until 3:15 a.m. but decided to make an earlier try. If they caught him at the door he would claim to be lost, in need of directions. Under the seat in his van was yesterday's mail from two doors down. Mr. and Mrs. Dennis Rhodeman. He would say he was looking for the Rhodeman house. They would know the name and that would erase any doubt about his legitimacy. So he punched the code and ever so softly depressed the handle mechanism and held it down, in the open position, until he was certain they wouldn't hear it click when he released the pressure.

He listened again. It was a TV program. He moved through the foyer until he could make out the words the actors were saying. He heard no other voices. Retreating back to the stairway, which was just inside the front door, he tested the first step for any creak. The house was new enough the stairs were silent. So he kept going up.

At the top landing he stopped and listened again. He had the switchblade in his side pocket, just in case he was discovered and there was a struggle. At the very least he would get away and escape the neighborhood in the van. The freeway was but two blocks away and he would disappear. The whole caper would be called off and he would disappear to Costa Rica with the mobster's advance payment. The money was already there; the only missing ingredient was his smiling face on a long warm beach.

He counted slowly to 300 and then began tiptoeing down the hallway. This time of day her door would be open. He felt the plastic bag in his hip pocket. It contained a washcloth soaked in chemicals. Sleepy-bye medicine. He smiled. This was unbelievably nervy, but this was how you made the big bucks.

At the third door he paused. Just the slightest sound, the softest breathing sound possible. He leaned across the doorway and peeked inside. She was face-down in her crib, head turned to the side. She was half-covered with a pink sheet patterned in flying Dumbos. He knew the print. He had had children, before they were taken away and his parental rights severed.

Ever so quietly he slipped the plastic bag from his rear pocket and removed the damp washcloth. He turned his head to the side and held his own breath. Mustn't breathe the fumes or they might find two of us unconscious. Now to place the washcloth at her nose and mouth—there we go. Doesn't move. Big inhale, nose twitching and then slowing the in and out. Very light breathing. He removed the washcloth. Can't give her too much or the whole trade goes south.

He quickly folded the washcloth, reinserted it back inside the sandwich baggie, and stuffed it in his rear pocket. Carefully he placed his right hand up against her diaper and slowly increased the downward pressure. She didn't move. She was lightly unconscious.

He leaned, taking care not to brush up against the bars of the crib and risk leaving DNA behind, and lifted her bodily from the bed. He cradled her in his arms and looked into her face. Olive skin, wide eyes, mouth that looked like rouge had been lightly applied to the lips.

She was wearing a T-shirt, diaper, and white socks. Perfect.

As carefully as before, he made his way back down the long hallway.

This time the stairs were taken one at a time. This was to make extra sure he didn't lose his balance or lunge and make some kind of sound.

At the bottom, he stopped and listened again. Security would still be about on the rear lot line, beating the bushes.

Then he disappeared out the front door.

He laid her in the passenger seat and, unlike her doting parents, didn't bother with a seat belt.

Ever so slowly he pulled away from the circle drive and started rolling down the street.

At the secondary street he took a left, went up a half mile, and then entered the freeway on-ramp. The little girl hadn't stirred. Once he was up to freeway speed he glanced over at her. He wondered if her parents would ever see her again.

"Twenty," he said. "I think. Or was the last girl twenty?"

A flash of anger. He honestly couldn't believe how many

it had been now. Some families had paid up and gotten their kids back; some hadn't. Some of them had been hookers, some hitchhikers, some he had met in singles bars. Always it was the same. There would be pleading, there would be desperate tears, there would be bargaining, there would be cries of pain. He glanced again at Sarai. This one presented no problems at all. Too young. Just lock her in the cupboard and walk away.

It was that simple.

They had until noon tomorrow to wire the money, the parents. If not by noon, Mountain Time, then his job was done. He would be finished with what he had promised. He could leave the desert, climb aboard the Greyhound, and head south, or maybe east. Wherever there was an international airport that accepted forged passports.

The child would be forgotten.

"Put you on a milk carton," he said to his prize.

SHE CAME to at North Las Vegas, saw where she was, and immediately erupted into paroxysms of crying. "Mommy," she sobbed. "Daddy."

He refused to look at her. He had smelled her on the stairs and that was all she was going to get out of him.

He wanted to hit her to shut her up, but couldn't, because he had his orders.

Until noon tomorrow she was to be kept alive and free of bruises or other marks.

After that, anything went.

53

S cout was so named by his father, a huge Harper Lee fan.

Scout was fourteen, honest and trustworthy and all the other characteristics revered by the Boy Scouts of America. Because Scout was one. A Boy Scout.

The Aviation Merit Badge was almost within reach. After that came the Eagle.

Aviation Merit Badge Part 3 required that a Scout: "a. Build and fly a fuel-driven or battery-powered electric model airplane. Describe safety rules for building and flying model airplanes. Tell safety rules for use of glue, paint, dope, plastics, fuel, and battery pack."

His Scout leader said the plane, in free flight, should cover no less than three miles. Scout looked over the rules, both in the book and online, but could find no such additional requirement—footnote or otherwise. He ran a hand through his tousled blond hair and just for an instant thought reflexively of biting his nails, but remembered again. A Scout does not bite his nails. So, he refrained.

The plane was a Sky Chief 1001x, built painstakingly

from a kit he had purchased with his paper route money. He delivered for the *North Las Vegas Herald* and cleared $22.50 weekly. The kit was the equivalent of two weeks' pay, including model airplane engine. The engine was an 049 fuel-powered jobbie, that was broken in following thousands of nonproductive cranks on the prop, which resulted, finally, in the engine coughing, thrumming to life, whining like a banshee, only to be tamed by knowledgeable twists of the needle valve. Scout had done all that and more. Now he was ready for flight.

The tackle box contained a can of fuel, plastic line to connect fuel tin to gas tank, needle nose pliers, and assorted odds and ends that only a fourteen-year-old Boy Scout would think compulsory.

Together with Rodney, his best friend since second grade, Scout hopped on his Kawasaki scooter and blasted out into the desert. Strapped to the handlebars was the plane; the wing was safely placed bungeed to the luggage rack situated on the very tail of the scooter. The tackle box and equipage were safely stowed inside the rack.

Rodney clutched Scout around the midsection and hung on for dear life while they roared along the sandy back roads. Rodney was a black kid whose dad had once played for the D League Maine Red Claws, the Celtics' farm club. Tall for his age, Rodney was also fully developed at fourteen, a young man, but a man nonetheless. In physique. Intellectually and temperamentally he was fourteen and, like Scout, in pursuit of the Aviation Merit Badge. They would be Eagles in about two more years, if they stayed on track. Which they fully planned to do.

They were dressed alike that afternoon, shorts with cargo pockets, running shoes with no socks, Celtics tees, and hats with the bills backwards. Oakley sunglasses completed the look for each kid, and it was a good thing because the temperature was about to climb past 110 degrees and the sun was blinding. In deference to the rattlesnakes that prowled the desert, Scout wore a .22 pistol in a quick-draw holster cinched around his waist. The snakes were all too common and there was nothing worse than a face-off with an agitated diamondback or sidewinder. There were merit badges about those guys, too, and the boys had nothing but the highest regard for the serpents.

Finally they motored down a long, sloping mesa and drove onto a flat plain that was a good twenty miles long, north to south. Here they would launch the sailplane, because they would be able to keep eyeballs on it no matter how far it went once it got out the range of the radio controls. RC was only practical for a short distance. If your plane flew beyond that invisible circle, well, good luck, buddy, because your aircraft had a mind of its own from that point on. The earthbound pilots could only helplessly follow behind from the scooter, while the plane wandered away and the fuel tank held out. So, that was the plan. The scooter had an odometer. Follow the plane from launch to landing and diary the miles. At which point they would own Part 3a.

Scout pulled the caliper brake, applied the footbrake, and slowed to a stop. He dropped the kickstand and stepped off the bike. Rodney had come around and was already taking the bands from around the fuselage, preparing to assemble their machine for flight.

"Easy!" said Scout. "For crap sake don't break any spars."

Rodney gave him a dirty look. "For crap sake, have you forgot I own one-half? You think I'm gonna break my own plane?"

"Our own plane."

"Our own plane."

"For crap sake."

"Crap, shit, piss."

"Wouldn't let Mister Eddy hear you cuss like that, dude. You'd find your skinny black ass kicked out of Scouts."

"And you'd find your skinny white ass close behind my skinny black ass. You're the one with the dirtbag mouth. Scuzz."

"Scuzz back."

"For crap sake."

"All right. Let's do this."

Scout grabbed the tackle box and unsnapped the lid. Rodney rubber-banded the wings to the fuselage by pulling an X series of loops around the top of the wing and hooking them into the transverse rod running through the upper portion of the fuselage, at the CG—center of gravity. It was all in the book and it looked good to the boys. "Mother's gonna fly," Rodney mused as he worked.

They put the model on a stretch of hard-packed sand, and attached the fuel hose. Two long squeezes and the model's fuel tank filled and ran out the overflow. They wiped off the overflow and put the fuel can back in the tackle box. They attached the wires and alligator clips from the twelve-volt battery to the glow plug and ground.

"Ready?" said Scout

Rodney pounded the ground. "So cool!"

With his index and middle fingers of his right hand, Scout flipped the prop through a cycle. Nothing. He flipped the prop again. Nothing. Once again. Still nothing.

"I smell fuel," said Rodney. "You got it flooded."

"Don't think so, fool," said Scout. "That's overflow you smell."

"Isn't."

"Is."

"Fool."

"Scuzz."

Scout retrieved the glow plug wrench from the tackle box and removed the plug. He blew lightly between the points until all fuel was dry. "Happy now?" he said to Rodney.

"You'll see," Rodney replied. He was sitting on the sand now, evidently preparing for a potentially long stay at that location.

After thirty minutes of cranking the prop, the boys gave up. They repacked everything, climbed on the scooter, and returned to their homes in North Las Vegas.

They agreed to try it again tomorrow, after Scout's father checked out the engine that night.

54

G inny Sumners was the branch manager and she responded to the call from the police at 9:03 p.m. Would she mind meeting them at the bank? There was an emergency with one of her customers. She double-backed, making sure it was the police. She wrote down the caller's badge number and then called the station and gave them the badge number. Yes, he was a detective, a lieutenant grade, and yes, that was him calling with that case reference number. The case number was new, the case having been opened just in the past hour.

THEY WERE WAITING for her at the branch. Two police cars and a third black car with black tires. He introduced himself as Lt. Koeller and the other man in shorts as Thaddeus Murfee. She thought she recognized the name but could not be sure. The police officer showed her his ID, Thaddeus showed her his driver's license, and she opened the bank door. "This will take about three minutes," she said, and

went to disarm the night security system. They all three
went into her office.

It was a typical branch manager's office, complete with
industrial carpet and veneer walnut desk with secretary
return, struggling ficus plant, computer terminal connected
into the bank's 2,700 locations, and poor nighttime lighting.
In the blue neon light, their skin looked translucent and
Thaddeus felt he was moving underwater, as if in a dream.
She flipped on the terminal and looked up to them. "So.
What do we have?"

Thaddeus spoke first. "They've taken my daughter and
demanded six hundred million dollars I received when I
sold my casino."

Her eyes widened and she looked at Lt. Koeller for some
sign, some indication of reliability. He nodded. "Checks out.
We've been over the closing documents online."

"How can I help?"

"I've got a hundred million on deposit with your home
office downtown. I need to wire that out tonight."

"Let me look up your accounts. I need your Social Security number."

Thaddeus recited his number and she punched it in to
the search field and hit RETURN.

"My," she said. "This is a flagged account. The system is
warning me that it will record my ID and all activity from
my keyboard. This must be big. Ah, here it comes. My.
Mister Murfee, there's a hundred fifty million in this
account."

"More than I thought. It's a start."

"A good start, I'd say."

"I need to wire it immediately."

"Do you have the receiving bank's routing number and
the account number?"

Thaddeus showed her the letter. "It's all right here."

She studied the document. "It says all funds must be received by noon tomorrow or you will never see your little girl again. We can do this with our bank, but I can't speak for the others. But are you sure you want to do this? That's an awful lot of money. Maybe calling in the FBI is the better way to go."

"He doesn't have a choice," Lt. Koeller replied. "Just get it done as fast as possible. Please."

"My God, I can't get anywhere near six hundred million wired out tonight. There's nowhere near that amount in this account."

Koeller nodded. "I put in a call to Lieutenant Ortiz. He's head of Financial Crimes at the department. He's on his way in to help."

"Thank you."

"Now, Mister Murfee, I'm going to need you to sign off on this wire transfer authorization. And Lieutenant, I'm going to ask you to place your signature right beneath his, as a witness."

Thaddeus signed without hesitation and slid the document to the police officer. He read it over and signed beneath the first signature.

"All right, then. Give me about five minutes and we'll have this on its way."

"Where's the account? What's that number mean?"

"This is the routing number. This bank is in...Grand Cayman in the Cayman Islands. Pretty place. Seven Mile Beach and all."

"Please," said Thaddeus. She returned her attention to her work.

Thaddeus was sweating profusely. A heavy damp band swathed his forehead. And the air conditioning was humming comfortably in the background. For the moment, he couldn't even stand to think about Sarai. But he knew he had to. No one else could make this happen; it was going to be totally up to him. What about the money that wasn't liquid? What to do about that? He began reciting in his head. He thought Fidelity was holding somewhere around $125 million. Another $200 million in real estate investment trusts he had purchased—which presented a huge problem because there was no way those funds could be made liquid by noon tomorrow. He said a silent prayer. He was saying another one when Lt. Koeller's radio crackled.

"Koeller," the officer said.

"You call for FinCrimes?"

"We've got a 1240 underway. Let me give you the location."

The cop spoke rapidly, but very carefully. The voice on the other end acknowledged and said he was on the way.

Miss Sumners looked up and smiled. "It went through. Here's your confirmation page."

Thaddeus accepted the pink copy out of the printer and stuffed it in is pocket. He looked at Lt. Koeller. "Now what?" he asked.

"Do you have any other liquid funds?"

"I don't."

"Anything you can think of anywhere?"

Thaddeus' mind was reeling. He felt as if he might black out. He forced himself to slow his breathing, slow his thoughts.

"I can't think of anything else."

"If we could get a Fidelity office open, then I could get more."

"Miss Sumners. Would you please Google and locate the nearest Fidelity office?"

She did as instructed. "Goodness. Not two blocks away. On Cherry and Blanchard."

"I've seen that," said the detective. "Any names on their web page? Branch manager, associates, anything like that?"

"Branch manager is Hans Mofford. Says call him anytime."

"May I use your phone?" the officer asked.

"Certainly. Here, let me get up and you come around and sit here. Should I make coffee?"

The police officer nodded. Thaddeus stood helpless by while the officer dialed the phone and then began speaking.

"Information, this is Detective Lieutenant Nicholas M. Koeller with the Las Vegas Police Department. We have an emergency and I need a phone number. Probably unlisted."

He listened back. Then he answered with badge number, case number, and type of emergency. Several minutes passed. Then he nodded. "Yes, connect me directly, please."

Thaddeus could hear the phone ringing through the handset. It buzzed several times and then, when it seemed like no one would answer, a voice said, "Hello? Mofford residence."

"This is Lieutenant Koeller with LVPD. I need to speak with Hans Mofford. It's urgent police business."

"He's not here right now." Thaddeus heard the voice, young, probably female.

"Who are you?"

"The babysitter."

"Where is Mister Mofford?"

"He and his wife went out to dinner and then a movie."

"What movie were they going to see?"

"I don't know."

"What movie theater do they usually go to?"

"North Vegas Ten Cineplex."

"Let me give you my phone number. Write this down. He must call me the minute you hear from him. Am I making myself clear, young lady?"

"Yes."

The police officer gave her his cell number and said goodbye.

"All right," he said to Thaddeus, "let's go."

They ran Code 3, lights flashing, siren screaming, and cars parted like a knife through warm butter. Eighteen minutes later they were pulling into the North Vegas Mall.

"Around back," Thaddeus said. "We come here."

The squad car sped around to the back, pulled up to the curb, and the lieutenant and Thaddeus ran for the box office.

The officer explained the situation, the cashier made an announcement to all theaters, and they waited.

Katy called his cell. "Not now, honey, we're running down some help here."

She said to please call her the instant he could. He said he definitely would.

A mid-thirtyish, sleepy-looking man hurried from the center theater doors across the lobby where they were waiting. "I'm Hans Mofford."

"Good," said the police officer. "You're wanted at your office. Come with us," and he grasped the man by the elbow and began steering him toward the door. "Do you need to leave your keys with the cashier?"

"No, Maline has her own set. But can't I tell her where I went?"

"The young lady at the cash register will do that. Right, miss?"

The girl nodded that yes, she would give Maline the message.

They were back in the car and speeding across town, lights flashing and siren wailing, slowing at intersections, crossing carefully, then accelerating and parting the seas once again. On the ride over, Thaddeus explained the situation to Branch Manager Mofford.

"I'm afraid I can't help you tonight if you're talking equities."

"Why not?" Thaddeus asked. He really wanted to shake the guy, but managed to restrain himself. "Why can't you help me tonight?"

"Those equities, to liquidate them means we'll have to sell them on the open market. And the markets don't open until tomorrow morning."

"That might be too late," said Lieutenant Koeller.

"You've got to do something tonight," Thaddeus said.

"I can call my regional manager. He might have some ideas."

"Good thinking. Let's try that."

They tore inside the office, which was downtown in a high-rise, sixth floor, above a bank and a complex of small shops and Starbucks. The place was of course quiet, as were the downstairs stores, all shuttered and locked.

Once inside, Mister Mofford took them to his office and had them take a seat while he began making calls.

Then the dialing started.

BAT COULDN'T REMEMBER anything about the license plate. The cops were grilling him, Katy was making frantic calls to hospitals and ER rooms, and Maria Consuelo was accompanying the police while they continued to canvass the neighborhood. Katy returned upstairs several times, usually to hold Sarai's crib blanket and smell it. She cried softly as she hugged the blanket, trying to imagine only good things happening to their little girl.

55

Ragman opened the van's sliding door and carried a box of items into the abandoned office. He had placed Sarai on the floor in the dark room, and she was crying again. "Up, up!" she howled, begging to be taken up off the floor. She didn't know this man, didn't know where she was, missed her mommy and daddy, had a wet diaper, and it was long past dinner time.

The man placed the camping lantern on the top of the cupboards that ran around the room, and hit the switch. A low, blue light entered the room like a waist-high umbrella of illumination. Which scared the little girl even more.

Ragman ignored her. He removed the switchblade from a side pocket and sliced open a package of beef jerky. It was pepper-flavored and tart, but it would have to do. For tonight, at least.

He bit off a piece and spit it into his hand. He waved it at the little girl, as one encouraging a dog to come close by. She only stared blankly at him, lip quivering as she caught her breath. "Come and get it," he said. "You better damn well eat, because this is it tonight."

She looked at him and flung herself backwards and began flailing against the floor and emitting piercing shrieks. He slowly shook his head. "If you were mine, first I'd do, I'd reach in there and cut those vocal cords. Stop the damn caterwauling."

She continued, oblivious. He turned and scootched himself up onto the cupboards. He watched her cry and flail about on the floor. Then it occurred to him. He could always go out and sleep in the van. Behind the bucket seats. "You're about to spend a long night alone," he warned her, "if you don't stop this dumb shit."

Nothing helped, nothing mattered, and so he took the lantern and found his way outside to the dark van. He left the office door open and wondered if she might wander off during the night. It wouldn't trouble him if she did.

Slamming the doors to the van and hunkering down behind the seats, he was instantly gratified to learn how quiet it was with her inside the office, him outside in the van. "Finally," he said, and propped his head back against the seats. Through the side windows he could see a huge rectangle of the nighttime desert sky. Stars winked and satellites moved. Jetliner lights circled overhead, making ready to set down at McCarran. Soon he was tired, and sleepy. He lay down prone on the floor and closed his eyes. He just could hear her wails. This just might work, he thought, I just might get in an hour or two of sleep tonight.

He violently came awake thirty minutes later. He was having a vision of slicing her throat open, the little girl's. He stumbled out of the van and went into the office. He heard nothing, so he returned to the van and found the lantern. Flipping the switch, he retraced his steps back to the doorway and peered inside. She was balled up, her head against the dusty cement, her legs drawn up to abdomen, sucking her thumb and staring at nothing. Eyes open, thumb sucking, and that's the way he left her until four hours later when he had to urinate and walked around to the end of the van. He peed all over the right rear tire and then checked back inside the office. The thumb was still inserted in the mouth but the eyes were closed. She appeared to have cried herself to sleep. Just for the slightest instant he actually felt a twinge of tenderness toward the little girl. He found a blanket in the van and folded it in half. He moved her onto the blanket and pulled the flap up over her torso. She didn't stir.

He checked his watch. 2:43. Almost time to call in. He waited another ten minutes inside the van. Then he selected one of the throwaway phones and dialed the number.

"Ragman," said the voice. "You got her?"

"I got her right here."

"Keep her alive. He's sent me over a hundred million so far, and counting."

Ragman said nothing.

The voice spoke again, irritated. "Did you hear me?"

"I heard you."

"I want her alive. Got that?"

"I'll do what I can." Ragman flexed his hand and studied the muscles in the lamplight.

"That isn't what I said. I don't need a kiddie murder mob of cops coming after me. Not to mention the father. That son of a bitch is crazy."

"Keep her alive. Check."

"I better read in the papers where they got her back, you want the second million."

"Keep her alive. Check."

"Man, are you just dumb or only stupid?"

No answer. Ragman clicked off the phone.

Keep her alive. Check.

He would think about it tomorrow. For now, she meant nothing to him, he would abandon her tomorrow, and that would be that. Maybe they would find her. But there would be too much heat to contact them and give her location. Only a fool would call them.

And he was anything but a fool.

56

F idelity Investments had a heart. A huge one.

The regional vice president was finally located, and he listened in as the branch manager, Thaddeus, and Lieutenant Koeller explained the situation. His name was Reynolds and he seemed very sympathetic as Thaddeus pled his case.

"So you need it liquidated tonight, bottom line?" said Reynolds.

"Yes," said the branch manager. "There's nothing in the manual of operations about that. It's your call."

"Here's what we can do. Mister Murfee, you can post the equities, and the REITS against the sale of the equities, and Fidelity will make one hundred twenty-five million available to you tonight. Mister Mofford will wire the money as necessary. Is that going to work?"

Tears came into Thaddeus' eyes. "I really don't know how to thank you."

"What time will the money be available?" asked Mofford.

Reynolds returned moments later from his computer

monitor. "Give it thirty minutes. We'll override the account and show availability by then. Have Mister Murfee sign the usual 2800 Series of indentures and we'll post those into his account as well. Then you're good to go."

"Thank you," said Thaddeus.

"Good work, sir," said Lieutenant Koeller.

"Thank God," said Mofford. "We'll wait thirty then wire. Got it."

"Right," said Reynolds. "And hold on. He's got about two hundred fifty million in REITS. We can take those down in the morning, turn them into cash, and you can transfer out another two fifty million immediately after. Does this conclude our business?"

"Honest to God," said Thaddeus. "Put me on your website as one grateful customer."

"We're here to help, Mister Murfee. Is there anything else?"

"I don't think so," said Mofford. "But if you could stick around your phone for a while in case I need to make a callback."

"Sure. We're in for the night, so I'll be here."

Thanks were again given and the threesome concluded the call. Mofford looked at Thaddeus, who was ashen but breathing again. Lieutenant Koeller wanted to know if there was any coffee. It was going to be a long night and he needed the jolt, he said. Mofford told him there was a Keurig in the kitchen, help himself. Thaddeus said he would like one too and Koeller said he'd get it. Mofford and Thaddeus talked obliquely after that, skirting the story around the little girl's disappearance. Katy called once on Thaddeus' cell and he updated her. Bat was still with the police and Maria had just returned from talking to neighbors along the block. One elderly woman had noticed a van around seven o'clock, parked in front of the Murfee's, but she couldn't remember the color or anything about the driver. Then she had seen it drive away, watched its taillights flash at the corner, then make a left, toward the freeway. That was the sum and substance of her knowledge.

Thirty minutes later the wire transfer went through without a hitch.

"Are we done here?" asked Koeller.

"We are," said Thaddeus. "But Mister Mofford, I really don't know how to thank you enough."

"Hey," said the branch manager, "I've got two little ones myself. I don't know what I'd do, in your shoes, but I'd definitely need a hand from someone too. Glad to oblige."

They said their goodbyes at the front door and left Mofford to close down the computer system.

"Home?" asked Koeller.

"Home," said Thaddeus. He was exhausted. He had wired every conceivable last liquid dollar to the Grand Cayman number. It was just a matter of time now. Her fate was in the hands of unknown people and he could only wait to see what tomorrow brought. He said a silent prayer as they ran at normal speeds back to his house. He didn't know what effect prayer had, but he was willing to give it a try. Any action was better than none, and prayer was all he had left.

AROUND MIDNIGHT he couldn't stand it anymore.

He went inside the office and picked the little girl up, blanket and all. He carried her to the van and put her in the back cargo area, where it was much warmer. He sat, smoking in the dark, and listening to her breathe. She must be hungry, he thought. He almost called for additional instructions but decided against it. He would decide at first light about the girl; there was nothing else to do now but get through the night. For the longest time the sociopath considered his actions, but by nature couldn't attribute any fault to himself. The introspection abruptly ended when the little girl coughed and turned over. He sat up and made sure she was covered.

An hour later he carried her back inside the office. He found a cardboard box, flattened it, and laid her down. With the blanket he tucked her in and watched her for several minutes. Finally, he shook his head and went back to the van. It turned right over and he spun it around, back the way he had come. He would be in L.A. before evening. As he pulled away he waved out the window.

It was the least he could do.

And the most he could do.

57

Saturday morning dawned clear and sunny. By nine a.m. it was hot in the desert, and chicken hawks were circling lazily in the sky, the sunlight dancing off their outstretched wings as they watched the ground for the next meal. Thermals bore them higher and higher then fell away, dissipating, and the birds glided further and further in concentric circles, seeking out the next updraft. It was going to be a scorcher and the birds meant to dine early and then seek out their shady shelter for the morning.

The boys assembled in Scout's garage and the father explained to them—again—each step to take before turning the prop. When he demonstrated for them, the engine immediately coughed and buzzed to life. The boys looked at each other. So what was he doing that they had evidently missed?

They loaded everything back on the Kawasaki and hit the starter. Minutes later they were off, headed for the desert and their first launch of the sailplane. It was hot; they were sweating heavily when they reached the city limits of North Las Vegas, but they were determined this time.

"Damn thing better fly!" Rodney shouted in Scout's ear as they turned onto the dirt road.

"It will. Dad showed me how it works."

"Well, just be sure you do exactly what he said."

"What do you think I am, stupid?"

"Hey, I'm just saying. Scuzz."

"Scuzz yourself."

Rodney reached up and flicked the driver's ear. His head shot forward and he emitted a loud curse. Rodney laughed so hard he nearly fell off the speeding scooter. It was going to be a grand day.

They roared down onto the long plain, stretching miles in a north-south direction, and parked the scooter approximately where they had made their first efforts yesterday. Scout lowered the kickstand and Rodney removed the wings from the rear bungees and went after the fuselage up front. Scout meanwhile grabbed the tackle box out of the cargo unit and off they went to a flat spot, clear of cactus and underbrush, where they would try again.

"It's not like we're the Wright brothers," said Rodney, as Scout made the preparations.

"What's that supposed to mean?"

"No reporters around, taking our picture for posterity."

"Dumb, Rods, dumb."

"Someday there will be reporters. And we'll be in the papers. 'Boys Take Flight and Win Aviation Merit Badges' they'll say—something like that."

"In our dreams."

Scout connected the twelve-volt battery to the engine's tiny glow plug. He wound the second wire and tightened the lid on the fuel. No accidents. Then all was ready.

He cranked the prop and on the first 360 it caught. The prop buzzed to life, spun hard, and sprayed a light dusting over the boys' hands and arms as they made last-second corrections to the plane: positioning the elevator in an UP position so the plane would increase altitude each second it was aloft, and giving the rudder a quarter turn to the right so that plane would fly in long circles, but not quite enough to cause it to stay in one place. They needed three miles and, of course, this was all guesswork and best estimates, but they were doing what they knew to make it work.

Finally, Scout stood with the whining plane in his right hand and released it. The plane shot skyward and began climbing.

"Holy shit," cried Rodney. "Look at that mother climb!"

"Unbelievable," said Scout. "We did it!"

"Quick, let's follow on the scooter."

Rodney was right, the plane was beginning to distance itself from the boys. It was flying southwest and its engine whine was diminishing in volume. They ran for the scooter, jammed the tackle box and supplies in the cargo box, and gave chase.

"How much fuel did you put in?" Rodney shouted into Scout's ear as they chased after the plane.

"Full. I filled it all the way."

"That should be good for about seven minutes," said Rodney. "By that time we won't even be able to see it anymore."

"I know," said Scout. "But it's red and nothing else on the desert is indigenous red. It'll stand out like crazy and we'll be able to see it on the ground from far off."

"You hope."

"I hope, you're right. My God, it's almost a speck now."

"Can't we go faster?"

Their teeth were chattering as the bumps and ups and

downs jerked the motor scooter from side to side, up and down, but still they pursued at top speed.

"Any faster and I'm afraid I'll dump it. My dad would kill me if he found out."

"All right. Then we'll just keep going same direction."

Five minutes later they came to a desert road, unpaved, of course, and began using it to follow the general direction of the plane. The road crossed several washes, sand running across the road perpendicular to them, and then evening out again.

Then they saw the plane. It had made a perfect landing a quarter mile ahead, not a hundred feet off the road, and was awaiting them. They pulled up alongside and turned off the ignition. "Eureka!" cried Scout.

"How many miles?" Rodney shouted.

"Almost five! We did it!"

They high-fived and broke into a run for the plane. They wanted to hold it aloft and cheer, which they did. Then the exuberance died out and Scout suddenly raised his hand for silence.

"There. Did you hear that?"

They listened in silence."

"Sounds like a little kid crying."

"Or a coyote. Maybe with its foot caught in a snare."

"No," said Rodney, "it's a little kid. My little sister cries like that when she doesn't get her way."

They stood listening, then moved further away from the road, following the sound.

The crying increased in volume when they topped a rise and found themselves looking down on a deserted site consisting of two outbuildings and a low building between the two. They listened hard. The sound was definitely coming from down there, so they broke into a run.

Rodney found her first. She was sitting up, inside the office, screaming.

"Shit," he said, "her diaper's filthy."

"We gotta get water in her," said Scout. "She's probably dying of thirst."

"She ain't dying," said Rodney. "But she sure'n hell is pissed."

"Sure'n hell is. Who could blame her?"

"Hey, who would leave their kid out here?"

"Let's run for it."

Rodney, the fully grown man, easily broke into a run with the little girl nestled in his arms. In fact, Rodney beat Scout to the scooter. Scout took his position on the front seat, Rodney threw a leg over the rear seat, and they walked it in a U-turn, heading back toward home.

The ride back to the house took all of fifteen minutes. The plane was all but forgotten, for they had found something much more imperative. Rodney cradled the little girl and touched her lips with his finger while they flew along. She studied his face and at one point smiled at him. "I found you," he told her. "And now I'm gonna find your mama."

"Hang on," said Scout, "I'm turning in."

They rolled into Scout's driveway.

The police were called three minutes later.

THE ER DOCS ran an IV and performed a complete physical. Tests were undertaken and vitals studied and recorded. The police texted her picture to the parents. The parents collapsed with joy. "It's her!" they texted wildly in reply. "It's our baby!"

Lieutenant Koeller, who had never left the parents' side and who had sat with them all night, ran them Code 3 to the North Las Vegas Memorial ER. They flew past Admitting and found her in a small room. She was wide awake, an IV in her arm, holding a bottle of milk to her lips that the nurses had supplied. Her eyes followed her parents as she entered.

They embraced her, kissed her, and Katy rubbed her arms. "It's mommy and daddy," she murmured.

The little girl pulled the bottle away from her mouth. "Mommy for Sarai," she said.

Both parents collapsed on her bed and promised to never let her out of their sight.

The doctors wanted to watch her overnight and keep the IVs going. She was transferred to a private room and roll-aways—two—were provided for the parents.

At long last Lieutenant Koeller shook hands all around, receiving a huge hug from both parents. "We couldn't have done it without you," Thaddeus told him. "And those boys who brought her. I want their names and phones."

"I'll put them on your voicemail, soon as I get back to the station," said Lieutenant Koeller.

"Both boys are going to attend college," Thaddeus said. "Oh my dime."

"Can't blame you for that," said the police officer. "That would be a nice gesture."

"I can't repay them enough."

"You don't need to. They're good Scouts."

"Thank God."

"So we'll talk again. Probably sometime tomorrow I'll give a call and we'll finish up some housekeeping. Oh, by the way. CIS found a damp spot where we're guessing the perp took a leak. Looks like we're going to turn his DNA."

"Incredible," said Thaddeus. "I just want five minutes alone with him."

The lieutenant smiled. "I'd let us handle that."

"We'll see," said Thaddeus. "I have to think about that. I want the guy's name when you locate him."

"It'll be in the reports. And you'll get those. Later, then."

"Later."

Katy gave the man a second long hug and turned away, tears flowing down her cheeks. "My God, I love that man," she said to Thaddeus, when the man was gone.

"Me too," said Thaddeus. "I love him too."

"HOW MUCH YOU GOT LEFT, BOSS?" said Bat. They were standing outside on Thaddeus' deck two days later.

"Probably a hundred."

"One hundred million dollars?"

"Give or take."

"Whatcha gonna do about it?"

"Get it back, liquidate somebody, enjoy life."

"Liquidate who?"

"One of my Chicago acquaintances. He was the last one around who hated my guts."

"What will happen?"

Thaddeus took a long drink of iced tea. "We'll have to see. I'm already working on that. We might be taking a trip. A long trip."

"Me too?"

"I think so."

"What about security around the home?"

Thaddeus drew a deep breath. "I've doubled BAG agents. Around the clock both inside and out."

"That'll be inconvenient."

"I've got lots of enemies, Bat. Lots of enemies."

"But you've got lots of friends, too."

As if on cue, Kiki came through the sliding glass doors.

"Back again?" Thaddeus said.

"Can't stay away. I'm so relieved, Thad."

Thaddeus encircled her waist with his arm.

"Bat was just telling me how many friends I have. Between you and him, how can I go wrong?"

"And don't forget Sparky," said Bat. "That guy thinks you walk on water."

"I walk on glass," said Thaddeus. "Tell him that."

"Let's go inside," Kiki said. "Katy sent me to tell you lunch is ready."

"Sounds good."

"And Sarai is looking for you."

"Then by all means," said Thaddeus. "By all means."

THE PEDIATRICIANS and critical care doctors monitored her over the next two weeks. At the end her vitals looked good and her health was fully restored.

The crime lab reported a DNA match from the urine. Now to find the guy.

Thaddeus hired a team of private investigators and went on the hunt. They scoured the U.S. coast to coast. Then the FBI reported that a name had been found. Thaddeus demanded the name. Sorry, they said, but that's an ongoing investigation. So he filed a *Freedom of Information Act* demand.

Special Agent Pauline Pepper called. She said she would meet with him in Chicago, that the investigation was an uncommon one, and she wanted to discuss personally what they had so far.

He boarded the jet and headed for Chicago.

He watched the plains slip by beneath the wing. Who was this guy that a special meeting was required?

Whoever he was, it was just a matter of time before Thaddeus would locate him. He only prayed that he would get to him before the FBI made an arrest. It was a simple prayer and a short one, offered up by a man who never prayed.

Lead me to him first, he repeated.

Lead me to him. First.

The End

UP NEXT: CHASE, THE BAD BABY

"A must read, plus Ellsworth incorporated another sideline story within this story...AWESOME!!!"

"Great psychological study. I found it interesting and factual about mental illness and birth defects."

"Do not mess with Thaddeus Murfee's family......he always finds the bad guy, even with the FBI watching him constantly!"

"Another winning book by John Ellsworth. I am so pleased he is retired and now writing books. "

Read Chase, The Bad Baby: CLICK HERE

ALSO BY JOHN ELLSWORTH

THADDEUS MURFEE PREQUEL

A Young Lawyer's Story

THADDEUS MURFEE SERIES

The Defendants

Beyond a Reasonable Death

Attorney at Large

Chase, the Bad Baby

Defending Turquoise

The Mental Case

The Girl Who Wrote The New York Times Bestseller

The Trial Lawyer

The Near Death Experience

Flagstaff Station

The Crime

La Jolla Law

The Post office

SISTERS IN LAW SERIES

Frat Party: Sisters In Law

Hellfire: Sisters In Law

MICHAEL GRESHAM PREQUEL

Lies She Never Told Me

MICHAEL GRESHAM SERIES

The Lawyer

EMAIL SIGNUP

Can't get enough John
Ellsworth?

Sign up for our weekly newsletter
to stay in touch!

You will have exclusive access to
new releases, special deals, and
insider news!
Join today!

Click here to subscribe to my newsletter: https://www.
subscribepage.com/b5c8a0

ABOUT THE AUTHOR

For thirty years John defended criminal clients across the United States. He defended cases ranging from shoplifting to First Degree Murder to RICO to Tax Evasion, and has gone to jury trial on hundreds. His first book, *The Defendants*, was published in January, 2014. John is presently at work on his 31st thriller.

Reception to John's books have been phenomenal; more than 4,000,000 have been downloaded in 6 years! Every one of them are Amazon best-sellers. He is an Amazon All-Star every month and is a *U.S.A Today* bestseller.

John Ellsworth lives in the Arizona region with three dogs that ignore him but worship his wife, and bark day and night until another home must be abandoned in yet another move.

johnellsworthbooks.com

johnellsworthbooks@gmail.com